THE AGNOSTICS

THE AGNOSTICS

A Novel

Wendy Rawlings

THE UNIVERSITY OF MICHIGAN PRESS ⌒ ANN ARBOR

Copyright © 2007 by Wendy Rawlings
All rights reserved
Published in the United States of America by
The University of Michigan Press
Manufactured in the United States of America
⊗ Printed on acid-free paper

2010   2009   2008   2007   4   3   2   1

A CIP catalog record for this book is available from the British Library.

Library of Congress Cataloging-in-Publication Data

Rawlings, Wendy.
    The agnostics : a novel / Wendy Rawlings.
       p.   cm. — (Michigan literary fiction awards)
    ISBN-13: 978-0-472-11625-6 (acid-free paper)
    ISBN-10: 0-472-11625-8 (acid-free paper)
    1. Middle class families—Fiction.   2. Long Island (N.Y.)—
Fiction.   3. Domestic fiction.   I. Title.

PS3618.A958A38   2007
813'.6—dc22   2007019358

An excerpt from this book appeared in *Tin House* (Spring 2004)
as a short story entitled "Berries on the Vine."

For my mother

One of the last great realizations is that life will not be what you dreamed.

—James Salter, *Light Years*

one

They had gone to high school together. But they had not been sweethearts, had not run with the same crowds. It would have been preposterous, back then, to try to convince them they would marry each other. After the winter recess Stephen appeared in homeroom and was asked to introduce himself. 1960. Stephen from Amherst, Massachusetts. He did not register with Bev; he had no fanfare about him. He played Tom Wingfield in the production of *The Glass Menagerie*. His Tom was a noble figure, with upright posture and a look of yearning that made people conflate Tom Wingfield and Stephen Wirth. Perhaps it was natural; he had offered them so little of Stephen. On stage the spotlight caught the lenses of his eyeglasses; it was not possible to see his eyes. When he graduated, the quote the editors chose to accompany his yearbook photo was "Avoid entangling alliances."

One day he passed her on a motorcycle. That same upright posture. She identified him by his back as he retreated. Another time in a boyfriend's car she passed him on a hill. This time he was running—no, sprinting. He was working the edge, nearly beyond his abilities. He had inherited the compromised lungs of his father; he would never be a runner of any note. He wore a white shirt and white shorts and didn't break his stride when the car veered in and passed close.

"That's Stephen Wirth." Bev looked in the rearview mirror. His face in the moment she glimpsed it seemed slack as the face of a man sleeping.

"He runs," her boyfriend said.

"For the team?"

He shrugged. His name was Richie Salerno. The discolored skin under his eyes gave him the look of someone tragically unhealthy. He would die young, a bad death, gasping in the street. "He just runs. I see him all the time on these back roads."

"Why would he do a thing like that?"

"Maybe he's got time on his hands."

She wanted to ask Stephen. But they traveled in different circles. She had a white sweater with a blue bullhorn sewn on and down the length of the bullhorn the letters of her name by which she was known.

"Have you noticed the girl everyone calls Binky?" Stephen asked his brother Parker. Parker was eighteen months younger than Stephen but a prodigy. He had skipped a grade and still scored higher on exams than Stephen did. He was known as a math whiz.

"You can do better than a girl like that."

Parker was lucky that he didn't have any sort of a clear vision of himself. He believed he was popular, a lady-killer, that anyone cared his intelligence exceeded most people's. He did not know how to dress. His haircut was wrong. Stephen did not figure this out in a way he could articulate, but he could detect about his brother qualities that put people off.

People assumed he and Parker were twins.

In their senior year it was unavoidable: he and Parker shared a car and drove to school together. In the parking lot he spotted Binky talking with Richie Salerno. They stood facing each other between two cars. Richie's hand went out and caught Binky's sweater and shook her. She stood trying to keep her head steady, her mouth set, lips pinched shut. Parker was still walking but Stephen came to a halt and watched Richie Salerno shake the girl, then pull her toward him and slam her against the car.

Stephen heard a noise issue from his throat. There should be a confrontation, he felt, between that man and us. He blinked and was no longer a neutral country. Still, he felt it was necessary to say as little as possible. Not clutter the event with words. Not even tell Richie Salerno he was wrong. Just get the girl away.

Parker was already at it. Stephen heard some of it: "nerve," "preying on the weaker sex," and so forth.

He hurried over to them, but he did not run. Richie had turned away from Binky. Stephen caught her under the elbow.

"Come this way." He wove them between several cars, until they were a distance from Richie and Parker. The two men gesturing at each other in different body languages, the brute and the squire.

"He's never done that before," she said.

"Of course not."

"I think he has a kidney stone. That's what's bothering him."

"He's certainly agitated."

"A kidney stone."

She held to that story and when he ran into her would embellish it; she would always make sure to mention the kidney. He began to see Richie Salerno's kidneys whenever she approached. They were brick red and dangled like earrings. If they shriveled, went defunct like stems once the grapes have been picked, an obstacle would be removed. She stood with an old textbook in her hand. As they spoke she put the textbook on her head, let it balance there, let it slide off. He could not pay attention. No, the focus of his attention was so profoundly visual that he couldn't catch and hold the aural. He looked at her mouth. Out of it came sounds. Yes, "Richie," "kidney," "hospital." It took a concerted effort for him to put the sounds together. Richie had gone to the hospital; he took olive oil daily; there was hope of a new treatment.

She turned up in school with a black eye, painted over diligently with flesh-colored makeup. It was not unusual to see a girl painted up to hide getting socked in the face. Or a broken finger swollen up like the finger of a baseball glove. Maybe their fathers did it. Some man.

She had a dancing chorus role in the spring musical revue. At rehearsals the members of the large cast lounged backstage between numbers, smoked illegally, fooled with their costumes and the racks of old costumes from other productions. A purple and pink hat like a cake, can-can dresses layered underneath with a froth of ruffles, the front and back ends of a cow. *West Side Story* had just come out; everyone would have preferred to do a production of *West Side Story*.

"Richie could play the thug."

It was Parker, getting into trouble again.

"There's more than one thug. There's a whole bunch of them, Jets and whatever, Sharks."

"Richie could play all of them."

"I should punch your lights out." Not Richie but a friend of Richie's. He wasn't part of the theater clique, he was a member of the crew, lived in the black pants and shirt crew members were required to wear, a pack of cigarettes rolled up in his shirt sleeve, an aptitude for car repair and passion for very little but cars. Was invisible and unthought of. Was both these things now as a kind of livelihood. Lots of students existed this way, unnoticed, invisible. Bev, existing first and foremost in the spotlight of other people's eyes, could not have understood.

"Then you could say you accomplished something today." One thing about Parker was the absence on his part of even a healthy measure of fear. It was the one thing that got him respect. Every time walked right into the fray. It was a thing to witness. He wouldn't even flinch.

Stephen and Bev sat on opposite sides of the room. It had checkerboard black and white tiled floors, mirrors on three walls, the racks of costumes stood against the fourth wall. "Commie," among other things, had been written on the mirrors with lipstick. Remarks about Parker—the size of his penis, unflattering adjectives—also on the mirror. If he found himself alone in the room Stephen would wipe or smear them. Never if anyone was around. It was better for people not to see you trying to do anything on Parker's behalf. Parker himself didn't seem to care what anyone had to say about his penis.

Richie's friend was muscular. He lifted Parker like a sack of grain—a small sack—and tossed him in the direction of the costumes. It would have been comic had it not been for the sound of Parker's head making contact with the cinderblock wall. Parker and some sequined dresses slumped onto the floor.

"You smashed his head!"

"If I did I did him a favor." Richie's friend stepped over Parker and stalked off. The rest of them had to hurry and kneel over Parker and confer. They would call an ambulance. Later it would seem to Stephen as if they had all taken their parts in a play none of them had seen but somehow all knew. He splayed his hand across Bev's back. They bent over him together. Parker was conscious but glassy-eyed and woozy. He had a concussion. Still he was able to take up a feather boa from the floor. Dramatic Parker.

"It's always worth it," he said to Bev.

"What is?"

"Being in the right."

She thought he was referring to the run-in with Richie's friend. She hadn't figured out that he had engineered an emergency to see whether or not she and Stephen would magnetize. See, it was not true that all Parker felt for his brother was antagonism. Parker wanted Stephen to be happy. And so, though he disapproved of Binky Cohen, he contrived to deliver her to his brother.

⌒⌐

May 1966. The day of Stephen's college graduation. Even from a distance, something about him is rumpled, asymmetrical. His mortarboard canted at a precarious angle. But it will not fall off; there is no fear of that. He has affixed it to his head ingeniously, if not symmetrically. He will receive his degree in mechanical engineering today. The degree is merely an official stamp. He has always had a knack for making things work, in the way others have a knack for language or decor. He designed the winning boxcar for the annual race down Broad Street; he is the sort of man who can build a bed, repair the heel of a shoe, take apart a dead radio and make it broadcast again. One look at a clock or a television or phone and he gets a picture in his mind of its guts. His failing is how confident he is that his knowledge will transmit easily to other people. How frequently his failing is demonstrated to him. How stubborn his refusal to see it.

"Everyone should know. It's our duty, if we're going to be relying on these things." In his commitment to technology he is almost an ideologue.

It's the mystery of the telephone that captivates. The invisible bridging those distances. And the way the picture tube comes to life, with the living, dancing, speaking people inside, miniaturized. Bev imagines an entire race of people, tiny replicas of everyone on earth. And inside the television many chambers, each filled with little beds.

"That's absurd," Stephen said.

"I know it's absurd, I just like to think it."

"That's absurd," he said again.

He was graduating summa cum laude. Bev liked the Latin, a parallel language, a secret way of speaking the important things. A gray day, May fifteenth, more rain threatening. The legs of the wooden folding chairs sink into the damp loam. It had been a record wet spring. The graduates in their robes serious men, most thin, still in the leanness of youth that would gradually over the years yield to accumulation in the midriff, forearms, jowls. Stephen among them one of the most serious of the serious. He drank shakes with raw eggs broken into them, he wolfed his meals, snacked on crackers in between. But still lean, his jawbone prominent, reminding you that a skeleton moved underneath.

Bev felt a great uprushing of pride, greater than any she had ever felt for herself. She did not know why she was proud. She could not say how she regarded herself in connection with him. He was only a man, he knew nothing of what she knew. That the miniature humans inside the television irked him, that he did not like to think of them in their miniature beds. Well. She had no patience for sprockets.

She was sitting on her own at the end of a row, the tips of her white pumps muddy. She was alone. She had white gloves balled up in one hand. She did not feel alone; she felt inhabited. Was it the clothes she had chosen that propped her up? A new dress, sleeveless, barely broken in, with a cropped jacket over, a bandeau bra beneath. All white. The bandeau bra not enough support for her breasts. She can feel them spilling out of it. And her hair beneath the hat, a falling wave of dark hair heavy as brocade.

His parents sat several rows back. Straitened, cautious people. The mother with a fulsome laugh and ornamental violets on the rim of her hat. Jew haters. So her own parents had said. Her parents elderly already, suspicious, their sight beginning to fail. A mistake or even a tragedy for people to marry each other and then for both of them to have their eyesight fail. How much better it would be if one would lose hearing, the other sight. And only one daughter. One chance.

Don't give our one chance to Jew haters.

They had not said it but she could hear it in everything they didn't.

When the ceremony has ended, when the mortarboards have been tossed into the sky and have shot back promptly to earth, when the disappointments of gravity and ceremony are concluded, some mortarboards catching in the spring mud, they move toward Stephen and gather around him. He stands awkwardly, his arms too long for the sleeves of his robe, his hands oddly idle until they find each other, then twist and spindle the graduation program. Always the hands needing to do something. Later, a party at his parents' house, half an hour by car. A narrow winding band of a road leads up to the house. Fragrant Pines Road. Already at the house the ham is prepared, the pigs in a blanket, the mince pies, the cold asparagus and hollandaise. All is waiting, white tablecloths, flowers in vases, quivering, still. His mother is a consummate entertainer, and contemptuous, though in secret, of those who are not.

They had already embraced him when Bev made her way to the flagstones where they were clustered. Her white pumps smudged with mud. It was this that charmed him, that she had arranged herself like an angel and yet how her perfection at the edges had been smudged. It made her more perfect.

"Beverly. My parents." Then the handshaking and nodding. As if they were the Japanese. Bev always felt an urge to curtsey. They would like that. By contrast Bev's own family gallingly physical in the way they extend themselves, the embracing, cheek-pinching, the back-slapping. It is a cliché often said of Jews but also now from what she has seen, true. Her cousins in Staten Island hug like bears.

She shook their hands, dry, almost powdery.

"Lovely to see you, Beverly."

The father mumbled something she didn't catch. He had a shock of silver hair that fell forward as he shook her hand and looked at the ground, a nose like the nose of a man in a painting and a mouth that declared itself the instrument of someone to whom others would listen. A thousand of him hung in government buildings, municipal chambers. None of her hung there.

Later, at the party, Stephen drew her to him in front of the fireplace. The others out back in his mother's garden, brimming with gladiolas and hovering bees.

"You look beautiful. A study in black and white."

"There's no black—"

"Your marvelous hair." He lifted and twined it around his hand. "It's so dense, it's like coal."

"Thank you, I think."

He suddenly knelt and pulled her down beside him. There was no fire in the grate. There should have been.

"Did you see him?"

She looked around. "No. What are you talking about?"

"At the ceremony. Did you see what he was doing?"

"My ankles hurt crouching like this."

His elbows on his knees, he held his hands in front of his face. "Click, click."

"Your graduation present? He got you a camera."

"Naw," he said. He took a boyish swipe at his forehead, which had begun to sweat. He said "naw" all the time and "jeepers" when he was annoyed, when something broke or confounded him. "All through the whole ceremony, click click. He was taking pictures of you."

"Me!"

"His study in black and white."

She thought of how Stephen's father would be soon; he was aging every minute. The shock of silver hair was distinguished. But there would be punishments: wattles, the cough shading into emphysema, the sad jowls of the elderly.

She saw him photographing her thighs and breasts, as if she were his morsel. He could see inside her body with that camera, to her muddy Jew core.

"That's ridiculous," she said.

When he told his parents of his plans to marry her they sat speechless as cats. This time a fire in the grate. His father in the easy chair, Stephen on the sofa beside his mother. His father reached under the seat cushion and retrieved the nebulizer. Rybarvin. He turned away from them to spray it into his throat. Bitter but with a cloying edge. A day had come when Stephen just had to try it, when he felt he could not go on knowing his father any longer without knowing what it felt like to spray that business into this throat.

"It won't be a rabbi. Her parents have agreed to a justice of the peace."

"A rabbi!" his mother said.

The small canister tucked back under the seat cushion. They were stowed all over the house. His father caught his breath and sighed heavily.

"You're a grown man."

But the photos, Stephen thought. The photos were proof of Bev's power, distilled to essentials, black and white. Were his father to bring them out it would take no more than a glance at that coil of hair like tar or dark oil from deep in the earth cascading or what had he called it when they knelt by the grate—coal?—and the wonderful figure, her calves strong from dancing and her dark eyes, two haunted almonds. Haunted almonds! What was he thinking? He nearly laughed aloud at himself. He was not thinking; he was half out of his mind.

"Do what you will, Stephen."

Their only endorsement.

His parents had a Chinese junk, *Hai Sing.* A rowboat tied and bobbing behind it like a duckling was *Low Sing.* The sailboat's hull was painted crimson and had an irregularly shaped sail the color of jute. It must have been a notion of the exotic that drew people. People in Connecticut were in need of the exotic. His mother wore a white cotton boating hat and one or another navy blue dress with white piping at the hem and neck. She bought them at Talbots; they were variations on a theme. His father paced, smoked his pipe, wore an emblazoned captain's hat that paradoxically diminished his authority. His parents would sail the boat across the sound from Connecticut and drop anchor at the harbor right in town. It was convenient. Their weekends were hijacked. Bev was already pregnant.

"It could be worse. We could be driving up there in wall-to-wall traffic."

Stephen was right. And yet something despaired in her as she stood at the edge of the dock and waved one arm and then the other out at them while they motored into the harbor. These were not her people. Or she not theirs. They were brittle with each other; she could not get close. Perhaps it would change when she had the baby.

His father motored in on *Low Sing* to pick up Bev and Stephen. Dried salt on the metal dinghy made it chalky to the touch.

"Your mother has a lunch made."

Bev watched the motor churn the water up white. Until now she hadn't ever been so silent. She had been a gregarious child, indisputably beautiful, the sort of girl upon whom adults comment in her presence. Then a sociable young woman, told so often of her beauty that it had become a fact she carried, distributed like a pamphlet. She had been voted Most Popular, Best Looking, Best Teeth. Teeth! Odd now how this man she has chosen, this family—they are not a family of beauties. To anyone it would be apparent, how irregular their features compared to hers, how irretrievable their teeth. Overbites, discoloration, and Stephen's father has developed an uncharacteristic habit of sucking at his teeth. As if to draw something out of them, fortitude or venom. An animal gesture. To be among the Wirths is to remember how humans are at bottom a species of animal. How among this family her beauty is prey. Or at least a candidate for. That is what separates us from the lower animals, Bev thinks. They have just prey and we have candidates for it. We conduct interviews.

⌁

She is uncertain if in pregnancy she has retained the looks that drew people. Some women of course grow even more beautiful, but of herself she is not convinced this could happen, she having reached already an apex of beauty.

She's ungainly, climbing out of *Low Sing* and onto the sailboat. She has to let the men take her hands and hoist her up. In this theatricality she might be the heroine of a long-ago play. Stephen's mother puts out her hands from on deck to help with the embarkation, though only ceremonially: she can't swim. Can't swim and so fearful of drowning she wears over her navy blue belted dress her orange life-jacket with the clasps tied. When she and Bev make their quick embrace there are these obstructions, Ann's damp life jacket and the curve of Bev's belly, hard as a nutshell.

Down in the cabin the oak booth's table top glossy with finish. A luncheon laid out on it nearly as elaborate as the graduation luncheon: triangular sandwiches with cucumbers and prawns, currant tea cakes arranged on a doily, shining fruit in a bowl. Fruit so perfect it gives the impression of being made of wax. Big toffee candies in a metal tin with a lid Bev pries open with the lip of a spoon. Inside the candies nestle in a bed of confectioner's sugar. Surreptitiously she licks it off her fingers. English toffees, imports from home. When

John and Ann go back to England to visit their siblings and cousins they bring back toffees, loose tea, tins of anchovies, Devon cream in a can.

"Can't they get anchovies in this country?" Bev asked. The grandeur of their departures and returns doesn't sit well with her. You emigrate, settle, stay. But if you have enough money, if you are that kind of immigrant—not an immigrant at all really but more accurately an expatriate, an infinitely lovelier word, as champagne is lovelier than beer—the overarching rhythm of your life can be that of leaving and returning. To return and then to leave again. To never have to claim fully any one place. A condition to which Bev aspires, though she doesn't know this yet about herself.

The stink of low tide. How smells can color utterly the mood of an event. How difficult it is to be dignified with such a smell coating everything. A smell of rot. For behind it, death and not just the impermanence but the way when things die they decompose and yes, rot. Horrible word. As the tide goes out the smell intensifies. Wrapping up the remainder of the sandwiches, Bev felt unaccountably sad so few had been eaten. So few for so much effort; Ann had cut off the crusts with the precision of one using a razor. Or nail scissors. She pictured Ann over the bread with nail scissors and felt not like laughing, as she would have expected, but a great sorrow welling up inside her, just beside the baby or even pushing the baby aside. Most of the currant tea cakes untouched as well. Semaphores on the curtains Ann sewed for the cabin windows. Semaphores too made Bev feel desolate, the way Braille always did. A world without the comfort of a written language. But Braille was written; they were just raised dots instead of strokes with a pen.

Her husband and his parents, a family, were above deck, no one speaking. They were not a group that felt much the need to speak to each other. Whereas her own father. Jewish. She stopped herself. Was it that he was a Jew? She chalked up to it everything that distinguished him from Ann and John and Stephen. His constant talking and eating, his opinions, the manic pacing, his remarks about anyone's weight or physical condition. He was going to lose his teeth; they were not well enough taken care of to last him his life. Even that wouldn't slow down the talking and eating the way you would imagine. A peripatetic life, running from something. He paced in the kitchen while he ate standing up, a barrel-chested man with what Stephen called chicken legs. Legs all muscle and sinew, with very little flesh. He kept all his flesh at his midriff, like something he was holding on to. His teeth were beginning to brown from smoking. His pate was bald and tanned, covered with liver spots and spots that were pre-cancerous. At the wedding, in her parents' living room and back yard, he had ricocheted among the guests. He reminded Bev of the silver pinball in the machine. By the time her children were old enough the pinball machine would be gone into history, something else she and they would not be able to share. This thought, too, sunk her lower. She sat down in the booth, rested one hand on the hard nut of her stomach. Still no word from above. That family in harmonious if separate silence. The stink would be cause for embarrassment. They wouldn't mention it. Three of them sitting there and all around them this smell of things rotting, organic matter that had once been alive and now was dead. It was a failure to acknowledge. They wanted to block out the essential things, death and birth and by implication sex. She held it against them. Her father would have pinched his nose and announced just what it smelled like.

She did not think she would see her parents as much anymore. Already it was understood she had gained entry into his family; his was the more desirable.

"We should take her out for a sail," Stephen said. The late afternoon light, poetic, would soon begin to mitigate the stink.

Soundview. Twenty-five miles to the city on the highway. They went in at the holidays. *Into the city*, as if Manhattan were a chamber or catacombs, something with depths and deeps. The impression strengthened by the means of arrival, the Midtown Tunnel. Its dim narrow tiled curves. At first *The Nutcracker*, at Christmas, year after year. Then, later, Alvin Ailey. From the stiff legs and tutus and sharp angles of the white bodies to the black muscular barefooted flow. They made Bev's heart hurt. In a tiered magenta skirt, she moved across the cold floors in winter, pretending it was spring. The community dance group was putting on *Hope for the Flowers*. She was a seed, a bud, then blossoming into a plant she imagined as tropical, something with fronds. Flowers always had to die. She liked the last collapse at the end, all of the women breathing together, their cheeks against the sandy floor. She was a broad-hipped woman with breasts too big for her. A woman for whom it had become customary to curve her shoulders inward, from early on aware that the size of her breasts discomfited. The physical fact of her a distraction. But she had been a dance minor in college. In ballet class, the instructor paused beside Bev, studied her thoughtfully. Bev stood erect, unsmiling, her head high. Her limbs ached. She was determined to be fierce, fiercer than the narrow dancers who came to this easily. She would work harder, eat less. Her face held the intensity of someone ill, someone who no longer thinks beyond the needs of the body. The instructor saw it. Her mother had perished with that look, a cancer death, in stages.

The instructor too was one of the narrow women, the knobs at her hips visible, the noble scapulae outlined under the skin. It wasn't useful for someone built like Bev to gather such intensity. She touched Bev at the hip, to adjust her posture. Then pinched her thigh.

"Not so many between-meal snacks, Miss Beverly."

Bev watched her face in the mirror, willing it not to register the remark.

At the kitchen table she sat with a scoop of cottage cheese in a Pyrex dish. Black coffee. *I am trying to lose.*

The towns that make up Long Island are not important. They are only satellites. The sea is the one amenity the city cannot claim. Soundview's downtown: a grocery store, firehouse, post office, card shop. Luncheonette, barber, butcher. A dry cleaner with an Irish woman and daughter who do alterations and seem never to leave the shop. Wedding dresses stiff and upright in boxes with cellophane windows stood on the shelves. Norm's Tackle Shop, with a dusty front window. Abe's for candy and magazines, cigars. Our Hobby Liquors. Hobby? Stephen Wirth had never paused to think about that. "Hobby" now a word dropped from common usage. At one

time men included hobbies on their resumes. Building model airplanes. Archery. Bowling. Years from now, this will occur to him.
He will wander, lose his footing and his nerve.

"You think it's a good idea to say drinking as a hobby?" He
ambles through the aisles as one might in a souvenir shop, lifting
bottles off the shelf, peering at the liquid. The worm lolls in the bottom of the tequila, gold flecks drift in the bottle of schnapps.

"Naw, this was my dad's second business. Owning the store's the
hobby."

The house for rent in Soundview isn't right on the water. But
close. At low tide the smell, rotting and alive, wafts up from the
muddy shallows. This is the creek side of town, where the tides are
sluggish, the bottom silty when stirred up by feet. Horseshoe crabs
are common. The shore is rocky and uninviting, weeds and cattails
preventing easy ingress. But someone has carved a path into the sea
for swimmers and lobstermen, who go out before dawn in rowboats
to check their traps. Someone, invisibly it seems, keeps the cattails
cut back.

The first time they swam, Bev got tangled in weeds. Ropes grab-
bing at her and pulling her down. She has a flair for the dramatic,
and she has never trusted the sea. On her honeymoon at the Jersey
shore, she went under a wave, tumbled, scraped her back in sand,
gulped mouthfuls. Stephen brought her up, his hands dug into her
armpits. Screaming, she heard her voice screaming even when she
was telling it to stop. But it's not like that here. There are no waves
in Soundview; the sound and the bay are calm waters. And this a
calm town. The Catholics worship at Saint Gertrude's, on a steep
slope overlooking the main road. And the Protestants in a modest
brick building on a side street. There are no blacks. There are no
Jews.

Bev is not anyway much of a Jew. Her cousins had been bat mitz-
vahed but she, the youngest of them, was not. The family less and
less interested after the war in setting themselves apart. And then
Stephen's Episcopalian family, British, with a horror of Jews.
Stephen's father in London during the Blitz hung black crepe over
the windows. Buzz bombs falling so close by, the next day there were
empty casings in the streets.

London, his city, cratered and ruined.

Stephen's father likes to start the evening with a drink. An evening can start at four, three. He draws from somewhere on his person one disallowed cigarette.

"The fault of the Jews. The Jews' fault."

It is 1968. Bev is usually taken for an Italian, sometimes a Greek. "Just go along with it," she tells Stephen. Easier, in this town, if she wants to blend. Sometimes, in the evenings, they hire a sitter and drive down to the strip of bars and restaurants along the beach. The amusements are thin, the Astroturf at the miniature golf balding, the paint on the dwarf windmills faded by sea air. An optimist will build an outdoor bar serving clams casino, daiquiris made from a red powder mix. Skirts of artificial grass taped to the bar. Lit torches, plastic masks with features meant to look carved in wood—the Tiki feel.

Bev orders a rum punch. She tells them how she wants it made. A drink makes her loosen; her self-consciousness lifts. Not so long ago she knew she was the most beautiful woman in the room. Most rooms. She can't lean on that anymore. She is a mother now; her belly is scarred, her breasts a comedy. Her bikinis sit in a cardboard box for the Goodwill.

A second drink makes her argumentative. That beauty she once leaned on, its loss: it must be someone's fault.

"*Tiki* means 'first man.' Or 'creator of first man.'"

A little noise from the back of her throat.

Stephen steadied himself. "Are you going to get all pissed about it?"

Binky *Wirth*, now. Beverly Wirth. Stephen thought of himself as the luckiest of men. The days were rich and striated; they took on hues: crimson, violet, a deep imposing blue that made him feel as if his sternum were a ruler implanted in his chest. Until now hadn't he been trying to pass the time? His days had been a burden. He had run as if training for athletic contests, tinkered with clocks and gadgets, the Morris Minor with the dead engine he bought for thirty dollars and got working again after months of collecting parts at junkyards. Now, when Bev got out of bed to use the bathroom during the night he reached to smell her pillow; he ministered to her like a slave who has been released and yet prefers to remain with the master, a planet in that orbit. To have a master gives one's existence shape. He knew he was indulging Bev as her father and grandfather had indulged her, yet to indulge her gave him all the pleasure. He was convinced hers, merely receiving his love, could not be the greater.

Winter mornings he rose early and hung a blanket in the doorway between the kitchen and sitting room. He ran hot water into the sink basin. They would bathe Louise together when it cooled.

"Do you want your coffee? Half a grapefruit?"

"In a minute, yes."

He was putting his hands out to her; he wanted to touch the folds of her robe.

"Stephen, pay attention."

It had not occurred to him that they would have a child so soon. It seemed an error or at least a failure of imagination that out of their passion the only tangible thing to come was another helpless body. He was helpless enough. What could he have been envisioning? A suspension bridge the size of his hand. Any kind of gadget, though one made from eclectic materials—gossamer, eggshells, strands of Bev's hair. But a baby: its poundage and ounces, its leakages, noise, the ammonia-smelling pink folds between the kicking legs on the changing table. The birth itself had stung and appalled him, Bev producing this thing she seemed to have been hiding from him. It was in his nature to think of a child as an invention, willed by its creator. Yet here, three months after Louise was born, how little Bev knew about her invention.

She had sat on his lap when she told him, ruffling his hair. "What did you think was going to happen? We'd make a little carburetor?"

She who didn't know for sure which part the carburetor was.

She was kissing him. She was getting fingerprints all over his glasses. "Little carburetor with a bow in its hair."

He tickled her. It was still just the two of them; he held to that. Though Bev already turning inward, toward herself. She contained parts that could address other parts, could consort inwardly as he could not.

He stretched tentatively toward what he had been planning to say. "Weren't you using those inserts?" He stopped. "Inserts" hung in the air like a dirigible.

"Not always."

"Oh."

"There wasn't always time."

He saw himself crawling across the bed to her with the begging look on his face. "Kiss me kiss me kiss me kiss me kiss me." Whispering like someone with a problem in his mind. Delirious with fever. He had descended on her, over and over again, muttering his idiot words. As if he was a martyr moving along the pavement, a bed of nails, bed of fire. He had not been interested in sex. He had been nearly a virgin when at last they lay down together, in the dorms.

Years from now, on an anniversary trip to Madrid, in the Plaza del Sol, the two of them will come upon a body supine on the pavement, even the face covered with a black cloth. From beneath it only a hand holding a chewed-looking Styrofoam cup. The hand with enough life in it to rattle its coins.

The people in the square step over the body. This is a heavily trafficked area.

"I can't."

He took her by the elbow and hauled her along with him.

They stopped at the corner to wait for a bus to pass. "I could have kicked him in the face."

"Well, you didn't."

She was digging in her shoulder bag, already heading back the way they had come. When there was a lull in the foot traffic she dashed to the body and knelt. He heard her say "dios." Still there was no movement under the cloth.

Later they sat in a dark bar and drank *chatos*, the small glasses of cold sweet red wine. There was a soup made with pork and tomatoes. To a wooden board propped on the bar the leg of an animal was tied with a length of hemp rope, the hoof in the air, a piece of aluminum foil wrapped around the meat at the other end.

"If it was a man or a woman, old or young, alive or dead. That was the worst part," Bev said.

"You couldn't tell from the hand?"

"No."

They drank a great deal more. Varieties of olives they had never tried before were set out in carved wooden bowls, prompting them to speak, as they had every time olives were laid out, of the superiority of Spain to their own country with its bad olives and salty snack mix. The bartender performed a trick in which he held a wineskin an arm's length from his body and guided the stream of liquid along the grooves in his face. All led to his mouth; he laughed as the rivulets coursed in.

He felt a surge of love for her standing there in her yellow bathrobe, soaping his infant daughter's head.

"I could hook up a sprayer you could use to rinse her." He lunged to show where he would install it.

The child's head slipped out of Bev's hands.

"Jesus!"

"I got her, I got her." Stephen wiped the startled face, the face of a guppy, an innocent. A face like a piece of cheese. He thought that. Later he would bond to her and not think of her as cheese or guppy. "It doesn't look like she's going to cry."

"She's an Aquarian." Bev swabbed the soap from Louise's ears with a washcloth. She spoke of astrology as she spoke of nutrition, biology, psychology. For her everything systematic was a kind of science. Stephen saw himself living comfortably among her assertions, as one might live among several different kinds of pets. He would not quarrel with her or try to make her understand what made the television work. He was convinced of everything by her beauty, and that such beauty should ally itself with him.

When Louise began sometimes to struggle for air, Bev suggested that they should start her on a regular swimming program.

"I'm sure it's inherited," Stephen said. "My father's asthma was terrible when he was a child, before he ever started smoking. He was in an oxygen tent the day he met my mother."

"Oh, I don't believe that for an instant." Stephen's father was a brisk commander of himself; he ate up all the air in a room.

"Did I never tell you this? He was a patient on her ward in her nursing days. She had her eye on his brother, a thoracic surgeon. So she was being especially solicitous. Then word got around the surgeon was engaged to one of the other nurses."

Later he was sorry he had told her that story. Wasn't it obvious Bev had simply settled for him, as his mother had for his father? There must be for Bev the equivalent of the thoracic surgeon somewhere. Someone Bev had known at the University of South Florida. She had left after one semester, shocked at the drinking fountains right beside each other marked "Colored" and "White." Right beside each other, the "Colored" one smaller or otherwise inferior, the drain often dotted with chewing gum.

If she had been black she would have spat in the white fountain.

"Not if you knew you'd get your lights punched out for it," Stephen said. Bev underestimated the costs of political resistance. She was too willing to open her mouth or to try to get others to open theirs; she didn't anticipate the consequences. At the university she had complained about the different curfews for male and female students and quickly gained a reputation. But she didn't take the care to organize a resistance, plan a strategy—she just shot off at the mouth. A rumor that she had been caught out late with a professor began to circulate. That she was very possibly pregnant by him. But she claimed these rumors were not why she'd left; the patent unfairness of the curfews and drinking fountains was why. And yet, maybe she had been thwarted by her thoracic surgeon there. Maybe there was a professor. Maybe he had a wife.

Bev's resemblance to a popular movie star was profound enough for it to be not merely vanity. It was fact, not a resemblance fabricated from a wish. Men openly remarked on it when they met her. Women were more circumspect, waiting to see whether Bev would be snooty or aloof. Then, when she was warm, when they were engulfed and could no longer resist, they would confide the observation to her proudly, hand it to her like a gift they had been concealing until the right moment. Bev accepted the compliment with a surprise that was incredulous and disinterested, muted, a slight smile playing on her lips. Like Natalie Wood, she underacted.

"You think . . . ?" A vague stare out into the middle distance. Perhaps a film still from *Rebel Without a Cause* projected on a distant piece of sky.

"Oh, absolutely." For proof, then, the woman making the claim would remark upon Bev's coloring, her hair, the similarities between the mouths, the shapes of Bev's and Natalie Wood's faces (this likeness the indisputable proof; it was not merely the superficial similarities of eye color and hairstyle).

"Doesn't she, Stephen?"

He smiled. "I suppose I can see a slight resemblance."

⌣

The shank of winter, the sky an unchanging white all day. There are no gradations except at dawn and dusk. The days long and blank as socks. Were socks blank? All of existence seemed woven together by ordinariness—laundry, bread, washrags, water, the bills that came in through the mail slot. Everything a surface to be buttered or wiped clean. When Stephen pulls away in the Morris Minor all falls still in the house. He won't be home until after dark. Bev launders the cloth diapers by hand; her hands seem to smell always of the pee of a nursing baby, pungent but inoffensive.

Elsewhere, in Washington, in Vietnam, the great antipathies of human existence are playing out, the irreversible decisions. What does it feel like to hold a gun? To end a life? To give orders to end a life? She has no frame of reference; the milk courses through her. It's exhilarating and humiliating for her body to be making such demands. The milk leaking out of her. Then she has to bring herself to Louise for a feeding, make the feeling go away. Pressure, then release. Does it feel like that to hold a gun? It must in some way, an impulse born of pressure, a need to release.

She washes her face with pHisoDerm, its odor sulphury as she dispenses the white liquid into her palm. She washes her hands, too, with pHisoDerm, though it's meant for the face. Upends the green bottle and dispenses long lines of white liquid up each arm, which she then rubs to raise a soapy film. In the bedroom Louise is napping, an episode of *General Hospital* playing low on the TV. A nurse named Audrey with a cap pinned to her auburn hair; she has a brisk life, look how often she moves, how frequently she speaks! Where does she live in real life? Bev imagines Audrey stepping out on the street from a television studio in Midtown, her nurse's cap and crepe soled shoes left behind in the dressing room. Even her name is different now, as she heads out into the city lights; it changes twice a day.

She regards her face in the mirror, her soapy arms. The weight she gained with Louise will be with her for the rest of her life. She cannot think of it as benign.

Still the doe-brown eyes, the delicate mouth. But no one, now, would mistake her for Natalie. It would only be flattery to make such a comparison, and she is not interested in flattery.

Natalie, the name she wore in sunglasses, on the city streets, cultivating the similarity to the real Natalie as one might cultivate a friendship.

Now that resemblance gone. Now these pendulous, leaking breasts.

She mourns the loss alone, foolishly, as one mourns the death of a celebrity.

Their second child is born, also a girl.

A striped afghan across Bev's lap, knitted by her visiting aunt. Stephen sits on a stool beside her in a corner of the room that gets sun.

"Are you disappointed?"

"My god, what a thing to say!" He was whispering, as if in a library or church. "She's beautiful."

Aunt Beck prepared dinner in the kitchen. She worked with scallions, Napa cabbage, fresh ginger that she grated onto the middle of a large plate. She would tilt the plate to display it, as if this were jewelry on velvet, or arrowheads she had found in the ground. When Stephen cooked he made the wartime dishes his mother had served in London during the rations. Cauliflower with melted cheese, broccoli with the same. Often turnips, indulged with lumps of butter that had been rationed when he was a child. From Beck he would learn how to make curries, stir-fries, all the dishes to which Deborah would later object. Now Deborah was asleep in Bev's arms. She has not yet tasted solid food. Her eyes don't even work properly. Her fair hair will change color, the eyes turn from a milky blue to brown. What had he thought he wanted? His mother had each time she was pregnant knelt to pray for boys. Why had sons been so important to her? There had been tears in her eyes when she cut his and Parker's hair, the fine blonde curls so many young children outgrow. She saved them in an envelope. This was when they were five, six. People mistook Stephen and Parker for twins. Out of nowhere his mother would make a declaration, while he or Parker examined the notched plate on the back of their father's pocket watch or played with Dinky Toys, the small metallic cars they collected. "You'll have your own money." Her eyes would be brimming. More than once: "You'll go down your own lane." Maybe she had been drinking. He tried to remember if there had been a glass.

He had one vague and entirely pictorial memory, like a photograph found in an apartment recently vacated by the previous tenant: They were on the threshold of a room, his mother made to look like a Japanese woman with dark lines redrawing her eyes and pancake to whiten her face. Her kimono shone the green of an emerald. His father looked to have dust or ash in his hair, a pot belly made with a pillow, a sword at his waist and a dark coat with epaulets.

"I'm Yum-Yum." Her voice was high and cracked, as in one ill or afraid.

The photo began to move. His father made broad gestures with his mouth and hands. Flourishes. He could have been singing in the opera had any words come out. It was all pantomime. Stephen remembered it being extremely quiet. Though this must have been in Connecticut already. He might have been mixing it up with the time of the war, when he was very small and had a hand pushed over his mouth for bawling during an air raid drill.

His father pulled the sword out of his waistband. Another flourish. The neighbor who had been looking after them poised to move quickly, the way one moves when a bat has gotten in and is circling erratically.

Beside the man with the sword the Japanese woman cringed.

Later, the makeup came off, his mother sitting at her dressing table. One eye was still Japanese, the other English again. His father in the bedroom was snoring, sleeping it off. "Have sons," his mother said. He stood behind her and met the reflection of her eyes in the mirror. He thought she was playing her character; it seemed like a Japanese thing to say.

Beck. A diminutive of Rebecca, curt and efficient as the woman herself, and sexless in a way that is, unexpectedly, comforting. In the presence of Beck, Bev can feel how much energy is sapped by gender. The way the bodies of men must be reined in and contained. None of the rules applied to Beck. Stephen thought her by far the most competent of Bev's relatives. Her mother, for instance, was useless, burned dinner, could barely cook at all except, Stephen joked, charbroiling. Bev's mother's repertoire was Mary Kitchen hash and scrambled eggs or hotdogs and canned beans. Or a piece of liver in the middle of a plate. Louise was her grandmother's cooking's only aficionado. It was cooking a child could relish.

But Aunt Beck. She made potato latkes, pirogis, soufflés. This evening a crabmeat quiche. Aunt Beck had a repertoire of songs. One went "Relatives stick together," that was the one she always sang. Others were by men with plaintive voices and guitars. "Here's to Cheshire, here's to cheese, here's to the pears and the apple trees. And here's to the lovely strawberries. Ding dang dong go the wedding bells." That was Pete Seeger. Louise had no idea what it meant. She taught Beck the only one she could remember well enough to sing for a stretch, the one about John Henry. "I'll die with a hammer in my hand," the refrain went. Beck would heft an imaginary sledgehammer over her shoulder and swing it through the air in an arc. You could believe she had the strength for it.

Aunt Beck lived in Sandusky. Usually she made the trip to New York alone by car. There was some unspoken disagreement between her husband and Bev. It was her husband who was Bev's blood relative, her father's brother.

"What say we take this dinner outside and eat it on the front steps?" she asked Louise.

"Aren't we supposed to eat at the dinner table?" Louise was five. She favored rules.

"But we always eat at the dinner table. No more alwayses."

Stephen stood and watched the two of them, a plate for Bev in one hand and one for himself in the other. Aunt Beck was a blessing, Bev said. A blessing but a tiring one.

"No, we eat under the ping pong table!"

"Okay, under the ping pong table!" Through the swinging kitchen door Beck went down the basement stairs. Louise trotted after her, protesting nobody ate their dinner under a ping pong table, she had just been making it up. That was the thing about Beck: she called your bluffs. Whereas Stephen would say no and no and no, getting into battles. He would have to remember that.

God knows what Beck did; she must have just hunched over and ducked her head when they got under the ping pong table. Stephen got the stool from the kitchen pantry and sat on it next to Bev in the living room with the baby. He had named her Deborah in his mind as soon as her head crowned, and when he said it aloud to Bev she agreed. Deborah. His parents perceived the name as overtly Jewish and thus as a slight.

"We should have named her Penelope according to them. Or Georgina."

"They sound like names of princesses," Bev said.

"British names."

"The last thing I need is princesses."

An irony of sorts, if one thinks of who Bev was in high school. Head Cheerleader, Homecoming Queen, Best Looking, Best Teeth.

"But I was never a princess. Remember how that boyfriend hit me?"

Aunt Beck always stayed for as long as she wanted and no longer and no less. Sometimes Bev would beg her to stay on, but Beck would say she had to get back to Leon and her switchplate business. What she did was dry and press wild flowers, then shellac them onto the plastic plates that went over light switches. People went crazy for them. Recently she had expanded to shellacking favorite images such as dog breeds, flags, and beach scenes. The idea of which she was most proud was using the Sunday funnies, Andy Capp and Dick Tracy and the Lockhorns. She and Leon had developed a categorizing system and arranged the switchplates in wooden boxes. These they kept in the back of their Cutlass Supreme and drove all over the Midwest attending craft fairs. Des Moines, Fort Wayne, Topeka.

"I draw the line at Jesus, though. Jesus shouldn't be on a switchplate."

"They put him on dinner plates, for Chrissakes. They put him on bumper stickers."

"Well, I don't want to be a party to that."

"They put him on a crucifix; I can't see as it would matter if you put him on a switchplate," Stephen said.

"I would make a lot of money if I used him."

"Organized religion is behind every great bloody conflict in the history of the world," Stephen said.

"We're talking about switchplates, not religion."

"Here we like to talk about both."

Beck sat forward. Her dark eyes glimmered; there was something she wanted to say. "I'm just trying to think through a business decision. Do I want to drive around the Midwest selling Jesus switchplates? Because if you start doing something word gets around and then people start requesting it. A few months back, well maybe it was more like half a year now Leon came home with some Playboy bunnies. The bunny symbol, and then some copies of the magazine from friends of his who keep them around and make, well, I don't know what you call it. Yes I do. Pornographic switchplates. Only Leon says they're not really, the spot where the woman's crotch happens to be in most cases gets cut out by the opening for the light switch anyway. There are still breasts, but there are plenty of photos of girls wearing little tops and things that cover the nipples.

"I know the two of you think the sorts of people who go to craft shows are women with their hair in braids and macraméd vests, but let me tell you something. I sold every last girlie switchplate I had. Leon was taking orders for the next two shows up near Dayton. Now I have to do this. People have put money down. I have to figure out, do I want to do him with the apostles, the Last Supper, by himself on the cross or what have you."

"Jesus and a Playboy bunny," Bev put in.

"Someone wanted a Playboy bunny playing golf."

"They play golf?"

"They don't have to play, they just have to pose with clubs."

They sat on the green sofa in the living room, Aunt Beck on the brown floral-patterned easy chair across from them. She was in her traveling clothes, boots that looked oiled and gauchos and a dark turtleneck and wool poncho she had knitted for herself. She was an imposing woman, with wrinkles radiating out from her eyes. It was difficult to see her eyes when she smiled.

Louise whined and hung onto the poncho.

"I can't understand you when you talk like a baby."

"Can I go?" She looked from parent to parent.

Bev didn't say anything. Deborah was her only province now. The baby was a small country she lived in alone. Stephen thought of Vatican City. He had once believed the pope lived by himself among the tapestries and the great Michelangelo mural with its glances and dramas. To care for a small baby is to renounce those glances, those sorts of dramas. A drama was the yellowy crust that formed on Bev's nipples and hindered nursing. He had been enlisted to get salve for her from the health food store that had opened in a residential house. The wood floors creaked; behind the cashier the wallpaper had a pattern of lanterns and teacups.

"Sure, go ahead. Pack a bag."

"Really?"

"Make sure you take your wheezy medicine."

"I'm taking my bear."

"But also your wheezy medicine."

She was halfway up the stairs.

"Now what are you going to do?" Bev asked, once Louise was out of sight.

Beck shrugged. "She can come back to Sandusky with me for a little while."

"She has kindergarten Monday."

"I can teach her that business."

"Really?" The thought of having a house without Louise in it for a while, in these early days with Deborah, drenched her in longing. She thought about her pillow. She would be able to sleep.

"I can bring her back next time I come. Say in a month."

"That's crazy," Stephen said.

"It'll be good for her."

"What, to make switchplates?"

"There are other things for her to do." Beck had a sort of giant adult tricycle. She had never learned to ride a two-wheeler. "We can go blueberry picking. I can take her to the Alexander Graham Bell house."

"It sounds marvelous," Bev said. She felt as if she might laugh hysterically and hurl the baby off her chest. Yank the nipple right out of her mouth. *My* nipple, she thought territorially.

Louise came downstairs with a duffel.

"You're sure you want to go with Beck?"

Louise looked pointedly at the baby. Little usurper.

"Do they have Good Humor in Sandusky?"

"It's not Bora Bora, Chicken. Of course they do."

Louise didn't know what Bora Bora was or why Beck called her Chicken.

"I like toasted almond or the one with the gumball in the bottom."

They got as far as the New York State border.

"I have to go home. I forgot the wheezy medicine."

"They told you three times to bring the wheezy medicine!"

"Two times."

"I thought I saw you put it in your bag."

"That was the other wheezy medicine."

"You have more than one?"

"There's one if you're going to be wheezy and one if you already are."

It was starting to rain. They had been on the road for maybe eight hours. Beck had been thinking she would just floor it and get them home to Leon. She'd popped a NoDoz to keep everything moving. At a quick clip. She felt very nervous, very alive.

"You want me to turn around?"

"Maybe we could fly. Is there an airport around here?" She was craning her neck.

"And what am I supposed to do, abandon the car? It doesn't drive itself, you know."

Louise toyed with her seatbelt and hummed. The car was not her problem; that was a problem for adults. She might get peanuts on the plane. She had been on a plane exactly once, when she was too young for peanuts. The only reason she knew about them was that her father brought the foil packets home for her from business trips. Those and little soaps the right size for her hands.

"I don't think I brought any extra panties, either."

"They have panties in Sandusky. They also have your wheezy medicine."

"Not *my* wheezy medicine."

"Well, if you buy it you make it yours."

"But I want mine. The one Daddy got me."

"It's all the same stuff in the little canisters."

A Howard Johnson's near the interstate had a vacancy. There were two beds but Louise refused to sleep alone. In the night she wet the bed and when Beck questioned her she denied it.

"Now when will you come ride in my tricycle basket and see the Alexander Graham Bell house?" Beck asked as they headed east, retraced the previous day's drive.

"And pick blueberries."

"Blueberry season will be done."

"When?"

"A few weeks from now. You'll have to try to catch it next year."

"When I'm six?"

"Yes, you'll be six by then."

Louise put her Macmuffin down in its clamshell. The morning sky was a tedious white.

"I hate myself."

She was prone to making such pronouncements. How early it starts, Beck thought. Though she herself had never been susceptible.

In Manhattan Bev saw a painting that upset her. Some women on a train. Or people, at least, wearing heels and dresses and hats. She stood looking at the painting for a long time; the museum was fairly empty. Maybe it was only that she looked at it so long. But the faces looked like the faces of men. She remembered in college seeing some detail views of the Sistine Chapel in a textbook. How Michelangelo had painted bodies of women that looked like men's with breasts. But the breasts an afterthought. This painting was in a way the inverse. Women's bodies under those clothes, but the faces with angles, chiseled, and with the hard eyes of serious men.

Stephen couldn't see it. He had Deborah on his back in a carrier, was sneaking her pretzels from a baggie. He liked the Natural History Museum best. Even the Metropolitan was better, with the mummies and masks. He wasn't much for paintings. They didn't seem real to him; a painting wasn't a thing. Whereas mummies, masks, even vases or broken pottery or arrowheads, all those were real.

"A painting is real. It's as real as anything else."

Stephen had taken Deborah's carrier off his back and was stooping to wipe her nose. "I know what you're saying. It's just a painting doesn't do anything."

"That doesn't make it less real."

"It makes it less real to me."

"Go try to put your hand on that de Chirico. That'll make it real."

"Why would I even want to touch a painting? You can't do anything with it. All you can do is make the alarm go off. Or if I actually could get away with stealing it I could sell it on the black market."

"And buy a boat."

"And buy a boat," Stephen said.

Bev dreamt about the painting. In the dreams the men's mouths moved but she couldn't hear sounds were coming from the throats. It was already a very green painting—the interior of the train, the upholstery on the seats—but in the dream the painting got greener. Grass and shrubs grew from it. The men dressed in women's clothing were tracking her through the tall grass. One engulfed her. She woke before ascertaining whether it was a man dressed as a woman or a woman who was mannish.

Blood seemed to be coursing down the face; that was how fast it was moving. It was impossible; she wanted to stanch it with her hands. Bev swung the car to the side of the road and put it in neutral.

She heard herself calling her daughter's name. Saw her hands lift Louise and felt her legs hurrying along under her. Good legs. She was still shouting when people started to emerge from the school building. Pricilla Barnard, Ivan Fiedel and then Roz, in gypsy skirts and ballet shoes and bangles, some kind of tchotchka on her head. Were they actually called ballet *shoes*? Or something else? Slippers. Later she felt she must have been trying to remind herself not to slip and fall.

Ivan had his arms out to receive the child.

"She's bleeding from the head."

"I was just getting sprinkles," Louise said, blinking away blood. She wasn't crying and seemed not to know what all the fuss was about. She didn't like that her hair was sticky.

She was rushed inside, an ambulance was called, she was fed into the back of the van along with her mother and taken away.

Crouched beside the ambulance attendant Bev prayed to God to spare Louise's brain. They could have anything but the brain—a wrist, a whole hand. She put her hands together, prayer position, and held them under her chin. She tried to make the gesture look ordinary. For a long time she had professed not to believe in God. It was natural but immoral to go asking for help from someone you didn't believe in.

"You probably don't have to pray too hard," the ambulance attendant said.

"What?"

He was a young kid, religious himself, from the Midwest. He had great faith in Jesus; that was one of the things that enabled him to do his job. This was only his tenth time out on an ambulance run as a full tech rather than a trainee.

"It's a superficial wound. Heads just bleed a lot."

"I was just getting the sprinkles," Louise said again.

"In your eyes?" Bev wanted them to do something about all the blood.

"No, on the floor. We had cookies with the colored ones on Monday."

"Oh, *sprinkles*!"

"Like jimmies." Louise was trying to sit up. The attendant gently prevented her. "I wonder why they're called jimmies."

"You don't jimmy them on, you sprinkle."

"You jimmy a lock."

They smiled at each other. Similar smiles might have been exchanged elsewhere when two people traveling in a foreign country discover that they speak enough of a third language in common to have a brief conversation, about the food or weather.

Louise hadn't been wearing her seatbelt. The gash in her forehead was fairly deep.

"I wouldn't think a seatbelt could do that kind of damage." As she stood holding Louise's hand Bev couldn't look. The surgeon was putting in stitches.

It had been when she drove over a safety bump in the narrow drive leading to the school. Bev never slowed enough. The metal seatbelt leapt up and hit Louise squarely in the forehead.

"Ironic," Bev said to Stephen. "The safety bump." They were all home together for the evening, Louise parading her bandage and three root beer lollipops she was committed to flaunting for a time before she ate them.

It was the kind of school that believed in abacuses and round praise. Instead of gym, Ivan took the students out on nature walks to collect rocks and robin egg shells and leaves. Occasionally a toad, who lived for a while in a terrarium in Ivan's office, where he also had a grand piano. Ivan said the toad liked Rachmaninoff in the morning. Roz and Ivan ran the school out of a grand dilapidated old mansion covered with ivy, the brick washed white. The manner in which they ran the school was not at all unlike the manner that they kept the building and grounds. Benign neglect, generous indulgence, a disregard for details that Bev felt was permissive rather than irresponsible.

"The roof will fall in on that place one day," Stephen said. "There's algae growing on the back patio. Someone'll slip and break a bone."

Bev had to disagree. Ivan smoked a pipe that moved him into and out of rooms swathed in aromas of cherry and maple. He was the sort of man whose lap you wanted to sit on. Stephen raised an eyebrow when she mentioned that.

"Not like a kinky thing. Like Santa." She couldn't explain it, how there was a whole class of men who in her mind existed to comfort people, in the manner of stuffed animals.

"Well. I can assure you Ivan Fiedel doesn't think of himself as a stuffed animal."

She would never be able to explain the many valences in her relationships with men. Men of all varieties. Lust wasn't the only valence available.

"Let me tell you a few things about men." Stephen's standard response.

She wondered whether it troubled him that she had knowledge of a few things about women, inaccessible to him.

⌒

Inverary. She kept thinking she knew what it meant, something like infirmary. But it wasn't even an old folks home. Bev's parents had suddenly moved south, after living all their lives on Long Island. It was 1973, a year after Deborah was born.

"That's what Jews do," Bev joked. Alone with the idea she was crushed. Her mother had helped so much with Louise. Had made it possible when Louise was two for Bev to go back to work. Now if she wanted to keep working what would she do with Deborah? Stephen's mother was an hour and a half away if the traffic was light. And aside from that she had a fear: If she left her girls with Stephen's mother they would be trained to turn away from her. Her Long Island accent and loose cotton clothing, Indian print skirts, the easy casualness of their household, sitting cross-legged on the living room floor, Jim Croce or Don McLean playing on the turntable. That would become anathema. The girls would learn to resent the friends passing through who slept on the sofa, meals taken at odd times or eaten from pottery bowls with chopsticks or sometimes cereal for dinner. Puffed rice. Ruffed pice, Stephen and Louise called it. Muddy baba ghanoush, tabouleh, curries Stephen makes in an electric fry pan. That is their life; they do not want any formality or glassware. They can drink their wine from jelly jars, Welch's grape with cartoon characters on the sides.

Her parents lived in Fort Lauderdale now, in a multistoried concrete building beside a golf course. Now once a year they'll fly down with the girls to visit. The girls will come to think of their Florida grandparents as a once a year event, like a holiday or the beginning of school.

An interminably slow elevator took them from ground level up to ninth floor. The first time she exited into the concrete tunnel that led out to the balcony walkway Bev found the other word she'd been thinking: penitentiary. A crippled woman lived in the apartment below her parents. She walked with metal devices that Deborah called canes, Louise crutches. There were cuffs that enclosed her forearms.

The first thing Bev's mother did was pound on the floor with the end of a broom. "A Visit With Denise," Stephen labeled this part of the trip. He had labels for the various segments that were replicated precisely each time they visited. "A Trip to the Bagelry," "A Drunken Pre-Dinner Interlude," "The Dying Talk," and "An Excursion to Publix" were others. Bev's father always bought a case of Fanta and Rocky Road ice cream. "For the kids," he said. Though the kids preferred vanilla.

Bev's parents were Saul and Evie. They quarreled. Stephen saw them as characters out of a Jewish novel.

Bev shrugged. "They're characters out of a Jewish *life*."

Stephen only encouraged them in their excesses of character. The way they quarreled was probably typical. Saul made an announcement directed at no one in particular about a shortcoming of Evie's. He might be announcing this from the bathroom or while bent over to retrieve a can of Fanta from the fridge. Then a few minutes later Evie on Saul. The remote control had food on it. Saul had left the butter out. It was lonely theater.

Denise hobbled up from her apartment. She too was a character, tragic and maimed. She was a Canadian and said her vowels differently. She had had scarlet fever as a child. Now she had MS. Her clothing seemed deliberately, willfully dowdy, a combination of items that had to have been culled from Evie's closet and clothes Bev believed could only have been copied from a child's wardrobe, enlarged for an adult. Gingham patterns, pinafores, coy white socks and saddle shoes. But then sometimes a silk scarf around her neck, or if she was feeling poorly, beige polyester slacks like Evie's, a cable knit cardigan over her shoulders.

"Here I am, still here, still here," Denise said as she advanced into the room, her crutches ahead of her. She greeted Evie's parakeets, knocking the rubber tip of one crutch against their cage.

"Ring a bell, Tonic. Ring a bell."

The other bird's name was Gin.

"He has a bad personality," Denise reported.

"He has a bad personality around you," Evie said.

Denise was young enough to be Evie's daughter, almost her granddaughter. Yet they played Rummy-O together and went for manicures. Denise was de facto invited with the family to dinner. She and Saul were the cutups, making requests and overtures to the waitstaff at the restaurant. Everyone at Scarlett O'Hara's knew them, was used to tolerating their hijinks.

"Bring us three vodka martinis on the double! Or at least three double martinis." This from Denise.

The restaurant brimmed with *Gone With the Wind* paraphernalia, hoop skirts and plantation photos and studio shots of Vivien Leigh and Clark Gable. There was a Confederate flag in the foyer. The fish was neutral in taste; it could have been anything in thin sauce. The girls had Shirley Temples.

"I wish I had lived then," Denise said.

"Why?" Louise said. "You would already be dead."

Denise lowered her voice. "Then I could order around the darkies." She frowned demonstrably. "I'm just kidding, for Jesus sake."

Stephen wished he could clout her.

But Saul and Evie and Denise were different people, they lived in a different world. Florida was slow and hot. Evie no longer drove. Alligators came up on the lawns. You couldn't walk on the grass; it was St. Augustine grass and stabbed at your feet.

"Let it go," Bev said to Stephen later. They were on the pull-out sofa bed in the TV room.

"It's funny how they call it the TV room. There's a TV in every room."

There was even a small black-and-white on the kitchen table.

The TV room smelled of full ashtrays but Bev couldn't find them. Her father's books crowded the coffee table and the desk where he sorted the mail and paid the bills. Mystery novels, metaphysical tracts and long books about the true religion of the self, *If You Meet the Buddha on the Road, Kill Him!* Did Saul really read these books?

Stephen found a diagram on a piece of notebook paper in Saul's hand. It was a diagram systematizing the universe, with God at the top and aspects of the human spirit below.

He handed it to Bev. "It's done as a flow chart."

She sat up in bed and examined it. "He has Lust on here."

Stephen looked over her shoulder. "Right in the center."

After Stephen fell asleep Bev lay alert on the sofa bed, resentful of the easy way he had dropped out of consciousness. She wanted to. She couldn't. Did her parents still make love? The way the grass punished your feet and the alternating blasts, outdoors and in, of hot gusts or frigid air, the rough skin of the crocodile, the cans of Fanta and of beans. Her father was always opening a can. It seemed they never used their stove, only the microwave. She felt sorry for her parents. Late in life they had embraced the technological age and in the process had evicted, she felt, everything good. She heard low laughter from behind their bedroom door. A laugh track. Her parents laughed, too. Their world now was television; it was how they planned their day.

～⌒～

The Bicentennial. Bev couldn't get excited about it. She didn't have a patriotic shred.

Their consciousness-raising group had been meeting for three years. Bev, Eileen Grizer, Meg Buckbinder, Pattie Jankowski, Sylvie Cooperman. A sixth sometimes showed up, Franny Miles-Johnston. The first to hyphenate her name. But she was a wedding photographer. She was often out in the Hamptons shooting a do. Her term for it.

"You've seen one wedding, you've seen too many weddings."

Franny was cynical and thin, the only one among them.

"Still and all I have to say I like weddings."

There was always one of them who couldn't resist.

"Even if they are a tool of patriarchal oppression."

No one took the bait. Enough of the patriarchal oppression.

"What they should do is have me shoot the divorces. That would bulk up my business."

Nobody missed Franny too much when she didn't show up.

CR group was wine drinking and ease, it was camaraderie. No one watched the time. Children weren't allowed; Louise lay on her stomach to spy on them from the top of the stairs. As a group of married women they felt during these evenings a little bit reckless, their feet up on the furniture, their hair loose on their shoulders. Some of them were braless; it was a time in the history of women when to go braless was to say something about the culture at large and your place in it, not just about your breasts.

There are parades planned for the Bicentennial. Cannons have been procured for the green at the center of town. In the center of every town, cannons and flags.

"They've just been stockpiling this stuff, waiting for an opportunity. All of Soundview will be a monument to warmongering."

Meg Buckbinder was an artist. She lived in a mural-painted mobile home in Sea Cliff with a glass blower. He was not her husband; he was her Man. He would tell you that if you met him, the way another person might inform you he was from Massachusetts. Meg had a difficult daughter who didn't belong to her Man. The daughter was from another time, when she had been married to an insurance agent. Years ago.

The daughter shouted a good deal. Exhausted herself shouting.

"So George says it's his cereal, if she wants some she can go buy her own box. He didn't mean in general, he meant right that instant. And she's on her way to school. So I say you're going to let her go to school on an empty stomach and he says it's not my stomach to worry about, right in front of her."

They are languid and feline on the sofa or the floor. This all is familiar, the rhythm of pouring and sipping wine is uninterrupted. And slices of cheese on a board, and fruit, and port wine cheese, and bread.

This seemed like the right moment so Bev said it. "I'm thinking of going back for my master's in social work."

Someone else was about to speak but then Eileen Grizer did. "Gus hit me."

Later Bev wondered whether Eileen had blurted that out thinking anyone going to get an M.S.W. would naturally be interested in assisting someone who'd gotten hit. But in truth, Eileen just blurted it at that moment because she couldn't have it working around inside her anymore. All of a sudden it seemed as if women had lost the ability to keep these secrets cloaked; they all came tumbling out.

And yet they are not so far along as they like to think. No one has asked Eileen about the yellowing bruise. Now everyone contrives not to look.

"What will you do?

"You have to leave him."

"Take the kids."

Where would she go? The children loved Gus, they doted on him.

They were practicing lines from a script. But not their script. The lines didn't convince, they were just mechanical movement. Gus was an easy man to get along with when sober, a whole other story when drunk. He made bets, wagered anything. Once he had wagered his car windshield in an Irish bar in Queens. He had wagered his leather wallet and everything in it, his social security card, all of it. When sober he had time for the children, he sang and played kickball, he knew randy limericks.

"I can't believe he'd do a thing like that." This from Pattie Jankowski.

"You're not supposed to say that." This from Meg.

"I mean I believe it but I don't *believe* it. You know what I'm saying."

"I know." Defensively.

"There must be a solution."

"There's no solution to Gus," Eileen said.

Gus was a dermatologist. Everyone wanted to be married to him and have Eileen's great skin and the big house in Locust Valley. Eileen had an English garden. Her children went to private school and camp in the summer.

"It's probable Gus will go on being Gus."

"And you?"

Eileen's lower lip trembled. "And me me."

Pattie stayed back at the end when the other women left.

"You want to go for a nightcap?"

"Why you talkee like that to me?" Bev was cleaning up the cheese board and plates. "Nightcap" made her think of cocktail dresses and swaggering men and waltzing. She'd had a lot of wine, probably too much. A headache would be next.

"We could go over to the Full Sail Inn."

"That place? That's the bar of the peg leg sailors and the town drunk."

"We have a town drunk?"

"Well, Gus."

"Gus doesn't drink there. His place is Reinhardt's."

Reinhardt's was up the other end of town, right on the beach. "Swinging Singles" went there, and cops, and people who worked for the town, some sad secretaries and office clerks.

It was true that mainly men patronized the Full Sail.

"What are they going to do, throw us out?"

It seemed reasonable to write Stephen a note. From the basement he heard the car ignition.

They bought a pack of cigarettes from the machine in the foyer. Winstons. Neither of the women had smoked since her first pregnancy. They sat at the bar and ordered whiskey sours.

"Girl's Night Out," someone remarked.

"Girl's Night Out."

It gave the patrons satisfaction to say it, repeatedly. When another one of the regulars showed up—

"Girl's Night Out."

Why was it the patrons objected to them? Perhaps that they were dressed wrong, that they were braless. And Bev with her big breasts. Oh she was a spectacle and in this dark bar there was no room for spectacles. Or that they are alone, for two women together are nonetheless women alone.

"Another whiskey sour," Pattie says.

When they leave they tip the bartender big but even he resents them.

The Matsuokas were the only foreigners who lived on their street. But Bev and Stephen were the only renters. On the first of the month Stephen would drive over to Mr. Clifford's house to drop off the check. He brought Deborah with him this time; she wanted rice pudding from the deli.

"It looks like the president's house."

He had never thought of that. It was true that the house was white, with twin columns and an expanse of lawn.

"Your tenants are here," the woman who answered the door shouted over her shoulder.

"You can give the lady the envelope."

Deborah handed it over solemnly.

She had questions. When Stephen explained it to her she cried. He had not known it was important to her that the house be theirs.

She and Louise liked to pretend that the half bathroom downstairs was a rocket that took off and flew to space. Some peeling wallpaper near the floor just outside the bathroom supported this illusion, and Louise, too, swore it was a result of blastoff. Now Deborah wanted nothing to do with the idea. She gathered her important possessions and kept them on her bed, as if physical contact with Mr. Clifford's house, his floor, would threaten her ownership. A Fisher-Price airport, a stuffed elephant, a peanut butter jar filled with blue and green sea glass, her "anky," a faded pink rag of a baby blanket: these were the things she valued. They were not to be given up to Mr. Clifford.

"Why don't we just buy it?" she asked at dinner.

Stephen shrugged and bit into his falafel. "Your mother's in school now."

Deborah didn't see what that had to do with anything. And her mother didn't even have a satchel like Deborah's plaid one.

"It's not for sale. He thinks he might want it someday for his daughter," Bev said.

They had made a policy of being honest. But what they did not understand was Deborah's incapacity to understand. Her mouth hung open. She was thinking, where is Mr. Clifford's daughter going to sleep? There were just three bedrooms and Louise didn't have bunk beds in hers.

She didn't know that Mr. Clifford's daughter was a seventeen-year-old girl. The house wouldn't be something she'd want until she was nearly thirty.

For a long time Deborah would worry about Mr. Clifford's

daughter. The daughter would hover in the hallways. Louise came home from school with a library book about ghosts and poltergeists that had a vaporous presence floating down a flight of stairs on the cover. That was Mr. Clifford's daughter.

One day Deborah becomes a girl who is no longer afraid. One day, or almost as suddenly as that, she takes up the stance of the older sister, Louise the timid younger. It is almost as if they have been waiting for this exchange. Deborah becomes athletic, she displays a smile full of strong white teeth. Whereas Louise's are weak, Louise needs braces, her teeth are an investment. The orthodontist is a woman in Locust Valley who works out of her stately home, ivory and shuttered, with a circular pebbled drive.

"I bet *they* don't rent," Deborah said.

It was a Saturday morning. Stephen was with them. He said nothing. In the waiting room he inspected the wainscoting.

The orthodontist wore emerald shantung, an authoritative rectangular pocket over each breast. She always wore a single strand of something—amber, pearls. She shook everyone's hand; she smelled expensive.

Sometimes Louise would whimper. They heard it from the waiting room. She had sucked her thumb for too long, for years. Now at bedtime Bev applied a bitter liquid to her thumb. But it didn't last. Louise would creep to the bathroom and scrub it off. She didn't mind the taste of soap. It went away after a little while.

Dr. Whalen had her arm around Louise's shoulder, as if the two of them had cut a deal. Louise swiped at her eyes with a balled tissue.

"She'll need something special. We've talked about it already."

Stephen leaned forward.

"A palatal expansion device." The orthodontist opened her own mouth and showed them. She would be installing it across Louise's upper palate, a little metal footbridge. Each day a small key would have to be inserted and turned. That would widen it.

"The whole palate?"

"Yes, the upper one."

Bev and the orthodontist talked off to the side. "It helps if you have some rituals around this." The same time every day, a routine, rewards.

Deborah watched the proceedings from her perch. She was coming to understand life as theater: that there are the lucky figures and the unlucky.

She was happy with her role.

Louise would run into her room and bar her door. Then Bev would lean against it, outside, reasoning, resting.

"If you postpone it'll just be worse at dinner."

On the sofa Louise cried and held her head. Silent tears worked out of her eyes. She was allowed to watch television. Deborah was expected, then, to help in the kitchen.

"I'm only eight."

"You're old enough."

She peeled potatoes and carrots, meted out the spices in measuring spoons. In this way, too, Deborah came to seem like the elder. Louise curled up, fetal, on the sofa and then, led by Bev, to her parents' bed. But Louise was learning things, too. *General Hospital, Edge of Night*, talk shows hosted by a woman named Dinah and a man named Merv. The orthodontic vise and teenage misery had hold of the inside of her head, but she was paying attention nonetheless. All this adult life flickering past. Ephemeral but she was catching it; she was storing it away. Deborah learned the nuts and bolts of adult life, paying rent and putting together a lasagna, but Louise was learning the submerged business, adultery and other, smaller betrayals, litigation, disappointments, the fine calibrations of emotion in adult life, when tantrums are no longer part of the repertoire. The two of them would pay attention in that selective way forever, Deborah noticing the pleasures of the potato ricer and the mock Tudor, Louise setting out after the complicated business of chasing after what the heart wants. The heart and the consumer both always wanting something else, or more.

Mrs. Qwee. She was barely as tall as Deborah, though would have been taller if she could unhunch. She stepped cautiously, as if on eggs. Stephen claimed it was fear of land mines. He had read a lot about the war, had kept watching TV after Bev said she was tired of watching, it was making her anxious. Whenever they mentioned

Mrs. Qwee in conversation they included how she was one of the boat people. It was a neighborhood novelty. The Jankowskis put her up in their TV room; the children had to move all their toys out. Mrs. Qwee owned nothing, only the clothes on her back. People from the neighborhood visited with gifts: slippers, a toothbrush, Ragg wool socks, a cactus. She couldn't make much of the toothbrush. Most of her teeth were gone.

"We should take someone in," Bev said.

Stephen was trying to fix a problem with the eight-track tape player. "We don't have extra room."

"The girls could share a room. They could sleep in Deborah's bunk beds."

"That's unrealistic."

"Why? It would be good, we'd be doing something."

After a few nights Mrs. Qwee came to the Jankowskis, Ed and Pattie, with a request. At this time she knew so little English and they so little Vietnamese that everyone resorted to hand gestures, nodding. It was determined she had a problem with the bed.

"She wants it on the floor," Pattie told Bev. "She's not any trouble."

"But what?"

Pattie had to think about it. She was a pale woman with pale hair. Later she developed a condition that would cause her to lose her skin pigmentation, her fair skin giving way to skin that was rabbit nose pink, nearly albino. "But I can't anticipate her needs. I try to make her more comfortable, but then it'll seem like I make it worse."

"She doesn't like creature comforts."

Creature comforts. Chocolate chip pancakes, central heating, central air. The shower nozzle had Pulse and Massage settings. The Jankowskis were proud of these things. Pattie made strudel.

"She's different than us, I guess."

"She likes to bathe her feet. I got her a little bin."

There are no Vietnamese in Soundview except for the boat people. You see them sometimes in Gristedes, or at the post office. Maybe half a dozen families in town have taken in someone; there was a push for host families on the part of both the Catholic and Methodist churches. The Jankowskis are Catholic. But they believe in the validity of all religions, they are not interested in holding Bev and Stephen up to a standard for the casual or non-adherence to their faith. At Passover, Bev likes to have a seder. It's the only vestige of her Judaism that interests her, this ritual. She arranges a tray with the bitter herbs, the salt water, the shankbone, the egg. It seems wrong that the egg is the food of mourning. She makes the charoset happily, chopping apples and walnuts that Deborah mixes with the sweet wine. Then the cup for Elijah. The Jankowskis are invited across the street for the seder dinner with Mrs. Qwee. And Stephen invites two engineers from work who are visiting from overseas, England and India. The men's names are Graham and Pradesh. They live like Stephen does—all engineers must be born from one engineer womb or strand of DNA, there must be a lathe or press that manufactures them. They take their bottles of beer and go down to the cellar. The hot water heater lurking and dusty, Stephen's computer console, sink leaks. These things interest them. Seder doesn't interest them.

Mrs. Qwee is small as a doll. She has to hoist herself up on the furniture. Bev gets her a low stool Stephen bought for Louise to sit on in the shower when she broke her ankle and had to keep the cast dry. Bev and Pattie eat crudités from a plastic sectional tray and talk about their children, who are out in the neighborhood together. What does Mrs. Qwee think about? The cut up carrots and celery and especially the pieces of cauliflower suddenly look strange to Bev, crude and naked. Improper. Maybe they don't eat crudités in Vietnam. There was always the joke about the Chinese eating dogs. Bev and Pattie drink sidecars, their tradition at seder and at Thanksgiving. Hot tea for Mrs. Qwee. She has the face of a sphinx. Of course Bev would think that, as the woman is ancient and foreign. And so silent she is like a venerated tree. Around her there is the kind of elegant silence that Bev imagines would be around the redwoods in California. It makes her uncomfortable, in the presence of such a person, to be discussing Louise's teeth, Deborah's inexplicable spate of bed wetting, the second mortgage Stephen wants to take out on the house. Shrapnel, nerve gas, mortars, killings off of villages. Whole places obliterated. The Jankowskis were told when they picked up Mrs. Qwee that the rest of her family was missing, presumed dead. She will never see them again. Here she is in a living room in America, about to have her first seder. She hardly knows what a Jew is.

None of the boat people came to live with them. But there were others. It was Bev who shepherded them.

Now they lived in a house they owned, Stephen and Bev's first. Louise made a commemorative plate in Studio Arts and Crafts. Maroon glaze, but in the center a studious, asymmetrical representation of the new house. Below that the date: March 30, 1979. The first time Bev saw it she didn't notice the tiny cat's head etched in one of the windows. Their cat, a tabby. Their cat had six claws, the extra one in the hollow between, in human terms, thumb and forefinger. For this the cat was thought to have special powers.

"Now we have a house that's our house," Deborah said. No more Mr. Clifford's ghost daughter prowling around.

Bev would hear them bragging. It was a new house, yes. The girls had been allowed to choose the colors of their rooms. Petal Pink for Deborah, Sun Yellow for Louise. But the split ranch had been put up in no time; the construction was cheap, the walls and doors hollow. All the flooring downstairs was linoleum over cement. The house had been even more inexpensive than others the developer was offering. This stretch of road was rutted and pocked with deep potholes that filled when it rained.

In the room designated as her office Bev hung her framed degree, Master of Sociology. On the wall was a silhouette of Don Quixote and Sancho Panza, a watercolor of the flowers that bloom blue if planted in soil of a certain acidity. Hydrangeas. It was one of her favorite words and flowers. There were photographs of her daughters on her desk in Lucite frames, a photograph of herself in college when she had danced. Slim then. Or slimmer. She was not sure how the little Quixote had ended up on her wall. In the old house it had hung in the bathroom.

In her last year of high school her father had come to meet with her and the guidance counselor, a ruddy man, well-meaning. He also coached JV football. It was at this time, perhaps, that her mother had begun not leaving the house. The stockpiling began in the freezer, meals for weeks.

It was clear the counselor liked her. That was not the problem. She understood that he liked her but was not her advocate. That word would not have been available to her then; she had no way of protesting the gap that existed between fondness and advocacy.

"She's pretty; she'll get married," the counselor said.

Her father crossed his legs. "Anyone can get married."

Marry well, the counselor meant. A doctor or a judge, someone for whose career it would be necessary to have a pretty wife. Her good looks were not idiosyncratic. She had mainstream, pinup looks. Her face in high school even a little vacant. Not much worried her: that is what her face communicated.

Her mother had never worked at a paid job. Now in Florida she watched her soaps, cleaned the parakeets' cage, kept the freezer filled with ice cream, Howard Johnson's toasties, fish sticks, sherbet. There was always a carton of cigarettes; they too were kept in the freezer. If the supply got low there were reprimands. Once a week she went to have her hair washed and set. Her mother knew little of Freud, of Marx. Yes, Freud was a Jew but he had crazy ideas that in the end discredited all Jews. He had written about little boys and their mothers being in love or having sexual contact; he had put cocaine on his eyes. And her mother knew nothing of Erving Goffman, whose ideas had convinced Bev to get her degree in sociology. Her copy of *The Presentation of Self in Everyday Life* was densely underlined, the margins filled with notes, as if she were writing a book in response to his book, sociological midrash.

She dreamed of writing a seminal book, one that would make her last name common in the field. It seemed every important text in her discipline had falling behind it the shadow of the book that had not yet been written. It was the story of women. The researchers had told the story of men. In the margins of Goffman, in her fine clear cursive she wrote copiously the parts Goffman hadn't written; she conversed with him and appended and made the new distinctions. There would be female executives, women sitting at the heads of boards. That would change everything; it would not be only the women hurrying along the streets with their new briefcases that would change.

Yet she could not get the writing onto her own piece of paper. The typewriter ribbon sat unused. She had bought a replacement for when that time came.

"I am like my mother, with the freezer," she said aloud. Sometimes she pulled out strands of her hair and lay them on the desk beside the typewriter, beside the dog-eared Goffman.

All her clients were women. Some didn't have driver's licenses. They had lost their privileges or they had never bothered to learn. Others appeared not to speak; they entered the house and averted their eyes as one does in countries where one has not learned to speak even the rudiments of the language, who by some oversight or haughtiness has not even bothered to learn "hello," "please," "thank you." Anyone can learn "thank you," even in the most distant or obscure of tongues.

Louise and Deborah stood expectantly at the stair railing when the doorbell rang.

"Maybe don't greet them like that," Bev said. "I'm trying to run this like a business."

Now when the doorbell rang the girls ran for the back of the house. On a good day, they watched the after-school special. If the program was about girls, Louise and Deborah were glued. One featured a girl who drank scotch and milk out of a thermos she brought to school. She said the wrong things in class and nearly fell out of her desk.

Deborah, laughing, kicked against the floor with the heels of her shoes. "Oh my god," she said several times. She was smiling.

"It's not funny."

"Yes it is."

In another one the main character was a boy but they watched anyway because he took drugs and gained superhuman strength. He broke the glass in the school's trophy case and knocked all the trophies on the floor. This seemed according to the movie the very worst thing he could think of to do. Later he ran through a plate glass window on the second floor and was cut to ribbons. He was shown in slow motion running toward the window but not afterwards. The next time they showed him he was just in his casket.

"Mental," Deborah said.

Neither could have said what her mother did for a living, downstairs with those quiet women. When their mother went out they typed ransom notes on her Underwood. One or the other of them had been kidnapped, was being held in a basement. "Undisclosed location," Louise said, spelling "undisclosed" for Deborah. All over the news hostages were being taken, it was no less outrageous or common a part of the daily fabric of life now than a nuclear meltdown, something discussed at breakfast over a Danish.

They would place the notes. Sometimes then they hid for hours. Once they climbed the chain link fence behind the house and into a kind of wilderness, mulberry bushes and dense bramble. There were dolls people had lost, liquor bottles, Frisbees. They had a book of matches and lit some, stamping and panicking when some brambles caught fire. Deborah was being held at gunpoint in the desert. Louise had been abducted and sold as a slave. The envelopes sat in their mother's purse, their father's briefcase.

Bev came to Deborah. She had the sheet of onion skin paper. "This isn't funny," she said.

"We were just messing around."

"Louise and me did it. It was both of us."

"I don't care who it was. Knock it off."

Louise used the typewriter to compose notes to her cousin. This was Parker's oldest child, six months younger than Louise. His son was strong, athletic, but so dyslexic he could hardly be coaxed to read. Adam. His daughter was his jewel and prize. Her name was Petra; she had leukemia. For a while after she lost her hair to the chemotherapy she wore scarves. But she had grown defiant; often she went out now in public with a bare bald head. She and Louise wrote to each other in code, Z for A and Y for B and X for C. When this came to seem too obvious they invented a language of pictographs mixed in with the A's and B's and Y's. Louise liked the look of her code letters best when typed. She added in the line drawings of swans and ribbons after.

One of the clients was Evelyn. In looks she reminded Louise of

Petra. Looks but not at all personality. Even after she came down with leukemia, Petra remained ebullient. She played the piano; her favorite song was Abba's "SOS" played at top volume. She liked to lapse from Mozart to the Beatles without warning, and then maybe to a tune from *Annie*. She would start anywhere and switch anywhere and detour anywhere. Whereas Evelyn made Louise think of grass or earth. Something always there that you didn't think about.

Evelyn would arrive at the door in clothes all of the same color. She was taking courses at the state university at Farmingdale toward a degree in horticulture. Her clothes were most often brown. She knelt in dirt, let it run through her fingers. There was a feeling she would like to dig herself a big hole with that spade and climb into it.

One day she showed up when Louise and Deborah were home on their own. She lounged against the railing along the front steps. "Your mother here?"

"She's out getting dinner."

Deborah stepped out onto the front stoop. "Did you have an appointment?"

"Yeah."

"Well, she's not here."

"We were on for four."

Deborah and Evelyn eyed each other. They were the only match; Louise wasn't even part of it.

"Well like I said, she's not here."

"I had someone drop me off. They won't be back for an hour."

Indeed, there was no car parked near the house.

"You wanna come in and call someone?"

Evelyn stepped indoors. "No one to call." She was not disconsolate; she was merely stating a fact.

"You want a Coke?" Deborah was on her own now. Louise had completely retreated, had gone back to the TV in their parents' bedroom at the back of the house. Deborah and Evelyn sat down at the kitchen table.

"I'm not supposed to drink this."

"Coke?"

"Too much sugar. Do you have sugar free? A Tab?"

"My mother doesn't let us drink those. They kill rats."

"That's a good one," Evelyn said. She shook her head and hung it between her hands, as if she planned to stay for a while and talk. "Old Beverly. In all her regalia."

"It's the saccharin, is what kills rats."

Evelyn didn't like to think about rats. She asked Deborah not to mention them again.

"Oh, I know what you mean. Louise hates bugs."

"I hate bugs, too. Which is bad, since I'm always working in the dirt. You can train yourself to desensitize."

Deborah was only half paying attention. She wished Evelyn's ride would come back and get her. Probably there was something good on television.

But Evelyn was still there when Bev came home from the market. "I needed to see you," she said to Bev. Her voice was too loud.

Deborah walked out of the room. Down the hall. She heard old Evelyn as she left. Old Evelyn, Old Bev.

"My brother's moving to Santa Fe," Evelyn was saying. "Now I got nowhere to live."

Evelyn liked to do things boys did and she looked like one. Her clothes were baseball caps, T-shirts, baggy jeans. She resented jewelry; she resented skirts. She worked in their garden; she made a garden along the side of the house where there had been weeds and untended dirt. Pebbles were trucked in. She and Bev collected sea glass and mussel shells from the beach. The shells were a dark, opalescent blue, mysterious in piles, like things recovered from a shipwreck. Evelyn lived in the spare room downstairs. Other than extra baseball caps she owned almost nothing. Louise looked in the closet and drawers. There were some undershirts, a necklace with a pendant of a saint on it that Evelyn didn't wear, hiking boots and Ragg socks, *Zen and the Art of Motorcycle Maintenance*. A title that made no sense. She had become a snoop. She was on her way to becoming the sort of woman who has one very close friend and who speaks to the friend every day, tells her everything she is thinking, gossips about people she can barely count among her acquaintances. Whereas Deborah would have many friends, a gregarious crowd of both sexes. Even as an adult Deborah would go on vacations, ski trips or camping, in groups.

There was a Degas print of ballet dancers hung over the bed in the guest room. It belonged to Stephen. Evelyn mentioned maybe he would like to hang it over his drafting table, in the ping pong room.

"I'd prefer to keep it there."

"You got it, Mr. Jones."

Why Mr. Jones? Nobody bothered to ask. Evelyn could only be counted upon to be Evelyn.

How long would Evelyn stay? No one knew. It would be easier to predict the path of the next nor'easter or the probability of Venus being visible from their back yard than it was to say how long Evelyn would live downstairs.

"Is she bothering you?" Bev asked.

"No. I don't mean she's bothering."

"So just that she's staying here bothers you."

That he had to explain it to her. That it couldn't just be understood and accepted that having this person living in the guest room indefinitely was anomalous, a discomfort, from a social perspective. People could come to stay but then in a week or month they would leave. He couldn't get that across.

"She has nowhere to go."

"You're her therapist. I thought you were supposed to help her solve that problem."

"She needs some kind of subsidized housing. Probably also a degree of supervision, to make sure she takes her meds."

"Okay, well."

"It doesn't exist right now. She'd be living on the street."

"You can't be their hotelier."

"I can do something."

You could not say Evelyn was appreciative. There was an air of resentment that traveled through the house with her. The fact of their family, the predictable smells of rooms and contents of cabinets, the predictable notations on the wall calendar in the kitchen. *Louise—orthodontist—4:30, Stephen—checkup, oil change Volaré, oil change Datsun, Deborah b'day.* This routine was cause for estrangement. Evelyn had not known the reassurance of routine. Her mother had been a drinker, her father erratic, a gambler who up and left.

But she liked having her feet massaged. And she liked Louise's *Mad* magazine.

"This thing is funny. It's for kids?"

"Kids and grownups."

Evelyn had her feet in Bev's lap. It was a Saturday, late morning. Stephen was off at his checkup. He said his doctor was obese and smoked cigars; it was hard to take advice from such a person. But Stephen's eczema had been very bad. So he had no choice.

"There's a corresponding organ for every spot on the foot."

"My Achilles tendon is killing me," Evelyn said.

"We'll have to look that up."

Louise wanted her feet rubbed. Evelyn volunteered. "Lie on the floor here and put your feet up."

Deborah was off elsewhere in the house, looking for something to do outdoors. The road outside was too rutted for roller skating. Her front bicycle tire had gone flat.

Evelyn wanted to be one of them. Therefore Evelyn was a threat. Though Deborah would not have been able to say in what capacity Evelyn wanted to be one of them. A parent? A child?

A son. That thought whistled through Deborah's head but of course was crazy. Evelyn was a woman, nearly old enough to be Deborah's mother, though small and fast, with the baseball caps and her disregard for her hair. She smelled not dirty but like dirt, like soil.

"You have to cut those back. Be stern with them."

She was at her best in the garden, with gloves on, squinting at her handiwork. She knew what to plant next to what, what to separate, versions of all the things she didn't know in people. She was disastrous at a dinner party, couldn't make conversation, sat and scowled at her food. Even Mrs. Qwee was less of task, especially now with her rudimentary English in addition to her willingness to smile.

"Imagine that she's your teenage son. That's how she's best related to."

"She's a thirty-year-old woman."

"I'm just telling you."

He showed Evelyn how he had arranged everything in the garage, explained what he was doing as he changed the brake pads on the Volaré. She was dexterous and unspeaking. All her questions were gestures and raised eyebrows.

"Like this."

And then she would imitate him, and he would signal his approval.

One day her stuff was gone. She had also taken the bed sheets.

Stephen went back to teaching Deborah. Her questions were manifold. She took all his patience.

The Search for Meaning. A representation of the cosmos on the cover. But it didn't matter. Everyone might end up as mulch.

He put the book down.

"What's mulch?"

He had not anticipated the question. Louise was developing breasts. He could see the outlines of her training bra through her T-shirt. He didn't want to see.

"Mulch is, well mulch is what makes new things grow."

"What does that have to do with God?"

Who knows if there's a God. There's us, now, and caterpillars and other insects and mulch. But he didn't say it. Bev wouldn't forgive him and then he'd have to do all the work to retract his statements. Retracting, when you were dealing with children, was the most difficult thing.

They were at the public library. At one time the buildings had been stables for a great landowner. You could still see it in the architecture. Though now the interior filled of course with books. The mint green water tower loomed overhead, bulbous metal, dropped down from another world. It cast a large shadow.

The town was Catholic, Saint Gertrude's bulk and cross resting on a high hill in the shadow of the water tower. On Sundays, cars inched in an unbroken line toward the church. Tuesdays the public school released children early for religious instruction.

Louise loved Agatha Christie, especially the Miss Marples. But she would read anything; she read the newspaper and Bev's self-help books and a book Bev had called *Memoirs of an Ex–Prom Queen*.

"There's a part in it where she has a baby into the toilet. Only it's not like a whole baby, it's just bits and blood."

Deborah covered her ears and made as if to scream. But it was playacting. What she wanted was an explanation.

"She had a miscarriage, sweetheart."

"What's miscarriage?"

"The baby couldn't live in her womb, she expelled it."

Deborah had pigtails, the tips of which bounced on her shoulders when she bobbed her head. "It doesn't *live* in there, it just grows. It doesn't live till it's out."

He had been the one so insistent about teaching them this. If he'd had a stick instead of words you would say he had beaten it in. His daughters had friends right up the road and friends that sat next to them in class who were being taught *life begins at the moment of conception*. The Minicozzis, the Salernos, the Imhof twins. A bunch of parrots parroting their parents.

He was trying to be a balancing influence. At least until they were old enough to investigate and come to their own conclusions.

"Well believe me this one wasn't living when it came out," Louise said.

"It wasn't *swimming* in the toilet bowl," said Deborah.

They were laughing.

He wanted to shelter them. Even as he let them read the likes of *Memoirs of an Ex–Prom Queen*. Louise was twelve, Deborah eight.

"It's not that I want to limit them," he said. He had let Louise read the Stephen King books, *Carrie* and *The Stand*. *The Stand*, for God's sake, was a rendering of the apocalypse.

"This, I assure you, is not the apocalypse," Bev said.

"But still."

"But nothing."

They were talking about a divorce. Everyone got divorces. Even the Matsuokas. Their daughter Lorraine ate toasted seaweed instead of Fritos as a snack. They were that traditional and yet they had gotten a divorce. The husband's name was Ots. He had a squint. He was dating a red-haired woman now. They played golf.

"It's not the divorce," he said.

"I know." But there was nothing else to be done now. She could not control it. She could not control who she loved.

Cannot control *yourself*, he thought. But didn't say it.

It was Pattie Jankowski. What surprised Stephen was how he had misguessed—he had worried it was Evelyn. But this was in some ways more ludicrous, a comedy. First the CR group and then Bev and Pattie had been on the committee to organize the Bicentennial Parade and of course most of all they were neighbors. Pattie's two boys who had walked in the parade with fife and drum. Louise and Deborah had been two of fifty children walking beside the flower float, each child wearing the banner of a state. Louise was North Dakota, Deborah Delaware. Pattie was a schoolteacher. She had taught them a song.

What did Della wear, boy, what did Della wear?
She wore her brand new jer-her-zee, she wore her brand new jersey.
Why did Wiscon sin boy, why did Wiscon sin?

Della wear made sense but not the part about sin. Wiscon wasn't any kind of a name.

So Bev and Pattie had gotten close folding paper flowers or something, he didn't know. And a germ of something had grown between them. Coffee and then lunches and then blam, they were eating each other's pussies.

"It's not like that, Stephen. There are things other than sex." She was very calm. Giving him the old eye roll.

"How do you like eating pussy? We could compare notes."

He was very angry.

It was Bev's conviction that they should just tell the girls all at once.

"Double whammy it. We're getting a divorce, your mother wants to eat pussy."

He was looking to get her angry, too. It seemed only fair.

"Wants to eat pussy; *ergo* a divorce."

"Jesus Christ, Stephen!"

They were both agnostics and had raised their kids agnostic, if "agnostic" is an ontological state of which kids are even capable. Kids *believed*. Though without instruction they probably wouldn't come up with the fire and brimstone. And most without instruction wouldn't figure the creator as a man in robes. The universe itself was both creator and created. That's how Stephen remembered thinking about it when he was a child, before his thinking got tangled up with Episcopalianism. The lilac was in and of itself proof of God's existence. The lilac, the ocean, the edible berry growing on the vine. There was no need to look beyond any of these things for their creator. It was enough that they existed.

His girls believed in all the wonders of the world. Though their wonders were of course different than his had been. As far as he knew there were no berries on the vine here in Soundview. But Italian ices were proof of God's existence. There was a place called Augie's in Oyster Bay. The great florid Augie himself made real lemon ices. You could tell by the pips. Italian ices, toads, the makeup counter at the department stores, Boogie Boards, tambourines, fish. He had taken them once on a fishing boat. Bev had objected but he'd wanted them to see the great breadth and width of the tuna as they got hauled up and over the side of the boat, the great moving gasping gills. And they had. Though they both had puked from seasickness. But even the puking had amazed them, afterwards, when they were sipping from a can of Coke and feeling better.

"I projectiled," Louise said.

"So did I." The pigtails bobbing.

But now they might need some religion. Something to fall back on, if their mother wanted to divorce and eat pussy.

God he was angry.

"But it's *empty*," Bev said. She was wearing some sort of scarf that covered her hair. She had a turquoise head. "It's just a crutch."

"Don't tell me about crutches," he said.

She gave him a quizzical look.

"Oh, you know." He was stalling. He had no idea what he meant. But he felt he did mean something.

He called it a field trip. They just walked over one Sunday morning when Bev was out at the Farmer's Market. He made them put on nice pants but said they could wear their tennies. If they combed their hair.

He had to help them open the heavy wooden door.

"Ooh, spooky," Deborah said.

"You're not supposed to talk," said Louise.

They were interested in the pews, the kneelers, the censer, the book of hymns and psalms. They pointed and whispered questions. Why did Jesus have to hang on the cross? Wouldn't it hurt? And then when the parishioners went to the front to take the Host. What was it? Bread? Could they go do it? Why not? What was a resurrection? How did it supersede woods, planets, the fireflies that dot the bushes at dusk, the underside of the sea where the corals breathe water and the lobster with its meat-filled claw drifts against the wooden slats of the trap the fishermen set? His girls had no cosmogony. Nature was their only explicator.

When you have been raised without religion, all religions become the occult.

He was startled. He had not thought their education, especially Louise's, would have been as secular as all that.

"You're not allowed to go up front for that. Not unless you're a Catholic."

Deborah stood up. "I want to be a Catholic."

Louise lifted a hymnal and placed it on her lap.

On the way out they ran into the Jankowskis. This was Pattie's family, though luckily sans Pattie. Maybe she was out at the Farmer's Market, too. *Getting some zucchinis.* He almost laughed out loud.

"Hello, Ed."

"Hello, Steve."

There was no way not to be awkward in each other's presence. *Eatingpussyeatingpussyeatingpussy.* That was right underneath. He was trying for it not to be; he knew that was not all it was, that it was a lot more complicated. He and Bev had never had very much in common. Getting married was just what you did at twenty-two in 1968. They had gotten married and started having kids just before the big paradigm shift, Janis Joplin et al. That may also have been the case for Ed and Pattie.

How inadequate he and this man were. Their flaccid penises tucked inside their corduroy pants. They hadn't been enough. Sometimes recently Stephen pictured himself with a giant penis, stiff as a newel post. It was easier to think about the circumstances in terms of the penis than it was to start broadening and generalizing. They were men.

Ed's two boys stood and looked at the two girls. He got a glimmer of Louise and Ed's older one noticing each other. Two colts. The way colts could nuzzle or kick. How they were at the pre-beginning of everything, knew next to nothing about the other sex. And then his youngest and Ed's knew nothing, nothing at all. When they were on the road, Deborah still asked to stop for the bathroom by saying she "had to go wee wee's."

Their mother and Pattie. He felt it would blow the lid off to tell them. Blow the lid off what? Off childhood? Off something here that was in a state of equilibrium.

"Did you just start attending?" Ed asked. "I didn't know you were Catholic."

It's Louise who speaks first. "We're not anything. We're nothing."

"We're trying it out," Stephen said. He couldn't meet Ed's eye.

He knocked on the bedroom door. He had begun doing that.

"You can come in."

He stepped inside and stood with his back to the door, almost leaning against it.

She was putting earrings on in front of the mirror and glanced at him sideways.

"You don't have to do that."

"What?"

"Knock. It's your room too."

There was a giant almost sculptural yellow plastic butterfly affixed to the wall above their bed. That would come down.

He went to his dresser and opened the top drawer. In it he kept all the flotsam that didn't belong anywhere else. Coins, screws, nuts, back issues of *Machine Design* he couldn't bring himself to throw in the garbage. Tie clips. Cuff links. He never wore tie clips but they were something people thought you needed if you were a man with a white-collar job. It was comforting to sift through these things, this detritus. Oh and recently he'd bought an issue of *Playboy*. He kept it among the *Machine Design*s. Gerry's suggestion. His friend Gerry. Gerry was kind of crazy. He had divorced his wife a while back. He had a salt-and-pepper beard already, at thirty-five. He had a pilot's license. One thing he did was pick up waitresses and barmaids, get them interested in him when he was eating or drinking at their establishment. Then tip well and hold out the promise of going for a plane ride.

It was Gerry who said "Get yourself a little porno. Feel like a man again."

"I never liked that stuff."

"We can go to a club. I know a place out by Roosevelt Field, the tits are huge."

He wasn't sensing this was the way his life would go. But where else? He saw no path.

"Do you want to talk to me about something?" Bev stood in the middle of the room, her hands on her hips.

"I'm having second thoughts about that Montessori school."

"So that's what this is about."

He stopped fussing with the detritus. "It doesn't give them enough structure."

"They like it just fine. They don't need that much structure."

"Now they do."

He broached the subject of parochial school.

"Are you out of your fucking tree?"

"Chaminade's got a very good reputation, among some people."

She was livid. But he felt very calm. Supremely. With enough concentration, he could almost control his own peristalsis. That's how calm he was.

"I'm not sending my kids to school with those fanatics."

" 'Fanatics' is laying it on a little thick. Don't you think, Bev?"

They came around to a compromise. They would send the girls to the public school in town.

He didn't get to use his trump card: "Pattie's kids are being raised Catholic."

They make us walk in lines. Boys on one side, girls on the other." Deborah threatened to go back to the old school, the teacher she liked, a woman named Priscilla. At the old school they called the teachers by their first names.

It was too far to walk, he pointed out.

She would take a taxi.

"We're not allowed to talk until they say we're allowed to talk. Like if we're working on maps or handwriting we have to be quiet unless they say."

Louise was more sanguine. For one thing the middle school had a better library. She was reading a big book about Karen Ann Quinlan, a brain dead girl being kept alive on a machine.

"What's brain dead?" Deborah wanted to know.

"Your body's alive but not your brain." He felt tears behind his eyes. It was the other way for him, his mind going a hundred and eighty miles an hour all the time, his body limp, penis flaccid as a sock in a drawer. He had tried to get something going with the *Playboy* and had gotten nowhere.

She came to him when he was at his drafting table.

She picked up one of the ping pong paddles. "Will you play?"

First he made them Bloody Marys.

He was a better player than she was. He had the eye-hand coordination. He played furiously, the drink in his left hand. Red splotches appeared on his side of the table.

"Let me get in a couple of shots, for Christ's sake."

"It's a fight till the death," he said. For a moment he actually imagined himself a gladiator in a winged hat, with a breastplate.

She put her paddle down and approached him around the side of the table.

"Hark! Declare yourself, forsooth!" He didn't know what he was saying. He held up his paddle. He was just pulling words out of somewhere.

Upstairs, the heels of the girls' shoes made their familiar clacking noises. They were in the kitchen, fixing tuna-on-toast sand-wiches.

This was their life. There was relish in the refrigerator, a bowl of red Jell-O, more than one jar of marmalade from his mother's trips back to England.

Why was he thinking of these things? What mattered relish, marmalade, Jell-O? What did they have to do with a life, his life, any life?

He thought of the blue Karen Ann Quinlan book on the end table in the living room. Louise on the sofa with a blanket over her knees, reading.

"Dad, I never want to finish this book." So quietly he had hardly been able to hear her.

Bev was standing close. Too close to the gladiator. "Stephen," she said. "I don't want to leave."

He felt suddenly as if he had been walking in the desert for days, among the saguaro and brush. He had an image of himself like Jesus, walking with a piece of lumber canted across his back. Maybe not a cross but definitely lumber.

"What about Pattie Jankowski?"

"It was nothing. It wasn't what you think."

"I'm not asking." The gladiator was not asking.

"Stephen, please. I know you're humiliated."

He put down his paddle. He allowed her to embrace him.

"I'm not so humiliated."

Just like that. The question of other women faded. Questions can. Fade, fade, and then submerge. Go deep under the sea with the detritus and tuna. For the duration of eighteen bottles of relish. Maybe more. They were able to go on like that for a while.

TWO

The turn of the decade. Now something different will happen. Bev had a fervent wish. But for what? What sort of change, upheaval, realignment? It was a time of great unrest inside of her. Though not the country as a whole. The country as a whole was settling down. The country as a whole was climbing up on Ronald Reagan's lap. Capacious. What of Stephen? He had changed somehow. She couldn't tell whether his core had ossified or dissolved. For she believed in a core at the center of each person if not a soul, the core structural and nourishing.

The phone rang in the middle of the night.

In the dark of their room Stephen gasped. Not passionate, but anguish often sounds like passion.

The phone returned to its cradle. She heard him settling his body back into the bedclothes.

"Petra died."

"My God."

"Parker found her. She had some papers with her, some of her writing."

They lay in their bed and did not speak. She wanted morning to come because she didn't like bad news in the night; she didn't want morning to come. Louise would have to be told. Deborah wasn't of any great concern—she had not been close to Petra and more importantly, she accepted death as a ritual. When their tabby had died the eulogy and burial had been of solace and interest to Deborah. She liked holidays; she liked spring cleaning and autumn bagging of leaves and send-offs and homecomings. Whereas Louise hated ceremony. If permitted she would have skipped the first day of school, the first day of all things. There are some people, people unlike Bev and Deborah, who do not like to be reminded of the continuity of days, of heritage and time passing. Louise lived as if each day were a clean tablet, the tablet wiped clean as clouds each night. As if nothing ramified. She would never, Bev predicted, raise a family.

And yet she was the one who kept a journal. Like Petra.

"It's in code," Stephen said suddenly.

"It what?"

"Petra's journal. It's all in some kind of language she made up."

"Parker'll crack it. If anyone."

"That's what he's betting on."

"Is he okay?"

"He's talking straight but he's not there. Once he comes to himself they'll have to sedate him."

It was autumn, an appropriate time. Death was consonant. When she got up that morning the girls were already in their Fair Isle sweaters and corduroys outdoors, taking running leaps into piles of leaves. It was Saturday. The day of the apple festival at the deaf school.

Louise was wearing mittens. Her hands were always cold.

It should not have been a Saturday. Had it been a weekday, they would be somber, disoriented, pleased to be kept home. It was only special to be home when everyone else was at school. They would be allowed to put their pillows on the sofa, Bev would give them magazines and soup. Not on a Saturday, it didn't work.

They couldn't absorb "dead." They did what others had done; they fumbled and fixed on "dying." Louise saw her cousin on the top bunk in her mint room, mint sheets, mouth in the "O" of pain or sleep, hands restless. The picture she got was not of Petra dead and therefore Petra was not.

They had bits of leaves all over them, in the weave of their sweaters, stuck to their corduroys.

"Come sit here, Lou." Bev patted her lap.

"We want to go more in the leaves."

But they understood. The mourning ritual was about to begin. They just did not yet know how, they were waiting to be told. They were waiting for the hearse and the casket; they had seen death on TV. What came before that they didn't know. They didn't own any black clothes.

They had hot cider with stick cinnamon and played "American Pie" on the turntable. A favorite of Petra's. But it went on forever, more than twelve minutes. Bev got down on the floor and lay on her back. The girls didn't seem to want to be touched. They walked around the living room, putting their hands on books, a decorative plate engraved with the words "Health, Love and Wealth and the Time to Enjoy Them," tiger-striped shells Bev had arranged in a dish, the clay mandala on the wall with a stunned-looking face at its center, a large cylindrical candle with dust on the rim. Stephen paced and got himself something clear in a glass with ice. The song still went on. "Helter skelter in a summer swelter"—and suddenly Bev joined in. She would have liked to smoke a joint.

"It's about Buddy Holly, who died in a plane crash."

"It doesn't say anything about planes."

"It says 'the day the music died.'"

"It does talk about planes. He mentions planes flying in the night."

They were just talking, to fill space.

Now they had ruined the song for themselves. In this phenomenon music is perhaps unique. Writing or painting can't be infected the way a song can be. Now they had woven Petra into it. None of them would be able to listen to the song again without being slammed against the fact of her death afresh. A child had died, she had barely been a teenager, her wheaten hair hadn't gotten the chance to grow back. She had died bald. In her casket they would give her a wig, something to which she would have strenuously objected. She had been gravely ill since she was ten, about a quarter of her life.

Louise chewed at the bitter wood of the cinnamon stick. She planned not to be a child any longer. In this she was only more of a child: to be an adult, she believed, was to leave fear behind.

How people are hard on themselves. There is a constant self-flaying and hatred. Among the four of them only Deborah was free from it. She was fond of herself, she rode her bicycle into the center of town on excursions to buy herself little presents at Abe's. Abe sold penny candy and magazines. The store was dark, the floors scuffed, he was said to keep his ancient mother in apartments at the back. Deborah liked the candy in the thick glass jars better than the newer candies in plastic containers with twist-off lids.

You got a small white paper bag from Abe and filled it yourself. He was a man who seemed preoccupied with unresolvable trouble, disappointed in himself, his livelihood. The salami hero he was always setting aside was always merely filling, never a satisfaction. He wore an eye shade and rumpled plaid shirts.

She had retrieved two Everlasting Gobstoppers, cherry and watermelon Jolly Rancher sticks (the cherry to torment Louise, to whom she might finally grant it), Necco wafers, a Mars Bar—and then she was out of money.

"Nothing else?"

"Maybe I have some change for Bit-O-Honeys." She fussed in the pockets of her windbreaker. "I hope so."

She came up empty handed. What money she'd spent already was change from the bottom of Bev's purse.

"For being such a good customer we gif you some Bit-O-Honeys." Abe worked his way around the counter and over to the table crowded with glass bottles and plastic jars. Deborah met him there. She was charming; she coveted things and knew not that she coveted, her eyes naked and glassy as they blinked and took in everything. She would develop into a very promising woman.

"Bit-O-Honeys is your choice?"

She considered. "Maybe also some Tootsies? Could I mix them?"

"Do whatever you want to do, half this, half that."

She was lifting the stopper off the glass jar.

"Let me do that." He reached for it, he reached, he ran his hand down the arm of her windbreaker and felt in his mind her lambent skin! He saw himself arranging her limbs on the sofa where now his mother was parked. A black sofa, black was very unusual for a sofa and what a contrast against this girl's limbs. He would show her secrets, he would open her with a single thrust.

"Ow, gettoffa me, you." She was batting him away.

She was just a kid. Abe, you crumb. He was sweating as he walked back behind the counter.

She swiped her bag off the table and hurried out of the store. She rode her bike several blocks and then stopped and got the bag out of her pocket. Three Bit-O-Honeys, four Tootsies. She knew she was electric to that man, she felt the force of her childish power.

These are easy days for Deborah. Louise is in high school, miserable. And there is something wrong with Louise, as regards numbers. She can't do any of the math on her own. In the evenings, after dinner, Stephen and Louise sit at the dining room table with Louise's arithmetic in front of them.

"Where's your scrap paper?"

"I looked. There is none."

"Then get some new paper." He won't give a single directive until Louise procures a stack of paper and some sharpened pencils. Then the long evenings begin. Tears, begging, whimpering, Stephen's patient silences. Sometimes Louise stomping off loudly to her room. She will never learn, numbers are stupid, numbers aren't anything in the world, they're just stupid. Her math teachers, these years, are men. She hates them equally. Mr. Pedulla, old and swollen-nose, white hair growing out of his ears. All Mr. Hagelin's word problems have to do with Glacier National Park, which is far away and west and has nothing to do with math. Mr. Marcario is the soccer coach; she can't learn math from this guy who wears soccer clothes to class. And his accent, Italian. He was talking about DeMorgan's Law and she started wondering whether it was really DeMorgan's Law or if it was in fact The Morgan's Law, because with his accent he said "de" for "the." Then she lost the thread of the lesson; she didn't learn DeMorgan's or The Morgan's Law.

"I *am* studying," Louise says. But her marks are 70 percent, 75 percent, 68 percent.

In the afternoons, when Bev and Stephen are still at work, Louise puts on her sweat suit, pale blue with dark blue and white racing stripes down the shoulders and up the legs. It's the dawn of the fitness era. Bev goes to Jacki Sorenson aerobics in the rec room of one of the churches. The only time she steps foot in a church. But Deborah's still in the body of a girl; her tongue is blue from the Everlasting Gobstopper.

"Don't bother me." Louise stands by the front door, on the landing between the flight of stairs up and the flight down.

"I'm not doing anything. It's a free country."

But Deborah leaves her and goes into the kitchen. Archway iced oatmeal cookies and a glass of milk, that would be about the size of it. She arranges the cookies in a pattern on a plate and puts a napkin in her lap when she sits to eat them.

Clonkety-clonk-clonk. Then the other way, Louise gasping and clumsy, pausing each time at the foot of the stairs to catch her breath. She writes what she has accomplished in her journal. Eight times. Ten. Then twenty.

And calories. How many in four ounces of cheese, in melba toast, in a tablespoonful of peanut butter.

For breakfast: cottage cheese, raisins, half a glass of juice.

At the end of the produce aisle in Gristedes, across from the deli counter, there's a shelf with self-serve pots of coffee with stirrers, milk, sugar, cream. The women who are beleaguered, the house-wives in curlers and children, they are the ones who drink it. Also Louise and Deborah, who are sent on an errand for an item or two, Worcestershire sauce or half a pound of butter. A splash of coffee in a Styrofoam cup. Then milk and two or three spoonfuls of sugar. It's free; it's practically dessert.

No more of that for Louise. No more drinking coffee like a baby; now the women in curlers are cohorts, following their slimming programs, drinking their coffee black.

Black Coffee: 0 calories.

Number of Pounds Lost: 2

Numbers were good for something.

⌣⌣

In August they still drove out to the end of the island. Amagansett was a whole other country, the beaches sandy, tomatoes and corn sold from wooden carts at the side of the road by sun-hatted elderly women. Out this far the first of many vineyards were establishing their tenancy; the soil and climate were good for wine grapes.

Other years they had shared a rental with Parker and his family, Louise and Petra with their hair sunstreaked. Then Petra bald from the chemotherapy, boyish in her one-piece swimsuit, taking in stares from other beachgoers. Is there anything worse at twelve than to be mistaken for a boy?

Now, without Parker's family, they forgo the house and rent instead a room in the motel. Windows with glass slats one cranks open to let in the breeze, sun-faded upholstery on the furniture, linoleum floors in the kitchenette. The shower leaks, the floor is gritty with sand. There's a small mound of sand gathered in the toilet bowl. The linens smell damp; they have small rips in them. Little change since the early days, when the girls thought it a novelty to sleep in the same bed. When in the morning they woke to Deborah curled up on the floor, Louise whispering to Bev, "Deborah pished the bed." Now, no longer a novelty to share the sofa bed.

"You're sisters, for god's sake."

"She's a lezzie." Deborah is at a cruel age.

"I am not." Louise crossed her arms over her chest. Her pink Izod shirt with the alligator, the fashion now. *The Preppy Handbook* is what they read, instructions for how to be like the royal family, to wear madras and grosgrain, to aspire to horses and hunting dogs. Except for her braces and feathered hairstyle Louise could be one of the girls Stephen remembers from London, before he was sent away to a school for boys.

"Are too."

"Not." Louise always on the defensive. She does not attack; she does not even retaliate.

On the television, a man with the garish face of a geisha sways and undulates. His clothes were carefully arranged and they were pseudo-rags, deliberately. He had the thick and unkempt hair of a Rastafarian. But he was not a black man. He was very, very white.

They didn't have the cable channel that showed music videos on their home TV. In motels they were transfixed.

Stephen had a large drink. He had packed all the accoutrements, down to the Angostura bitters. He nodded at the TV. "What the hell is that?"

On the floor Deborah sat with a bag of potato chips in her lap. "Boy George."

"No last name?"

"It's like Madonna."

"Girl Madonna."

"Madonna's just Madonna."

He investigated the shower knob from which Louise claimed to be getting jolts of electricity when she touched it. When he turned again to the television, cartoon men were hauling large boxes, the painted Geisha man gone.

We have to install microwave ovens, custom kitchen delivery / We have to move these refrigerators, got to move these color teevee-ees.

There is agreement about Dire Straits, voted unanimously Favorite Video in a secret ballot Louise conducts on small slips of paper.

In the late afternoon, when the rest of them are having a late last swim in the ocean, Bev sits on the bed in front of the TV with a glass of Pinot Grigio.

This time it's "Karma Chameleon."

What could it mean? That one's karma is capable of changing? What of the girlish lips, the face?

She's not sure she believes in karma. It seems at once too convenient and too frustratingly beyond one's control. That you have to consider yourself responsible for things you did in a previous life seems unfair. What if you were Pol Pot? You couldn't be Pol Pot; he was still alive. But say Hitler.

She was sure in a previous life she wasn't Hitler. Maybe Hitler's aunt, or a cousin. She couldn't imagine herself any nearer than that. And not a man. In her former lives she was always a woman. Of that she was sure.

She had a lot of convictions. Stephen said they were skewed because of her work. Now she was counseling victims of abuse at a domestic violence agency. The stories she brought home were baroque, ludicrous.

so then what he does is back the car over her foot
sprayed Fantastic in her face
raped her with a

"Please, Bev, Jesus. We're trying to have a dinner conversation here."

"Raped her with what?"

"I said that's *enough*."

It wasn't so much the horror they dreaded as the probability of laughter. They would have to bite it back. When you heard a story of someone backing a car over someone's foot, someone being raped with a root vegetable or a kitchen implement, the impulse just rose up.

With a spatula. Then you couldn't look at anything without picturing. Kitchen tongs, even a fork.

They ate dinner at their favorite restaurant, Lunch. Its real name was The Lobster Roll but the sign that dominated announced only in tall red the midday meal. The girls were sunburned and battered from the sea; they got lobster rolls in plastic baskets. Bev had steamers, Stephen a steak. Shellfish made him sick; he was allergic.

"You know Joan that I work with?" This was Bev's third Pinot Grigio, maybe her fourth.

"The lawyer?"

"She's changing her name."

"To what?"

"Kellerperson."

"You're frigging kidding me."

"I'm not frigging anything."

Deborah was pulling at Bev's blouse.

"No comprendo," Louise said. She was taking Spanish lessons from someone who had come through the agency, a Mexican woman who had gotten away from her husband and needed work.

"Joan's name is Kellerman and she wants to change it."

"Why?"

For a long moment she hovered on the edge of answering, stumped. Why? Well, why?

"It's her husband's name," Stephen said.

"They're getting a divorce."

"Ha!" He threw up his hands and knocked a passing waitress in the hip. "It's not even her name!"

"It became her name."

"Well now she can give it back."

"She wants to change it. It's her prerogative."

Deborah didn't like celery. She was trying to get all of it out of the lobster salad. "Kellerperson's ugly. She should just go back to whatever the other one was."

"It's like Sony Walkmans. You would think in this day and age they'd find a more gender-neutral way of naming. You know, a way of naming." Too much or many Pinot Grigios. She couldn't explain herself. If she could remove the Pinot Grigios, the explanation would come to her. If she could suck the wine up out of her system, vacuum it out, play the evening in reverse only for a little minute, the force of her argument would return.

"I suppose you could get behind 'Walkperson.'"

"Maybe."

"It's ridiculous."

"Maybe they could just be called Walks. The way the chairman's now in some places a chair."

He would finish his steak. He would not open his mouth again until he finished it and until he finished the paper cupful of coleslaw and the last French fry. What were other families at other tables in this crowded restaurant talking about across their filets and bowls of chowder, across the rotating caddy of salad dressings and glasses of inexpensive wine? By what lottery had he been placed in this group of people? He has spent the better part of the last two decades living among females. A sense fills him sometimes that he's not much considered. In this constellation he might be a placeholder. He might more than anything else be a role. Father, husband. Which is not how he thinks of himself. He is an engineer. His charge is to lessen the daily struggles and confusions for people when they interact with the material world. Take for instance the salad dressing caddy. Who wouldn't prefer a dimmer switch if given the option? He wishes he'd invented the dimmer switch.

He has sometimes thought he might redeem himself, in Bev's eyes, if he could devise something that would prevent the litany of indignities parading through her office day after day. A force field, so you couldn't have your foot backed over. Something like those invisible dog fences. If you tried to hurl your pregnant girlfriend down a flight of stairs a jolt of electricity would prevent you. That was the real work of the world. Not the splitting of hairs over Walkmans and Kellerpersons.

Sometimes he fantasized. They would be sitting at dinner having a conversation about the mortgage.

A woman named Donna Harknett came to stay. Donna had a friend, also Donna, who came around the house for her in the evenings. Sometimes the two of them sat on the front stoop and smoked. At that time two things also appeared in the house that had never been allowed before, Fritos and Cheetos. The Donnas favored them. Bev brought the snacks out on the stoop in ceramic bowls.

"She lost both her parents this year. The bills were atrocious. That's the only reason she got evicted."

"She works for the I.R.S.!" Stephen was joking but not completely. If he worked for the I.R.S. there would be a lot of useful information for him to glean. It was inevitable you could be smarter about your finances once you had an inside view. What was permissible, what could get you caught.

"Don't go asking her to futz with your taxes. She's got enough on her plate."

On her plate. Well. But he said it to himself. Still, no one could fail to notice Donna's weight problem. She had the look of an athlete gone to seed; she reminded Stephen of some high school football players who stop sports abruptly and gain in the face and gut, the new flesh on the face making the eyes look small, piggish.

She ate a lot of those Fritos.

He had been enlisted to try to fix the reception on their old television, so Donna could have one for her room. He'd procured a set of rabbit ears but on the screen there was still only snow.

"Just because you work for the I.R.S. doesn't mean you can fudge your taxes."

"A little?"

"Her parents' illnesses ran up twenty thousand in medical bills."

"How long is she staying?"

"However long she needs a home."

She had a neighing, cackling laugh, whereas the other Donna's laugh was a guttural, dignified chuckle. The other Donna dressed like Little Lord Fauntleroy, jackets with epaulets and loafers, argyle socks. This Donna was no Little Lord Fauntleroy. She gave herself home permanents that made the downstairs bathroom smell of science. Acid, ammonia. Rubber gloves and the plastic cap in the trash, small brown bottles. Before her arrival Stephen had kept his shaving kit and the tarry medicinal shampoo he used in the downstairs bathroom. Now he moved these back up with Bev's things, pHisoDerm and witch hazel, vinegar douches, mascara. For reasons he couldn't understand he felt it would be stranger to share a bathroom with a lesbian than with a straight woman. He would have preferred cakes of rose-fragranced soap, pantyhose hanging on the towel rack, a satiny bathrobe on the hook behind the door. It wasn't the home permanent; it was the cologne. Green bottle with the polo player, same as his.

He felt nostalgic for Evelyn.

"Her?" In the kitchen, Bev was trying to flip something with a spatula. "I see her sometimes at the women's bookstore in Huntington. They wanted to have Wayne Dyer read and there was a big fuss. 'He's not a woman, why should we have him?' What, he has to go get a vagina to qualify?"

Bev had read *Your Erroneous Zones*. From it what she was most enthusiastic about was what to do if you were trying to park and there were no spaces.

"You invent one," she informed Stephen. She maneuvered the car up over the curb and halfway on to a grassy median between two full rows of cars and shifted it into park, deeply satisfied.

"You might want to put on the parking brake."

She looked at him quickly and then out the window. "They wouldn't tow me. Right? They're not going to tow me from the high school."

"I saw some parking spots over by the tennis courts."

This was the evening of Louise's spring musical at the high school. She had two lines and some dance steps in *How to Succeed in Business Without Really Trying*. This was the second year she had memorized a song to audition for a speaking role without success. She had no stage presence. She had not made cheerleading, either. Her failures were beginning to coalesce into a story she told herself about herself. She'd had to ask a date to her freshman formal; already she knew she was going to have to ask a date if she wanted to go to the senior prom.

"But that's two years away, you shouldn't project that."

Erroneous Zones terminology. Bev's EZ talk, Stephen called it. Though he didn't know if this business about projecting was in fact Dyer's. He hadn't opened the book, despite Bev's entreaties. The photo on the front, the man tanned and with a bald tanned pate and a fringe around his head and the groomed smile below the groomed mustache dimmed his faith in anyone but charlatans ever getting ahead in America. So Stephen was having trouble at work, yes he was. He had thought he would be a chief engineer by now, a senior vice president who would get to make forward-thinking decisions about contact lens technology. But he was middle management, he was mired in paperwork.

Bev had talked to Louise when she was angrily putting her costume together: an old plaid shirt belonging to Stephen, a tiered magenta skirt Bev had worn back in the late seventies, in her hippie peasant days, tennis sneakers, a kerchief knotted on her head, mismatched socks. In the script she was designated as Scrubwoman #1.

"I wanted a speaking part and this is what I get."

"You got something. You should be proud of yourself, you're not just dancing chorus this year."

"Basically I am. All it is, is at the beginning of act 2 I have to come out with a mop and make this joke I don't even really get."

"What's the joke."

"It's about Vassar."

"Vassar's a girls' school."

Louise shrugged. She had singed her hair with the curling iron; the ends were crisp.

Bev sat down on Louise's bed. She remembered her own high school days as if they had only just passed, how beloved she had been. Her adolescence had been the easiest time of her life, even though she had reached puberty earlier than so many of the other girls and the first time she got her period she had bled for seventeen days. Even so, her beauty had been a buffer. People were willing to go great strides for you if you were beautiful. And Louise was not. Almost stubbornly so. Stephen had offered to get her contact lenses to relieve her of the burden of her glasses with their thick lenses, but she had refused. Her braces wouldn't be coming off for another year, and after that she would have to wear a retainer almost until she went to college. Worst of all for her image was the way she slumped, as if she had no faith in herself at all. Bev was actually surprised she had gotten any lines in the musical. Well. Scrubwoman #1.

Deborah was where Bev's beauty would show up. It was already starting to happen. Donna had even remarked on it.

"She has your skin. But it's more than that; she has this way of being in herself that's like you."

It was true. And Louise lived in her body like Stephen did, as if she would have preferred to be a brain stem that could hold a pencil. None of the other business of the body interested her. Bev wondered if she had even discovered masturbation. If that would even be something she would bother to investigate. Probably she would rather read an Agatha Christie.

Inside the auditorium, they spotted Donna and Donna. Little Lord Fauntleroy and their Donna with the hair like Olivia Newton John's in *Grease*. Olivia Newton John was holding Fauntleroy's arm.

"What are they doing here?"

"I think Louise gave them her other tickets. Deborah didn't want to come."

Louise began to think about other houses; she began to notice how people lived. Houses were dwellings. How did people dwell? She was taking in the differences. They meant things. The Imhofs bent their heads and prayed at the dinner table, the Minicozzis watched TV. Or at least the TV on the kitchen counter was on in the background with the sound turned low. At the Matsuokas you took your shoes off. At the Kuhners the meals were clattering and chaotic and handed around on big serving platters. Later she would think it was like dinner in a mess tent; she had seen it on a show she liked, *M*A*S*H*. She wasn't sure how she wanted to live. Was this a sign she was growing older? The Minicozzis kept a clean home; Mrs. Minicozzi didn't work. She stood at the kitchen sink with a cigarette in her mouth, wordless. She would be looking out the window into the yard. She was the only mother Louise knew with short hair.

Mr. Minicozzi watched wrestling on the TV in the den. The living room was white and had hard bright furniture and a white rug with a plastic mat making a path from doorway to doorway, so you could walk through to the kitchen. No one sat in the living room; there were candies no one ate. Mrs. Minicozzi's father lived in an apartment in the basement. There was a Siberian husky tied up out back that way. It had eyes of two different colors.

Louise was afraid at Denise Minicozzi's. There was a bad feeling, something malevolent. There were lottery tickets magneted to the refrigerator door, cut coupons on the kitchen table, Mary Kay cosmetics on the counter in the bathroom. Traveling salesmen came to the door with appliances, red-penned sales circulars were scattered on desks and end tables, Mrs. Minicozzi reminding herself or informing Mr. Minicozzi of the imminent need for a Dirt Devil or china cabinet or address labels, whatever it was Mrs. Minicozzi needed. Louise couldn't say why any of this upset her.

At Julie Kuhner's there were six children. The stairs up to the second floor were crowded with clutter. Someone's shoes, someone's board games, someone's soccer uniform and school books. They had an above-the-ground pool out back that sometimes didn't leak. Julie was the youngest and the only girl. Her front teeth slightly overlapped; she had gold hair she was always being told to brush.

"Act like a regular teenager," Mrs. Kuhner said.

But Julie Kuhner had no use for the preoccupations of teenagers. She had an electric organ in her bedroom and tried to teach Louise, who learned in its entirety only one song: "On Top of Old Smoky." Next Julie wanted to get an accordion. She had a pen pal overseas in Asia. She wanted another one but American, from the navy, so she could send him letters on perfumed stationery. The Kuhners' house was ramshackle. Mrs. Kuhner never worried about serving a proper dinner unless she was in the mood, and if she was not in the mood several boxes of cereal would be arranged in a line on the dining room table.

Some homes were dark, some malodorous, some choked with furniture, the drawers clotted with mail or scraps. There were rooms people inhabited and others, well-tended, furnished with ottomans or velvet, that no one visited at all. Were there prohibitions on even entering the premises? Louise couldn't tell. At Rosalie Campanello's a grand piano stuffed into the front room nearly prevented ingress. Photo albums were piled on top, and framed photos of baptisms, communions, confirmations, weddings. No light came through the curtained windows. Only the kitchen was ever occupied, and the kitchen was located at garden level, below the house, like a bunker. Rosalie's father had been a cop, but he had been shot in the knee on the job. Now he worked on cars in the garage behind the house.

If you wanted anyone to hear you at Rosalie's you had to walk around to the back and knock at the kitchen door and yell.

He leapt out from behind an old Impala, his hands in the air like brown paws. Louise nearly fell backwards with terror.

"She's inside helping her mother with dinner. Go on in."

She hated how he would leap out at her and then not explain. Not go through with it, either. If he swiped at her or tried to chase her down at least he would attract someone's attention and then maybe could be gotten to stop.

"Girls shouldn't wear glasses."

He had picked up a wrench and was weighing one end of it in his palm. She was afraid he would thrash her with it though the other part of her knew he wouldn't. She would duck out of the way; she would run.

"I have to, for my eyes."

"I didn't think you were wearing them for your heinie."

What could she do? Tell on him? *Mr. Campanello said heinie.* She would sound just like the priss people thought she was in school.

She was smarter than he was, that was why he wanted to scare her. She had met a number of adults like that. He did not read books; even his penmanship was bad. Some of her teachers seemed to suspect the students could see through their bluster. Then they would use scare tactics. He was like that. Though the teachers would do nothing so crude as jumping out from behind a car with motor oil all over their paws. Mr. McDowell, the choral teacher who couldn't play the piano other than slamming the major chords at rehearsals, forced the class sometimes to remain standing for the whole hour. If you tried to sit he would make you come sing near him. You would be facing the whole class.

Rosalie had one brother who was going into the army and a sister named Carmella. Louise always thought of candy. She had learned nothing more about Catholics than she had learned the one day a long time ago when her father had taken them on a field trip to church. Crucifixes hung in odd corners at the Campanellos', on the hallway stairs, in the dim foyer and bathrooms. They were crooked on the wall, they had about them a sense of abandonment. As if someone hoped they would just go away, like stray dogs did. There was a statue of the Blessed Virgin out back near the cars. She was never Mary, always the Blessed Virgin. There was a birdbath near her.

There was a game Rosalie had invented. A sort of game, though Rosalie was dead serious as she explained what they would do, squatting on the floor beside the phone. Her room was under the eaves upstairs, the top floor of the house with its sharply angled ceilings. She had a phone extension in her room.

On the list Rosalie had made were Michael Lombardi, Anthony Jordan, Mike Caruzzi, Tommy Rozzano, Nicky Liantonio, Richie Sabatino.

"If they'll go out with me," Rosalie said. "Just see what they say."

Rosalie wanted to be a cop like her father. She wore clogs and jeans and silver-striped tops; she ran hurdles in track; she had a long solemn braid down the middle of her back like a squaw.

Louise didn't especially know any of these boys. They weren't in her accelerated classes. Though she was in a lower math with Nicky and Mike, who kept a comb in his pocket and during class whipped it through his hair.

"Just see what they say."

"*I* don't know what to say."

"Ask what they think of Rosalie Campanello. That's it."

Her heart was thrummeting with fear. She had a cool and pitiless sense of her own invisibility. How to these people she was a nonperson. She knew she was not a nonperson, that all this would come to an end. After the yearbooks were signed and the diplomas handed out she saw how she would take on her true dimensions; hers would be the moment in *The Wizard of Oz* when the screen lights up in Technicolor after a Kansas prairie black and white. But that would be later. She would stay in black and white until it was time for college.

She dialed the number beside Nicky Liantonio's name.

A woman answered the phone. She hung up.

"That was probably his mother!"

"What if it was his girlfriend?"

"His girlfriend wouldn't answer the phone at his house."

Louise hadn't thought of that. She didn't think of things. There was one boy she liked but all she had done was write him letters she didn't send. They weren't so much letters, for in them she had him speak, she invented conversations between them. In a way she was writing a script.

"Call back."

"You call. He's your boyfriend."

Of course they had things to talk about. They were athletes; they ran the world. He was Hercules and she in Louise's mind was Herculette. She'd had dreams in which Rosalie was an Olympian hurling a discus out over the plains, deflecting arrows with a golden shield. Those were the athletes in high school. They were presidential; they owned everything, Louise would have traded every cell in her brain to be them.

Rosalie was grinning when she hung up the phone. Grinning Herculette.

"He asked me to a beach party on Saturday."

Louise nodded.

"We'll have to get some wine coolers."

She was making her way down the stairs when she met him again, his paws in the air, his mouth a rictus. He crashed past her; she had to shrink against the wall.

Once out on the road, walking home, it seemed to her she always let herself out of that house.

Inside, Rosalie was getting the hiding of her life. She would not call boys, she would not. She knew the rules. Louise had never been hit. Once she and Deborah had been acting intolerable at dinner and Stephen had grabbed them by their shirtsleeves. She remembered what he said, his face pulled up close to hers. "Your rapier wit is making your mother cry." She remembered because she didn't know what rapier was and she didn't know rapier wit. It was one of the few times she didn't know a word and didn't ask.

⌒⌒

Stephen had worked for the same company for twelve years. Why did Bev have to keep changing?

The sign outside the building read Advanced Testing Services. Bulletproof glass in the windows, a receptionist in a sort of cage at the front. She sat straight as a knife.

"I'm here to see Bev Wirth."

The receptionist gave him a desultory up and down. "Who should I say is here?"

"Her husband." She didn't recognize him? Or was appearing not to.

"You have proof?"

He got out his driver's license.

"She expecting you?"

"I don't know. She might."

She looked up at him. He resisted clarifying. Briefly he considered making a remark of the tough cookie variety. That would piss her off more. She would think he was being patronizing or patriarchal, whatever it was they complained about. But he wasn't going to tell her. It wasn't her business. Sometimes it was a tradition for him to come and take Bev to lunch on their anniversary. Some years it happened, not every year. They weren't reliable about tradition. The girls were disappointed that some years their holiday plans for Alvin Ailey and sundaes at Rumpelmayer's came and went like clockwork, other years not at all, as if they had been forgotten. Forgotten was never the case. Every year he and Bev would discuss planning for the holidays, but there were years when inertia overtook them, when inertia, when doing nothing, was more satisfying than planning. The not planning some years was part of the tradition. It didn't make sense; he knew it didn't. It was a feeling not unlike the one after several drinks, when you know in some part of your mind you should cut yourself off, but who's to say why you don't. You don't. There would be too much volition.

It wasn't good to ignore tradition. They were bad parents, their children would be impoverished by his and Bev's failures.

The receptionist buzzed him in.

"Stephen!" Bev in the middle of her office, holding a pen and a file, wearing her trademark wool blazer. He always misestimated how short she was. "I'm right in the middle of something. Can you hold on? Is anything wrong?"

"No, no. The girls are fine." He was taking a guess; he had no idea. Louise might have leukemia growing inside of her like the cells that had killed Parker's Petra, Deborah might be falling down a flight of stairs. On the sly she had gotten herself shoes with heels. They were called Candies.

He sat down on a plastic chair. Where clients sat. Women whose feet had been run over by cars, arms pressed with lit cigarettes. And penetrated with god-all. Things beyond kinky. He remembered the woman in Connecticut, killed and fed into a wood chipper. A Scandinavian name. It had surprised him; you never thought of Scandinavians as kinky or violent.

"What can I do for you, sir?" She sank into her swivel chair and smiled at him.

Not a glimmer.

"For lunch. Our anniversary."

"Oh, god. Right! I'm sorry, I remembered then forgot." She was staring off at something distant.

"We could still go. There's a new Chinese place I saw on the way over, I saw the banners," he said dumbly. He remembered the banners very vividly, like the banners over a car dealership only these had Chinese characters. Nobody cared. He was the only one thinking about those banners.

"I made a lunch appointment—I was going to take a late lunch." She stood up. "I can cancel it."

"You could?" He had meant not to say it as a question.

"Wait here a minute."

It was one of the most awkward moments they'd ever had. He didn't understand. Either this was being married forever or their marriage was going to end.

She came back rubbing lotion into her hands.

"All set."

"Chinese?"

She didn't like the aesthetics, the metal trays with the clanging metal covers, the dim reds and golds. Even the faces displeased her, the flat planes and small eyes. She felt ashamed and tried to counteract her impressions; she searched their faces for other beauty. Not even the waiter made eye contact.

They had been married seventeen years.

He ordered shrimp egg foo young, fried rice, spring rolls for both of them.

He was getting prosperous in the way of men. He had begun to bring home bigger paychecks.

"It's a good time. We'll be able to afford Louise's college."

"What do you think about Fire Island this summer?"

"I think we could probably swing that."

She heard herself say she was grateful. Her head hummed. Louise would be allowed to go where she wanted to college. The brochures came in the mail, glossy, seductive, like vacation brochures, only the people were carrying books. Louise wanted to go where her father went.

"But Hartford?"

"I'm looking at the college, not the city."

"But that's part of it, which city. You could go to Berkeley. Then San Francisco would be right there."

"*You* could go to Berkeley."

The egg foo young was molded into an inverted saucer shape and swimming in oily gravy. Instead she cut the spring roll into many tiny pieces. There was duck sauce in clear plastic sleeves.

"Does it have duck in it?"

"It's called that because it's used with duck."

Stephen's mother cooked duck; it was his favorite meal. Bev couldn't bear it. When Louise was a child she had fed them at the pond near the public library. She had called them "qway-qways."

When Louise went away to college, she felt it all might just come apart.

And Louise knew. You thought your children didn't, but they did.

The first Fire Island weekend, Stephen pulled the car up near the entrance for the ferry and motioned for her to get out.

"Aren't you coming?" They had only packed one bag with their clothes and toiletries in it and then a canvas bag with a Frisbee, wine, Stephen's box kite.

"Just put my stuff on the back seat."

She left him his toiletries and the box kite.

"I'll come back and get you Sunday. I'll call you and find out which ferry."

"Okay."

"Have a good weekend."

"Okay. You too."

He drove away. They had done it. The first hairline crack had opened.

On the dock another of the time-share couples spotted her. They were already tanned, though it wasn't yet Memorial Day.

"Where's your husband?" They didn't even know each other well enough to have all the names straight.

"He wasn't feeling well. He's been having gastric problems."

She surprised herself with *gastric*. The word seemed to stand out, hang in the air. But stomach ache seemed too benign. Not enough of a reason not to come.

"He's going to try to get in to see a specialist."

The woman was adjusting her sunglasses. Jody, her name was. "God, I hope it's nothing serious."

"He's just been under a lot of stress, since he got promoted."

"Oh, that's great!" The man lit up. "What's his line of work?"

"Contact lenses."

That dead-ended the conversation. The man was a songwriter. He considered himself an artist. She had forgotten. He had written a hit song for someone who had been an unknown until this one song had made it big. Now he was trying to write another.

"It's a conundrum. You don't know whether to try and write something completely similar or something different. It's like striking oil, you don't know whether to go back to the same place."

They climbed metal stairs to the upper deck of the ferry. Right away the wind came up; it whipped the women's hair in their faces and put an end to the small talk. Bev remembered a story of a girl who had been rejected by the boy she was dating and had just walked off the ferry into the water. The boy had been up front with others and had reported, later, that the girl said she didn't want to be heard from anymore.

Not that she didn't want to hear. That phrasing had chilled Bev, the idea the girl didn't want others to hear her anymore, that she didn't want to put the burden of herself on them.

She did think of Louise, but then she often thought of her. At home Louise was taking bottles out of the liquor cabinet. It couldn't even accurately be called a liquor cabinet; it was a display cabinet, vaguely Pennsylvania Dutch, triangular so as to fit into a corner. Louise's commemorative plate was displayed above, and on shelves below there were ceramics made by Bev's friends and a gravy boat from Stephen's mother. And below that there was a small door that swung open to shelves on which were kept Baileys Irish Cream, Kahlua, ouzo from Greece, Grand Marnier for dessert sauces. All were dusty.

"Did you ever try any of this?" Louise arranges the bottles on the dining room table. She is acting the role of the host, drawing the notion from friends' mothers or television she has seen. There are seven people in the house; Deborah has been persuaded to go to a friend's. Somehow, through machinations Louise can't fathom, the boy she likes has been brought here. He's athletic, freckled, remote, drives a jeep with a Reagan sticker on the back. Against the backdrop of the interior of her house he's like the Statue of Liberty; that's how alien to her house he is, and how large. She's worried he'll notice the fat on the backs of her thighs, the crazy books in the living room bookcase. *Zen and the Art of Motorcycle Maintenance; Soma, the Healing Mushroom; If You Meet the Buddha on the Road, Kill Him!; Your Erroneous Zones.* She's fairly sure Neal Meehan would be disgusted by anything having to do with the Buddha, bald and fat with a stomach prevented from bursting by a cork in the bellybutton.

"I have a six of Molson in the car." Out Neal Meehan goes to get it. Surely Louise has failed. In addition to these drinks all she has is a six of pink Champale and some wine coolers Rosalie brought.

"What is he doing here?" Louise mouths to Rosalie, who shrugs. Nicky Liantonio is here, Susanna Bellino, Richie Nagle, Denise Minicozzi. It's an odd number; hopefully, another boy will show.

Louise knows nothing about drinking, nothing about boys. She's so naive not because she has been banished but because she has so often chosen books over television, her parents over friends. *General Hospital* is her only TV show; from it she has gleaned contradictory notions from two people who fell in love in the aftermath of a rape-seduction on the floor of a disco. She can't calibrate the distinctions between seduction and rape. The world of adults is theatrical and heated. What it has to do with Neal Meehan, dressed in primary colors, a polo shirt and jeans and white tennis sneakers, she is unsure. They don't seem the right clothes for a seduction. Nor this house. Nor herself in royal blue bib-front cotton pants and the wrong blouse. She hadn't imagined anyone would bring Neal Meehan. It might be a joke.

"The Baileys is the one. In these little glasses."

The little glasses are dusty. She rinses them, her hands trembling even up to her wrists.

They bring the bottle of Baileys and the Champale and Neal and his Molson go down to the family room. Here there is ping pong and Stephen's Texas Instruments computer with another version of ping pong on a TV screen, glowing green vertical lines for paddles. Neal sits on Stephen's stool at the drafting table and spins. Teams are formed for ping pong; Louise drinks one Baileys and then another. Agreeable sweetness. The Champale isn't as easy to drink.

"Who ever thought of putting beer in the same bottle with champagne?"

"Same dumb twat who thought of wine coolers."

Rosalie objects that she likes wine coolers; regular wine is too sour. "Well not so much sour, but it tastes weird."

"Jizz tastes weird, too, but you developed a taste for that."

"Fuck you, Nagle."

"In your dreams, Campanello."

On the old green sofa, legs tucked under her, Louise takes in the conversation. Some of it she'll remember later. She and Neal Meehan then are in the hallway, talking, strolling, he with a bottle of Molson and her with her glass of Baileys.

"This is a guest room but most of the time someone's living here." She thinks of Evelyn and then of Joan. Where are they now? What were they to her? It seems they were more than boarders. She remembers how one of them wanted the ballerina print out of there, though which one she's not sure. She remembers Evelyn's overalls, her little serious shoes.

"What's this called?"

"A daybed." She remembers saying that, and of how nearly certain she was that when he sat down on it he would pull her down with him, caress and seduce her.

"My parents have this place in the city. Most weeknights my dad stays there."

"Does he have a daybed?"

"Yeah. It's on Wooster Street. Do you know where that is? It's a studio on Wooster Street. There's a daybed and a little kitchen, barely big enough for one person."

She had not understood that moment; her and him alone in the room with the daybed had gotten tangled in the scenes she was remembering from the disco on her soap. Someone's Duran Duran tape blaring. Then the Champale and all the Baileys she drank began to afflict her. She felt a great dark wave of nausea and another of a need to black out ride over her and meet.

She next remembered being in the ping pong room again, on her knees by the sofa and heaving up into an ovoid trash can, diamonds on the sides. Rosalie was behind her, coaching.

Later Rosalie helped her into her bed. Cool sheets. A compress was placed on her head. She was given a Dixie cup with a gulp of mouthwash in the bottom to swish and spit. The cup was taken away.

"Take an aspirin."

Fingers pushed the pills into her mouth; other fingers helped her clasp the cup.

In so many ways she was not like her mother. The glamour had been reserved for Deborah. But in her preference to be cared for over caring for others, in this way she was like her mother. The directives, the giving over of oneself to another—in this way she resembled Bev.

Deborah, preferring at all moments self-governance, would never be a drinker.

⌒⌒

Summer. The crowded season, the noisy season, season of bonfires and litter. Louise's hair was brassy from a spray treatment meant to be used once or twice for highlights in the sun. The bottle was nearly empty. It was July; she went and bought another.

She lives in extremes; eating nothing for long stretches. Then, in her bedroom with a bag of bridge mix or a box of Nilla Wafers, she eats in rapid, unthinking handfuls, as dogs gobble their food. She fears herself capable of consuming everything, as cartoon characters swallow not just the food but the picnic table, basket, cutlery. As she walks through town or the mall she sees herself eating the brick and façade, concrete posts, metal mailboxes, mannequins, clothes in which the mannequins are dressed. There was an affliction that compelled children to eat plaster or dirt. The texture of different kinds of fabric would feel different in the mouth. She imagined chewing. In the dressing room of The Limited she pushed a pant leg into her mouth, in the mirror watched herself bite down. It tasted like industry, the way a drugstore smells.

In bed at night she saw herself again biting down on the pant leg. Her worst fears were of being socially inept and being bloated. College couldn't be a comedy of her getting it wrong again. She studied fashion magazines as if they were conduct books. She should have been studying conduct books.

All her mother's unspoken ambitions had lain in the direction of the mind, the desire to write a book. For Louise the ambitions were for the body. Yet she felt nothing; she had no desires other than to be thin. She was eighteen; her mouth and vagina were dry. That summer she had a boyfriend with blue eyes and blond hair, a face pocked by acne scars. He was from one of the large Catholic families. One of his older brothers lent him a car. They drove to the parking lot behind the primary school. There was no one on the blacktop or playground.

She didn't know what a hand job was.

"Like this."

Her hand began to get tired. It didn't take long. He was so grateful it pained her to look at him. His eyes, mouth, a collapse and repose that is evident in the body of one giving thanks. Jesus is often painted in this attitude, his eyes upturned.

His hands moved along either side of her head, shoulders, down her arms. "What do *you* like?"

"I don't know. Anything."

He would have liked to touch her breasts, but he was afraid of her. They had been in an English class together for a few days. But it was a mistake, she was moved up. There were different books for the honors and regular classes. In his they read *Ethan Frome*, barely a hundred pages, a book about a sledding accident. When he had tennis practice he saw her reading a big book. That was how he got talking to her.

"What do they have you do in honors, read the dictionary?"

She marked her place on the page with a finger and squinted up at him. "The Russians."

He didn't know any Russians except the little one who had won the Olympic gymnastics a long time ago.

He was going to enroll in the community college in the fall.

To grow older, to age and sag—the thought made the blood drum in her ears. If she died when she was still young it wouldn't be difficult for the mortician. He would be able to drain the fluids out, spackle her imperfections.

When she bends to pack her trunk for college, her spine stands out in her back like a piece of sculpture.

Bev moved out. That day Stephen was under his car, Deborah on the phone, Louise writing in her food diary. An apple, both halves of a Stoned Wheat thin, the new Diet Coke. She planned to keep cases of diet soda under her bed in college. Drink her Coke all night, all day, all night. Avatar of the century that would dawn next: her fantasy was to give up sleeping, make her life vast and continuously profitable. Bodily functions were inefficient; she tried to eat as little as possible. What a waste, sleep. You could read all of Proust's long book if you didn't, memorize the glossary in the Gleitman psychology text with Michelangelo's David's head on the front cover she would buy for Psych 101 in the fall, do umpteen leg lifts, follow the news.

The cottage Bev rented was at the other end of town. In the years since Soundview had been converted from summer rentals to homes for year-rounders, the town had taken on two distinct identities. In the geographic center, radiating out from the two churches, stood the most substantial homes, with yards and garages and aluminum siding, rose-covered trellises and old stalwart trees. It was at the far end of town that the spirit of summer renters still reigned, though for the most part these cottages, packed tightly together, warped and weather-beaten, their porches sagging, were also inhabited now by year-rounders.

Why had Soundview never become anything of the resort town in the manner of the Hamptons and Sag Harbor? Stephen puzzled it over one day while sanding the hull of his boat. You had to trace back through the pizzerias, mini golf, tiki bar with the faux straw overhang, flybitten drinking establishments along the shore. Back through the one gaudy and overpriced seafood restaurant in town with a water view. From the name alone you knew you would be disappointed. The menu featured Surf n' Turf, a Landlubber's Special, drinks with umbrellas. Why was Surf n' Turf as a category of meal always doomed? There was something in a name. That made him think about Kellerperson. You couldn't saddle anything, person or pet or even dinner special, with a bad name. It would curse the thing for life. His mother had once disclosed she'd almost named him Rupert. What kind of a name? He was grateful for Stephen; it wasn't trying to be anything beyond itself.

The rocky beaches were the first cause. The wealthy wanted snowy sand. Beside the inhospitable pebbles all touristy flybitten establishments had sprung. People spoke of "getting Soundview feet," toughened by calluses. With work you could acquire them and walk the beach with dignity, not having to totter and stumble on the pebbles. There was an arcade on the strip catty corner to Poseidon's. Stephen went there sometimes these days when he was in a mood. In a mood: a Manhattan or two at the Full Sail, a six of Heinie from the deli on the corner; his kids or some kids in town had named it Friendly Corner. Why he didn't know. The lugs who worked behind the counter, Italian-American, weren't friendly. They weren't not friendly but they weren't friendly. Still, they didn't say anything to him about his nearly nightly six. Sometimes he came back later in the evening for a second.

The arcade hadn't been there long, compared to some of the other establishments, Pig n' Whistle and the ice cream shop. Maybe five years. Shoppe, as if even a glimmer of quaintness. On the arcade's false front was the word in orange letters, jumbled as if to suggest hijinks within. But within was belatedness or obsolescence, he couldn't decide which. Pinball machines, Defender, Centipede, Pac Man, Frogger. How could these games already loom and huddle like has-beens? He thought of Alan Turing's early binary computers, large enough to fill a room. But he was good at Frogger, he liked it; his initials occupied the second and third high scorer spots. Some teenager always trumping him. Or maybe another man approaching his age, he too dependent on solitude and drink, came in to play the nights that Stephen didn't. If he played for a while he began to sweat. He wore his good clothes, a marled black turtleneck sweater, khakis or in winter gray flannels. He had foul weather gear from L.L.Bean he wore when it stormed. Not many clothes, but good ones. He would not be seen making the old mistakes, beiges that clashed, pants that were too short, unflattering attempts at high style. Nor would he be witnessed parked at the public beach, drinking his six in the driver's seat. He always made sure no one was around. If someone with a dog on a leash walked by, he stowed the can under the seat. He had a copy of *Machine Design* he perused convincingly.

So he thought. In a town of a certain size there are few secrets. Some laws transgressed inside the home can be kept quiet, but transgressions committed in public, even when the parking lot of the public beach is empty, are somehow known. And then this knowledge disseminated.

What is Stephen Wirth doing in the video arcade?

What's he doing in his car in the Ransom Beach parking lot?

Doing what?

Just sitting there. I don't know.

Pornography was a guess. Or prostitution. Lolita syndrome. There were claims he had been seen letting himself into a room at the Tides Motel just around the corner from the arcade.

He wouldn't do a thing like that. Upstanding citizen, member of the town council. He owned a house, a boat, he had one daughter in college, another on the honor roll. He wore wool, had a coffee cup with his name on it at the Soundview Luncheonette. Though the mug said STEVE and no one called him that. He was a Stephen, not a Steve.

But still, with everything going on with his wife?

So they knew that, too. The whole town knew, a souvlaki chorus.

"What are you talking about?" Gerry was staring at him. They were eating Thursday dinner together at The Barefoot Peddler. They did that now, and sometimes Indian buffet at the Bombay House in Hicksville on Sundays. There had been a renovation recently that Stephen didn't like. He preferred the old divey décor to this new vinyl and stained-glass approach, new plastic plants and faux marble in the foyer.

"I was just thinking about Greek choruses and then about how the only Greek thing in Soundview's that souvlaki place."

Gerry had never read *Antigone* or *Oedipus.*

"No one's walking around passing judgment on you and Bev."

"Plenty of people are."

"Well, not on you. Bev's the one."

Alternately he thought it was a big deal Bev had crossed over and then not at all. All these years he had known. And there were worse things a person could do; Bev could have stabbed him through the heart with a knife and put his body through a wood chipper. Only she wouldn't know how to operate it; heavy machinery. Okay, so he could have stabbed her heart and put her through a wood chipper.

"Don't think about that shit. You don't have to anymore."

It was true. No more did he have to come home after work and be demoralized by Bev's stories over chicken Kiev or curry. No more foot runnings overs and no more wood chippers. No more circling the house with a gun and no more threw her down the stairs when nine months pregnant. There were things to be thankful for. High score in Frogger today. This was another one.

The names of the streets—Beach Street, Beach Comber Lane, Sea Wall Lane. They marked a sharp division between the town's two aspects. The street names changed abruptly at the town center. To the west of Our Hobby Liquors the names were Madison, Jefferson, Monroe, Adams. The stately streets, the princely names. The privileged, the president streets.

The cottage she found was on Wall's Beach Lane. The street was choked with cars; there was at all times the sense of a party in progress, of people convening for festivity.

"It's the bar at the end of the street."

Stephen knew the bar. Not rough and mock-piratey like the Full Sail Inn, none of that drunken father figure rough and tumble. Wall's was a remnant hippie bar with a smattering of sunburned Vietnam vets cum clammers. For a time more than a decade ago Stephen had gotten in with the crowd some when he began a renovation project on a wooden boat he and Gerry bought for five hundred dollars. It was custom made, odd dimensions: fifty by eight feet, built narrow enough to get through the Hudson Locks. Stephen and Gerry had become a little notorious down among the boatyardies for their quixotic project. Among those who knew them their project was known not as renovation but as putting the boat into rehab.

Joan came over to help Bev hang pictures. She had triumphed in her lawsuit; the name on her driver's license was Joan M. Kellerperson.

"I always picture a divorcee like Jane Fonda, glamorous, with a neck scarf."

"Jane Fonda's glamorous?" Bev thought of Ann Bancroft as glamorous, Sophia Loren.

"Yeah, Sophia Loren. She wears neck scarves."

"You're not the type," Bev said.

Joan put on a glum face. "Never?"

"Not if you dress like a high school gym teacher."

"That's what you think I look like?"

"All you need is a whistle around your neck."

Easy banter, effortless. They wandered down to the end of the road for a look at the water, then stopped in for a glass of wine.

They recognized her everywhere, knew she was Stephen's wife.

"How's Rehab going?" This from one of the many crusty characters who lived in this town; that was one of the drawbacks of living by the water, unless you could afford to live in Bar Harbor or Laguna. The man speaking to her seemed to have shrunken wood planks in his mouth instead of teeth. A flash of memory revealed to her a trip she'd once made to the waterfront in Baltimore when she and Stephen were first married. A bar called The Wharf Rat. A man sitting in a wheelchair near their table, no legs on him, had pulled from somewhere a ragged Styrofoam cup and tucked it under the blanket across his lap. It had dawned on her in delayed fashion he was relieving himself.

"Rehab?"

"You think they'll name her that?"

"Who?"

"That goddamn pile your husband's got himself into."

"Oh."

She agreed with him, with Planks-In-His-Mouth. He could have been a soothsayer, had she met him a year earlier. She hadn't realized she could have put her foot down and stopped this boat project. Every one had thought she would put an end to it. Told him to buy something small and reasonable, made of fiberglass.

"They're something, the two of them," the man said.

She knew what he was referring to. Stephen and Gerry had built a temporary structure over this boat, a sort of shack. But they had equipped it with heat and electricity, and then some friends of Deborah's had asked if they could paint a mural on it. Now in bright purple and in yellow: RUSH, STING, DIRE STRAITS.

"Get someone to paint it in big red letters on the stern, REHAB, that's what I say."

"Sure. Yeah."

"Rehab on the side," he said again. The phrase was in some way entertaining to him.

"He's starting to annoy me." Joan gulped her drink and set her glass down.

"We'll pay and go."

Outside they walked in the relative Sunday quiet. Maybe it was the setting sun that subdued the usual boisterousness, the clamor for beer. Few people were out leaning on cars and only a few more sitting on the curbs with cups. Once when Bev mentioned to a client that she lived in Soundview, the woman tilted her head back, laughing.

"What?"

"Soundview's where you go to drink. That's where everyone learns. They serve the mixed drinks in *pint* glasses."

Mary Minicozzi moved through her field of vision, jogging by in yellow and green. Mary Minicozzi, jogging? The woman had been a cigarette ad. Glamorous, and so full of languor you had the sense she could barely summon the energy to lift the pack off the table. A type for neck scarves.

"You know everyone," Joan said.

"Almost."

Bottle caps had been tossed in drifts of sand in front of Bev's place. She stooped for them.

"Other than this I like this place."

She had one extra bedroom in the front of the house, though the floor here was badly buckling, warping from sea air, the salt. She had the daybed from the guest bedroom and above it the Degas ballerina removing her toe shoes. Louise had said she would ride her bike down this summer and stay some weekends. Deborah had pointedly said nothing. She would stay with her father; she would have none of this reshuffling.

⌒⌒

A hydrangea bush. Bev had always loved hydrangeas. He waited until late at night, then parked his car nearby at the public beach and lugged it along the block like the body of a sleeping child, dead weight. Long Island was famous for its iced teas; he wondered how the particular combination of seemingly ill-suited boozes had been invented. Maybe an accident. He'd had maybe three or three and a half. The last one mostly rum and ice.

Her windows were dark, her car in the driveway. He kicked the tires. Needed air. A woman did need a man. He still had her button collection. Not clothes-sealing buttons but political, worn to make statements. For a long time Bev had favored the lapel of a denim jacket for public display. Sometimes they were political, sometimes just jokes. Or a combination of the two, for levity. *Keep Your Laws Off My Body* and *I'm Not as Think as You Stoned I Am. The Moral Majority is Neither* and *I'm With Stupid.* She was capable of recognizing her tendency to be strident, morally superior, stubbornly black and white. Or sometimes she was.

They were displayed on a cork bulletin board, a record of Bev's varied and various commitments and outrages. *Anita Bryant Sucks*

Oranges. God is Coming and is She Pissed. A Woman Without a Man is Like a Fish Without a Bicycle. No Nukes is Good Nukes. Every Child a Wanted Child. He had moved them into the guest room, where they resided mostly alone, proclaiming themselves only to the full-length mirror propped against the wall. Why hadn't she taken them with her? Maybe she wouldn't be away for long. Or maybe she wanted to leave forever and leave her commitments and outrages behind with him.

He was forty-two years old. A bachelor again. He didn't see himself reclining happily into middle age a bachelor. If Bev wanted out for good he would sign up to date. There were respectable dating services now. You could date someone from the Seven Sisters or business professionals only. He had heard you could date members of Mensa; that was a whole category, people with off-the-charts IQs.

He found a good place and began to dig with a spade. Why hadn't he brought a shovel? To slow down the task, to humiliate himself for her. He was waiting for a point when he would be full of humiliation as if with liquid and would tip, pouring it all out. Hadn't Deborah and Louise owned a game called Don't Tip the Waiter? You had to load up a tray. Well now he was that tray. Each spadeful of dirt.

It was possible Bev would perceive his gardening as harassment. This occurred to him once the bush was in. He had dug in her soil. Would she turn a symbol, an irony, into a violation?

Still, he wasn't going to dig it up.

"Want to go somewhere for your birthday?" Joan asked.

In the dark, in the back bedroom, Enya on the cassette player. Bev called it her kinky music. Not kinky-kinky but instrumental, the instruments hard to identify. Maybe a sitar, Tibetan woodwinds. Music to help sleep. In their clothes they lay on their backs on the coverlet, their arms crossed under their heads, picnickers resting on a hillside after the meal.

"It's not an important one."

"Every one's important."

Forty-one? It was an in-the-middle-of-nowhere birthday. For forty Stephen had said he would get her a BMW but as forty approached they had as a couple gone precipitously downhill. You couldn't receive a BMW from your husband if the two of you were more often than not sleeping in separate beds. Stephen had gotten into the habit of working late at his drafting table or on the Texas Instruments computer thing and then crashing out in the guest room. Under circumstances like that, no BMW, not even your boss's wife's, used.

"Want to go to California?"

"I've never been there."

"Then we should go. We could drive through Napa, drink the wine."

"What, rent a car?"

"Sure, why not?"

Forty-one years old and she had never rented a car. Or she had with Stephen, but he'd always been the driver.

"Would you drive?"

"Sure. Highway 1's terrifying, it's narrower than your ass."

"You do the driving, then."

"Sure. Maybe. You might want to get in on the fun."

"I doubt it."

"California's magical, magic. There are orange groves and lemon groves, and the weather's good. You realize people are in bad moods here so much of the time because of the weather."

They dozed like that, arms under their heads, thinking of California. The gold rush. Bev pictured those long-ago Americans panning in the streams, believing any day they might bring up a pan of pebbles made of gold. What a place, California. And this woman beside her on the bed, that phenomenon too she considered as she drifted off, and as outside in her garden overnight a hydrangea bush grew.

Bev called in the afternoon, when he was at work, the girls at their summer jobs. Deborah was babysitting, Louise working customer service at his company. She wore a headset and sat at what she called her CRT terminal, a computer with bright green data.

"I'm going away." Then she had to sneeze. It ruined her composure. "I'm going to California for a few days." She felt herself losing steam and nerve. "For work. A week." She hung up.

She dialed the number again. So familiar, she would probably die thinking of that sequence of digits rather than something profound like what her life had meant or what moments were best. "Tell the girls to call me."

He already knew, Joan said. The hydrangea had been a last ditch effort. "You have to admit there was some desperation involved, for him to come plant that bush in the dead of night."

They were on the plane, ready to take off for their western adventure.

"Let's forget about the hydrangea bush."

College now, Louise's new home. Away from Soundview, the dissolute sunburned summer influx drinking their pints of Long Island iced teas. Away from her mother in cutoff dungaree shorts, a tank top with her chest spilling out of it and for Christ's sake a woman symbol on the front. The shirts were always purple, a color Louise associated with flouting convention. Women hippies.

The dorm was overcrowded, three roommates in rooms meant for two. A bunk bed had been put in; she slept on the top bunk. And a metal locker for an extra closet. As she'd volunteered for the top bunk one of the other roommates took the locker.

The three of them stepped around each other gingerly, polite. Their apologies were constant and in this agonizing. Louise got tired of making apologies, more tired of hearing them.

"If anything's in your way you can just throw it in the bottom of my locker, throw it anywhere."

"Same goes for me; you can just chuck it."

Of course it was laughable; the idea of them throwing or chucking anything. A half-filled soda can was treated with reverence, an empty envelope placed carefully on the desk of the person to whom it was addressed. They handled each other's belongings as if they were made of gossamer, of glass.

"It's excruciating," Louise told Bev. "They don't even mention their periods. If one of them needs a tampon she gets it out of her closet and goes off to the bathroom with it up her sleeve."

"I'm sure it'll all change once you get to know each other."

Were they knowable? The two of them, Margaret and Caroline, seemed a different breed than she was. To hear of their lives reminded her of 1980, when her father's relatives in England had sent a book of full color photos chronicling the life of the princess Charles had chosen. She was shown with horses and children, but there was something about her stance that indicated patronage. Though Louise wasn't sure what the thing was.

❖

"Public or private?"

She was wearing her aqua lenses; they made her eyes the color of chlorinated swimming pool water. But no one had known her before; they thought these were her real eyes.

Private, she wished she could say. But then she would have to come up with a name and someone else might have gone there and known she was lying. Agnes Irwin, Choate Rosemary, Kingswood-Oxford, Pomfret. The names were castles; names were everything. The names were incantations. Private was everything.

"Public," she said.

The privates were worldly, European; they had lost their virginity eons ago, they played lacrosse. Something in the netted woven stick they used struck her as tribal, ancient. They were a tribe; they had their own dialect.

"No one's a virgin once they get to college."

He had one good eye and one that wandered in the socket, unseeing. But a head like the David on the cover of her Gleitman text, noble, sculpted. In this he was the first man she'd desired. The others had been crushes, boys.

It had happened while he was playing ice hockey. But he still played, was on the team. His name was Joshua van Gelden.

"Aren't you afraid if someone comes up on your left side?"

"I have a sixth sense. I developed it after the accident."

He had a single on the first floor of their dorm. She lived on the fourth. The bottom floor was all male. "In case an intruder tries to break in," one of her roommates said softly. The downstairs hallway smelled of males; they lounged in their doorways and called to each other. A pyramid of beer cans was erected. And nicknames. Queeth, Rubber, Faggot, Jake. "Gras" for Mardi Gras, to a short, ill-humored physics major who cursed when he drank. "Walking Mardi Gras" was the expression.

"Why do you call Eric 'Faggot'?"

"He acts like a faggot."

She didn't understand the relations between them. Sometimes they hit each other. Then a case of beer arrived and they were cordial again.

"What is there to understand? He acts like a faggot so that's what we call him."

She couldn't explain. Neither could she mention her mother, Joan Kellerperson, any of it. He would call her a dyke and leave her; he would not want to make love to her anymore or sit on the floor in his room with his head in her lap, her hands stroking his leonine head.

She ran every day. Three miles, four, five. A case of Diet Coke under her bed. She was small, smaller, a nested doll. She wanted, as in a child's book, to be smallest.

It was announced: the running mate of the Democrat would be a woman. On the news Tom Brokaw remarked a size six. Louise was an avid fan; she wished she could be Italian and blonde, that articulate, with a voice that commanded. She took the train home to meet Bev; they went to see the candidate speak at a rally. They stood in the crowded courtyard of a school. Next to them was a woman with twins in a double stroller who got into a squabble with another woman.

"I didn't expect her to be the pro-choice one," Bev said later.

"Neither did I."

Dykes on Bikes rode by, revving their engines and waving.

On the way back to the train station there was less to say than Louise had expected.

"I like Psychology okay. We're learning about Pavlov. And the terrycloth monkeys."

"I always liked Psychology," Bev said.

They faced forward, watched the road, the feed of cars.

"I lost my virginity."

Bev turned to her, lit up. "Did you like it?"

She'd been expecting an admonishment. The question offended her, though it was a natural question, she realized later. Perhaps the kind of question other girls would wish their mothers to ask. But it wasn't a question you could answer without fear. Yes and Bev might press further. No and she might press further.

"You'll like him. I'll introduce him to you Parents' Day."

They hadn't discussed the logistics. Whether Bev and Stephen would drive up together and act as a unit or separately. Or just one or the other of them.

"He can only see out of one eye."

"Oh. Okay."

"I just wanted you to know ahead of time. Otherwise you might have been wondering."

"I see lots of different kinds of people. I don't judge them."

"I know you don't. I'm just saying. In case you would be curious."

"I'm only curious about whether he's good to you."

She had to wait for him at the station in Hartford. It was Sunday, late. "Geraldine Ferraro: It's About Time!" on her T-shirt. Her skin felt grimy from traveling on the train.

Caroline had come in the car with him. They welcomed her back, him calling her "Geraldine." The three of them were very often together, eating in the dining hall or lounging in the hallways. To Louise she already had the carriage and assurance of an adult. She carried a day planner and made dates in it—for coffee or tea, a cocktail, brunch. She dispensed of her schoolwork efficiently, at her desk, the textbook open and then shut. She did not loll over her books as Louise did, struggling with Kierkegaard for Philosophy 205, with *Hedda Gabler* for English.

"It was fine," Louise said as they drove back to campus. She should have lied about the day's activities. Should have said she was meeting her mother at the Met. For after that the nickname was hers.

"Okay, enough," she said to Joshua one day.

"But I thought you liked her. I thought she was your hero."

"I don't want to be called that anymore."

"Okay, Geraldine."

"I said."

"Okay, I swear, that's it."

Caroline with her lunch and tea dates marked in her calendar was in one sense an adult. But in other ways they were all teenagers. "I swear," Joshua said. They made promises, declarations; they broke them. They were trying out different versions of themselves.

He put his clock radio to an FM station, coaxed Louise to take off her pink oxford cloth shirt and khakis. His hockey and lacrosse gear scattered around the room, he was most comfortable living in an equipment room as opposed to someplace orderly and homelike. His bed linens always smelled of sports. "Put your legs up," he said.

"They *are* up."

She did not have orgasms; her pleasure was located only in knowing she had him; that she was the one he wanted to have. Out in public he sometimes shunned her, pretended they were casual friends. Certainly: it was a game. Falling in beside him as they walked down the muddy hill to Psychology class, she might or might not be acknowledged. She wore a bright anorak; she was still losing weight, she was growing her hair long, like Caroline's, up off her long neck in a glossy ponytail.

At parties the Privates snorted cocaine off framed school photos of themselves with their classmates and headmasters. Louise would try anything now. Jell-O shots, grain alcohol punch out of which wafted the smoke from dry ice. Marijuana smoke she inhaled from a rainbow-colored bong. One morning she woke with a steady throbbing at the side of her head. Her ear had been pierced with a sterilized needle. She showered in the hall bathroom with Joshua. He steadied himself against the tile and she stooped.

Her mouth filled. It was warm. She gagged and spat; she couldn't look up at him.

"You did the nicest thing in the world you can do for a man."

He rinsed off and lay a towel over her shoulders.

"Actually swallowing is the nicest. Then he knows you accept him completely."

⌒⌒

"'A nugget of gold in a pile of shit.' That's what Reagan calls us." James Hinderly poured her a drink. Behind him on the mantel was a photograph of the president and his wife, she in a yellow gown that made her thin as a sliver of butter.

Louise too was thin enough to break. She was admired for this. Sophomore year now. A couple of the girls in this dorm called her "Ana." Only the thinnest girls were. Better by far than Geraldine.

She saw Joshua from a distance. He lived now in his fraternity house.

"You need not stoop to the likes of him." Hinderly stirred the drink, dropped in a wedge of lime. Like Caroline he too was quasi-adult, middle-aged in his preferences. He sent his shirts out to be laundered, kept a full bar with Tanqueray and Boodles on a stainless steel tray with tongs and an ice bucket, had the New York papers delivered.

Stoop. She thought of herself in the shower. But that was a different Louise, heavier. Now she was light as air.

Everyone called him Hinderly; he was never referred to by his first name. He knew every beautiful woman on campus and every party; he had drinks in his room on Tuesdays at 5:45.

Like her he had a secret. Jewish on his mother's side. They didn't discuss it. How did she know? She just did.

They had a week off in October, to catch up on their studies. There was an exodus to Boston for the crew races. Bev called and asked if she would come home.

"We have something to report."

"'We,' who?"

"Your father and me."

She brought Hinderly home with her. Why she wasn't sure, whether to scare him or to scare her parents. He wore a bow tie, a navy blazer. He was portly and corporate and had a laugh she loved; it transformed a whole room. He was a Republican; his family contributed to congressional campaigns. That much of a Republican.

"My mother had moved out but now she's moving back," Louise explained as they drove to Long Island in his Jetta. "There's going to be a smudge ceremony."

"Smudge?"

"To sort of rechristen the house."

There was a bar he knew. He pulled off the expressway.

"Something to wet the whistle. A little summery drink."

"It's fall."

"Autumnal drink, then."

He was the kind of person who made the word autumnal arch, ironic. He made a friend of bartenders.

They drank Manhattans, up, very cold, so that her head ached.

"No more, I'll be sick."

"Attagirl."

At the house her parents appeared to be wandering from room to room, aimless. It was a dim day, rain threatening. The sort of fall day when the lamps need to be turned on against the gloom.

"Gin and tonic?" Stephen asked.

"Con gusto." He knew some Spanish and some French. Hinderly seemed absolutely comfortable in his bow tie and blazer, though her parents were in sweatshirts. He was in his element; everywhere was his element.

"When's the smudge ceremony?"

"Later on," Bev said. "Do you know smudging?"

"I have great respect for Native American traditions."

Bev sat down at the kitchen table beside Hinderly. Then she was solicitous; she got crackers and a wheel of cheese.

Louise managed half a gin and tonic. On top of the other drinks it made her woozy. She refused a second but Hinderly took it for her.

"Louise said she'd show me this beach I've heard so much about."

"Go, go. We have to shower anyway before dinner."

They navigated down the ivy-covered steps and onto beach straw. The tide was going out, the wind bringing in the familiar rotting smell. Louise walked ahead of Hinderly. The wind was in her eyes. He was right behind her. She turned abruptly to him, so that he nearly collided with her.

"Why did you do this?"

"Come here?"

"Yes."

He shrugged. "Something new to do. I like your parents."

"They hate people like you."

"They don't seem to hate me at all."

"I said people *like* you."

"Maybe they make individual exceptions, on a case by case basis."

She didn't say anything.

"Anyway," he said cheerfully, "What am I like?"

His bow tie. For Christ Almighty in heaven, he was wearing a yellow bow tie with blue somethings on it, sailboats, ducks. No one at the smudging was going to be wearing anything even in the vicinity of a bow tie. She thought of her parents' friends: Charlotte, always draped in lavender scarves and rose quartz; Chester, who often wore a headband with a feather tucked in it—a very serious caricature of an Indian. A bipolar poet named Angelina Miller-Conway who self-published her work and always wore belted sweaters. Jim and John, first cousins who were also a couple. John was British and never spoke, Jim American and sufferingly loquacious. And what of Joan Kellerperson, now that Bev and Stephen were getting back together?

"A nugget of shit in a pile of gold. That's what Reagan would say about you at my parents' party."

Hinderly laughed his belling, pleased laugh. "I'll be the token Republican."

"You'll be the token everything. Republican, capitalist, normal person, non-freak . . ."

They were having to shout over the wind. Then his hands were on either side of her face. "I'm not so normal as you think, you know. I have a capacity."

"For what?"

"I can fit in anywhere, Louise. That's my talent."

It had never before occurred to her that he might be in love with her. Never, ever, ever. She was not patrician enough; her mother had been (wasn't she? was she?) a dyke; her family did not have assets, country club memberships, villas.

"I don't care about villas." He was still holding her face. Her cheeks had begun to color under his hands.

"I'm not in love with you," she said. "I like you, but never like that."

He let his hands drop. "But you like that *oaf*?"

"Joshua?"

"The one-eyed one."

"I haven't seen him in a year. I mean other than that one time." At a fraternity party, Joshua had yanked on her ponytail in a corridor, caressed her neck and whispered to her. They had already stepped outside, to the edge of the property, when Hinderly detained her.

"He's just someone to go to bed with."

They walked back to the house, neither of them speaking the whole way. She had greatly surprised herself with her remark, had not known herself to be so mercenary about sex.

It was a pot luck, tabouleh and hummus and rice salad and tofu croquettes in handmade ceramic bowls. Everyone stood with their plates while Jim showed slides of his and John's trip to England. The British arm of the family was ruddy; they were sailors and lived by the sea.

"Croquettes," Hinderly said. Gamely he put a whole one in his mouth. "What are those on his pants?"

Jim clicked back to the previous slide and scrutinized John's father's corduroys. Everyone in the photo was holding a tomato juice drink. It was daytime.

"Whales, I think they are. Little spouting whales."

Later there was champagne. Bev announced that she and Stephen would be renewing their marriage vows that summer. It would be twenty years. There was applause from the guests; someone suggested reading from the *Bhagavad-Gita.* Someone else suggested *Jonathan Livingston Seagull.*

"*Have You Checked Your Erroneous Zones?*" Jim said.

"Yeah, right," said Stephen.

"That's why I wanted you here, Lou," Bev said.

"What about Deborah?"

"She's at a concert with some friends. We told her earlier today."

Louise was stunned. She felt she might collapse under the weight of not having to carry it anymore. Her mother was not a dyke? No Kellerperson? No divorce?

Hinderly was standing beside her. She felt how he was restraining himself from touching her. They would be friends.

"Everything back to normal," he said.

She had her own life now, who cared what they did? She joined a sorority; she went off the meal plan and used the money to pay initiation dues. Some of the girls were wealthy. You could tell by the cars they drove or one who kept at all times with her a large white dog, a rare breed, Alsatian. She brought it on a leash to class. Now this personage said hello to Louise when she came walking along with the dog. She had boots made of smooth, caramel-colored leather; they came all the way to her knees. Sometimes she was in riding gear; she boarded a horse nearby.

Fascinating were the ones whose wealth was only implied. What was it that marked them? It was invisible; you could never quantify it. Her only hope was to convey this invisibly as they did; she couldn't afford the dog or the boots.

Two of them asked if she would room with them the following fall. In the housing lottery they would go for a suite. One was Southern and in this alone terrifying. She had encyclopedic manners, a long neck like a swan's, a wasp-waisted figure that looked best in dresses. She was dating a senior, a Jew.

"It'll have to end when he graduates." Her name was Katherine; she was called Kat. Her parents would never let her marry a Jew.

Louise said nothing. When the Jew came around she wondered whether he could tell that she too was Jewish. He had the nose, the dark coloring and eyebrows; his last name started with a Z. Maybe she was giving off the infinitesimal Jewish clue, the way Kat's bearing spoke of wealth. Which behaviors might bespeak her Jewishness, which locution or tilt of the head? Some Yiddish expressions she'd inherited from her mother's parents and Aunt Beck. *Oy vey* and so on. She had never uttered *oy vey* at college. That was from another life.

On Initiation Saturday they had to wake early. It was forbidden to wear makeup to the ceremony, the way her mother and aunts had been pale at her cousin's funeral. The new initiates were given sheets knotted at the shoulder to wear, girlish togas.

"We don't look so ravishing now," Tracy whispered. She was to be Louise's other roommate in the fall. She and Kat were Frick and Frack, the way Louise and Caroline had been freshman year. Now they were in different crowds. This sorority was known for being the sorority for good-looking girls, though not the athletic ones; that was another sorority. Now here they all stood in togas and socks, their faces ashen as the faces of hospital patients.

The initiation room was hung from floor to ceiling with white sheets. Purity of purpose, purity of purpose. Something about true womanhood. Each received a single iris and learned the password and handshake. Later they would get drunk on bourbon and coke; their faces would be painted with the three Greek letters, they would sing on their knees outside one of the fraternities.

The sorority suited her. She craved order and systems; she ate only bananas and Progresso lentil soup, she went through a case of Diet Coke a week.

❖

"How many miles do you run a week?" the gynecologist asked.

"I don't know, ten, twelve."

She knew exactly. She kept notes.

"Cut down on the running a little, you'll get your period back."

She didn't want her period. Her breasts were tiny. She read some girls grew hair on their stomachs. Laguna, lunago? She didn't want to go as far as all that. The knobs of her hipbones were comforting; she did not think hair on her stomach would be comforting.

Great cacophonous dinners, drawn-out affairs were held in the dining hall of their "brother" fraternity. She came to dread Thursdays. The invitations came in their mailboxes on a Monday, cards engraved in black. *The Brothers of Delta Phi invite you . . .* Not everyone was invited; it wasn't an official event. The brothers of Delta Phi could invite whomsoever they pleased. But she was nearly always invited; she was attached now to Kat Taylor.

And Hinderly.

"You don't have to invite me. Use your invite for someone else."

"I want to invite you. I like your company."

"The token Democrat."

"No one's a Democrat."

"I am."

He gave her a look. "You'll turn around."

"What about Caroline Unger?"

He was offended. He thought nothing of Caroline Unger; she was a paper doll.

"She goes to the Gold and Silver. She's in the social register."

"She's not a good conversationalist."

"She's the best cocktail party conversationalist I know."

"Oh, Louise," Hinderly said. "Do you think I want to have cocktail party conversation?"

She could not talk about politics; she could not talk about her family. Her politics anyway were knee-jerk liberal; she couldn't defend anything except to say it was her morals, her belief. When she tried to formulate why she thought a woman should be able to obtain an abortion, why the government should help the poor, she dead-ended. To her it was all self-evident; she could not argue about things that were self-evident. It was a flaw in her intellectual makeup. When one of the brothers launched calmly into his own argument she got enraged, apoplectic, she could hardly speak.

"You in your position of—privilege!"

The brother would raise his eyebrows. "And where are you? In the gutter?"

She was truly skinny now and in this defenseless. She had surpassed fashionable and veered into unhealth. She looked Biafran; her eyes seemed to bulge out of her head.

"Mom's moving out."

"Again?"

"This time for good," Deborah said. Her tone implied she would be involved in the decision making next time; Bev would not be allowed back under Deborah's reign.

"She found an apartment in Huntington Station. They're bringing her stuff out there this weekend."

Huntington Station? There were three towns close together: Huntington, where the shopping was, shoe stores and stores to buy stationery, a little store called Scentsational with glass-stoppered bottles of essential oils in rows. You could mix a lotion with any scent, gardenia, vanilla, apricot, freesia. Stephen had gotten Bev the freesia in body lotion as a stocking stuffer. The smell reminded him, he said, of England. The town beyond Huntington was Cold Spring Harbor, residential and quaint, with a Talbots, red shutters on the shops, a cookery store with copper cake pans in the front window. People with pleasure boats lived in Cold Spring Harbor, the driveways were circular, the homes European in character, old and, in Louise's imagination, though she had never been there, French.

But Huntington Station. A street connected Huntington to the expressway. It was lined with bodegas, storefronts converted to ethnic ministries, lingerie shops with limp red shiny bodysuits dangling in the windows, pawnshops, liquor stores advertising sales on cheap vodka and whiskey, places that would give you a loan until payday.

Next there was a phone call from Bev.

"If you don't have too much schoolwork this weekend. I got movers—more for the moral support. You know Deborah—"

Secretly they called Deborah Nancy Reagan. Just say no to drugs, the complications, all of it, the immense complications of life. Deborah didn't believe there had to be immense complications. Certain people made them.

There was a paper Louise was supposed to be writing. *The Picture of Dorian Gray.*

"Pick me up at the station."

"Thank you, Lou. You're my girl."

"She's coming," Louise heard Bev say as she hung up the phone.

There was no one to tell. Though she tried to picture the reaction from Kat and Tracy. It was like the mashed banana and the lentil soup she ate every day. The circumstances were dire but in a holding pattern. Her mother and women. It was an emergency, but the flow of life went on around it, holidays and anniversaries, family life. As did her pursuit of thinness. She wanted to be a wafer, holy, made of substances that could dissolve.

Whereas for Deborah it could not anymore go on under the surface.

Bev's clothes were packed in boxes. Her toiletries, makeup and pHisoDerm, thyroid medication, were still mixed in with Stephen's shaving cream, dandruff shampoo, treatment for eczema. Deborah held a box against the bathroom counter and swept everything in.

"That other stuff is Daddy's."

"The which?"

Louise knelt on the ground and picked out her father's things. She formed an arrangement on the counter, tallest to shortest.

"We don't have time for that."

Their parents were downstairs with the movers, deciding on which sofa and which chairs. All this had been done before, when Bev had gone to the cottage. Now it would be permanent; Stephen was paying more attention to what stayed and went.

"I hate her, she's a liar. Dyke liar bitch, with that other bitch Joan Kellerwhatever." Deborah's voice was raspy. She was starting to get laryngitis. Louise said nothing; she had sunk into herself.

"Good, then I don't have to talk to her at all now."

Rage came off her in waves. Louise felt them like heat. But she was removed; she was watching it all from above.

"And why don't you eat something? You're like a refugee, there's something wrong with you."

"Nothing's wrong. I'm doing Fit for Life. You only eat fruit every day until noon."

"What, like one grape?"

Bev had rented the upstairs of a house. It was on a main road, across from a convenience store. People lounged in the parking lot, drinking blue and green thirst quenchers, kicking the curb. The men in baggy pants, gold chains glinting against their necks.

"I hope it's not like that at night," Bev said.

The woman downstairs came up to greet them. She was black and wearing an apron that said "Kiss the Cook." "Oh, it's like that," she said. "That's our twenty-four-hour general store." She was looking around the room as she said this, from one of them to the next. The constellation, the four of them, perplexed her. No one offered an explanation.

"Your daughters?"

Stephen had gone back downstairs with the movers, trying to figure out how to maneuver a sofa up the narrow stairs.

"Louise and Deborah."

"And down there's your husband?"

"Yes."

"And you all, all of you gonna live here?"

"Just me."

The woman had bacon on and something in the oven. She took Deborah and then Louise's hands in hers when she left. "I never make any noise," she said to Bev. "Across the street Saturday nights is worst."

The apartment had beige Berber carpet, flecked, so that it was hard to tell whether it was dirty or clean. It smelled faintly of pets. Louise unpacked some pans and put one on the stove. It seemed to have a tilt; maybe the floor was tilted. She thought of her mother alone making Egg Beaters in the early morning, drinking instant coffee. Or eating her little dish of plain yogurt with a tentative spoon. Smoking a joint in the bathroom. The bathroom had a claw-foot bathtub that required a 360-dgree shower curtain.

"The truck's unloaded, Dad and I are going," Deborah called from outside. They had come in Stephen's car.

Bev sat down cross-legged on the kitchen floor.

"You don't have to cry, Ma. It doesn't have to be bad." The words coming out of Louise's mouth surprised her. She had not been aware of any reserves of strength. She suggested playing Steely Dan.

"There's not even a tape player."

"It's around here somewhere." But the boxes weren't specifically labeled according to content; they were only labeled by room.

She felt if she could find the tape player and the Steely Dan, she could ward off the terrible. It was the way sometimes she felt if she could get a Diet Coke or a black coffee.

She found the tape player but not the Steely Dan. Her father had kept that. The music left was Janis Ian, Chris Williamson, a group called Sweet Honey in the Rock. Deborah had from the first time she heard it hated Chris Williamson.

She dug deeper in the box and found Donna Summer, the sound-track to *Saturday Night Fever*, Joan Baez.

They worked in silence for a while, the music the only thing covering the awkwardness. Louise arranged her mother's cutlery and spices; she lined up the crackers and boxes of cereal in the cupboards. It was not unlike what her mother had done for her freshman year in her dorm. Noodle ramen, instant oatmeal, sugar-free hot cocoa.

Hot stuff baby this evening. Maybe the music would flow over them, maybe it would drown out the people at the convenience store, more of them gathering now as the sodium lights in the parking lot went on at nightfall.

This was it once and for all; Bev felt her other life, life as wife, break off. An ice floe floated away from the larger formation. The larger formation was who she was now, the life she was living, Joan. Even to her it was a surprise that her former life, the one she had lived until now, was such a small part of it. She watched it float away. It was only a thin sheet; it wasn't so vast or durable as she had believed.

"You want chicken or salmon on the grill tonight, babe?"

They weren't officially living together, but the elderly woman from whom Joan rented a room was in the hospital. She'd had a stroke. The woman's grown children had flown in from out of town and were staying at their mother's house.

"Nora warned me about them. They wouldn't take kindly to her extending charity to a big ol' dyke. They don't know about their mother's 'tendencies.'"

Joan had been cleaned out by the court proceedings with her ex-husband over the name. She had fought for Kellerperson and she had won, but not without a costly fight. She had lost her house. She said she didn't care; it was worth it. Houses were nothing; life existed in the moral victories, intangible rewards.

"You're out of your mind," Bev said. The center of life was its capacity for comfort. Not to be lazy, but to be comfortable, in this life where disease and other discomforts of the body lurked around every corner. She had torn her Achilles tendon trying to play racquetball with Joan; the pain had been excruciating. And then the other kinds of pain, shame and loss of living in Huntington Station. Out her bedroom window were the red, white, and green of the convenience store sign and the deadness of the parking lot, the expanse of asphalt and litter. She remembered the house near the beach, the blue mussel shells in the garden, beach straw, salt smells. Would Stephen even appreciate it? He would sell the place; he would get himself a houseboat covered with barnacles.

"We should buy a place." Joan shook tamari, salt, pepper, lemon on the salmon. She'd bought a little outdoor grill for Bev; they cooked their food over fire on the cramped landing at the top of the stairs. The inconvenience was romantic, as all inconvenience is when one is in love, the material world merely an obstacle over which the greater mysteries—the ineffable cause of love, what makes it grab two people and cast them at each other's feet—can hurtle.

"Us?"

"We could get a mortgage. People do now."

"I know people do." She hated being treated as if she needed an education; next she would be lectured on the Stonewall riots.

Joan sang to herself while she cooked. "People like us," was the beginning of many of the phrases. She had a fine strong alto voice with a raspy edge in the way of some black women, the best singers. Other than Rosemary Clooney all the other songs she played were sung by Aretha, Billie, Dionne, Ella. She spoke of them as if they were her intimates; she named her lavender bushes after them, her car. Her car she called Dionne. *And all the stars that never were are parking cars and pumping gas,* she often sang.

Did she love Joan? More than once she had startled awake in the middle of the night to find Joan looking at her. It was the beatific look on Mary's face as she cast her eyes on Jesus years ago, on the walls and hewn of the stone of Italy. She could not deny it. She was loved, voluptuously so, with the luminous glazed eyes of the devout. She had not been so loved and admired since the days when Stephen had cast his eyes on Binky, when she had flaunted her face and body, mistaken on the street for a movie star. Now the actress was gone, having fallen from a boat on which other recognizable personages milled and drank oblivious. Maybe they were all her lovers. The actor known for his face, long and flat like a wooden paddle, though one that could leap to life as if wood itself had become flesh. The sea had swallowed the actress, drink in her hand, toppling slowly and coming to rest alone in the deeps. An ordinary body would not sink but this was not ordinary, this was the body that had housed an icon. Bev couldn't see the drowning in its violence, only as elegant retreat. On Stephen's boat there had been times, among her in-laws and their friends. She had imagined herself gone from them, preserved by the sea as formaldehyde preserves, or as fish are preserved when buried in ice. Or hidden among the waving anemones and stolid corals (though of course no corals in these northern seas). What had she wished? For death? No. She had only wished her body gone before it would betray her. Now she was middle-aged, padded all over with flesh, her forehead marred by sun wrinkles. She was no Binky anymore, no Natalie Wood.

She would take it, this life. Now, at last, again, she would volunteer to be loved.

Joan owned softball gear, beach chairs, a plastic box filled with spools of multicolored thread, for her needlepoint. Some Yankees paraphernalia—a signed baseball, a full color photo of the team and one of the stadium.

"They can't go in the living room or kitchen. That's all I'm saying."

"What do you want from me? I grew up in the Bronx!"

As summer drew into fall, Joan sat on the sofa in the cramped living room and needlepointed while she watched the games. Bev learned the personalities and the rules of baseball. She liked best the stress-relieving rituals the players had, chewing on tobacco.

"Not tobacco so much anymore, it's sunflower seeds," Joan told her.

They were easy together; they both cooked and cleaned, read tips in magazines about decorating on a shoestring. Lavender grew generously in pots on the landing; they hung bunches of dried flowers tied with ribbon over the doorways.

"When the blender breaks and Joan takes it apart in the middle of the kitchen I don't get annoyed the way I did with your father," Bev told Louise on the phone.

"I'm glad you're happy." Louise was a robot, a Biafran robot. She was five feet, six inches tall; she weighed ninety-one pounds. Her clavicles looked like weapons or tools. Her family didn't know. That was the advantage of the phone.

"Are you liking school this semester?"

"I'll make dean's list. I'm doing almost all English courses this fall—Modernism, Jane Austen, the Metaphysical Poets. I've got reading up the wazoo."

She was taking NoDoz to stay awake. *Sense and Sensibility,* Faulkner, George Herbert's poems about God. With the NoDoz it all blurred; literature was one big stalled car in her brain, the engine trying to rev to a start.

"You can come here any time you like, stay for the weekend."

"I'll remember that." Her brain catching and chugging along for a moment, *my mother is a lesbian, my mother is a lesbian,* before it went back to Elinor and Marianne Dashwood's prospects in England.

⌒⌒

He sold the house on the water; he gave the beach away. It was foolish for him and Deborah to live in such a place. With some of the money he took Louise and Deborah that Christmas on a sailing trip to the Caribbean. They were grown up women now, Louise twenty-one, Deborah a developed sixteen. There was a T-shirt he said he would wear on their trip: "They're My Daughters." Deborah laughed genuinely; Louise, he saw, was less amused.

They flew to the British Virgin Islands on a day so frigid in New York the air seemed to suck heat from the body. They wore wool and parkas on the plane and emerged into a hangar like bears. Beamish was for sale at the makeshift outdoor bars on the several island beaches they sailed to: Cooper Island, the Bitter End.

"It's a British colony," Louise said. She was impatient, rummaged disconsolately through the contents of the cooler provided by the company that had rented them the boat. "They probably serve kippers, too."

Stephen wanted them to learn the crucial things about sailing. Deborah was interested but seasick. The Dramamine doped her; she slept for hours on deck, her limbs splayed limply over her face.

"Is she wearing suntan lotion?"

"I'm sure." Louise didn't look up. She was reading a giant paperback book. *Bleak House.* It seemed all Louise did at college was read giant novels. This spring she would graduate and go on into the flow of life. He thought of college as out of the flow, suspended, as if in dream. Twenty-three years since his own graduation from that same school. He remembered Bev that day, the mud on the chair legs arranged on the Quad. Her fall of black hair, all the intricate white parts of her outfit like sacramental garments. Where had that curtain of dark hair gone? Who was she now, in overalls, purple shirts, her hair clipped short? The two of them had so little now to say to each other. As a category he felt he was doomed with her; she had no patience anymore for men. He'd thought he might be exaggerating but Gerry agreed with him; she had decided to stop liking them on principle.

He was a skillful sailor, navigating patiently. The cords on his strong arms stood out. Fine wrinkles radiated from the corners of his eyes, from squinting into the sun. He was aging but he was aging well.

"Did you sail with Grandma and Granddaddy when you were our age?" Deborah asked.

"By the time I was your age I could sail *Hai Sing* alone."

"Did I go on *Hai Sing*?"

"All the time, when you were a little girl."

"I barely remember." She closed her eyes again. She had a faint memory, visual and arrested, nothing else, as if she were remembering a painting. The crimson hull, strangely shaped jute sails. As if instead of grandparents sailing toward the dock from Connecticut these were Orientals from across the sea, all the way from another part of the world, from China.

"You and Louise used to jump off the side. Granddaddy would catch you in the water."

"Before he was sick?"

"Before his asthma got bad, yes."

"I wish we had a boat like that."

There was hamburger packed in ice, peanut butter, corn chips. A fairly ambitious supply of Coco Lopez. Louise fidgeted on boats, in their cramped unstable spaces; she was irked with all transportation. She had gotten up to use the bathroom during the flight and had been ordered to return to her seat by the male stewardess. Flight attendants, they were called now. What a tremendous effort, all this transporting of bodies from one place to the next. She wanted only to sleep, lay about reading, run once a day on a preset course, five miles, ten. And food packaging, this too was an effort and an obstruction. Most of the food was encased in cellophane. When you saw it that way you wanted to leave it that way, it was like a painting in a museum, a sword or suit of armor in a case.

Deborah woke up from a long doze and made herself a bologna sandwich. She ate it in the tiny galley, chewing silently; she was still half asleep, chewing as if in a dream. Her face under the sunburn was unguarded, soft.

Louise had a can of Coco Lopez in her hand. Was studying the palm tree on the can. She looked up at Deborah.

"You better wear a hat now, you're roasted."

Deborah didn't say anything. But she acquiesced, still chewing. She wasn't interested in getting into a war. She was in a war with her mother; that was enough.

"You use a can opener on that," she said.

"I know."

December. It got dark early; even in the Caribbean, dark by five. Stephen rigged a lantern to a halyard, but the light seemed barely to penetrate the dark, it was so thick, thicker than a summer dark.

Dinner was makeshift, Stephen and Deborah fixing plates for the three of them from bits of this and that. More bologna, olives, anchovies, a loaf of bread. Louise did not eat at all. There wasn't the faintest pretense; the plate sat beside her untouched. She was treated in this with the deference allowed certain actresses. As if her craft would be endangered by an activity as coarse as mastication. Stephen ate the anchovies and bread, little else, though he drank prodigiously of the rum they'd gotten at Cane Garden Bay. The night was dark and enveloping. On a sailboat there was nowhere to go, no way to make the dark any lighter.

"What time is it?"

"Seven-thirty."

"That's all?"

They got more cups from below and shared the rum around. Even Louise. It made her lightheaded and happy; she told of one of the fraternity dinners with Hinderly, the ridiculous opulence, she had sat next to a king's or prince's son from the United Arab Emirates.

"The only minorities are royalty. You have to be a prince or like, a shah."

"A shah!" They remembered Bev's father saying his granddaughters were princesses; they would only marry princes.

"Or shahs," Deborah said. The word was funny enough to be repeated.

Not far from them was a restaurant built in an old schooner. "Let's go over," Deborah said. They climbed down into their dinghy, Stephen holding the lantern and steadying the little boat. He was high from sun and rum. But who cared. He steered the dinghy through the boats moored nearby. At the bar they ordered Painkillers. They were made exquisitely, the thick froth at the lip of the glass sprinkled with shaved nutmeg. There were other sunburned parties there, all fours and fives, families or intrepid friends. There was a sense they would do anything to enjoy themselves, anything to maximize the enjoyment. When they were old and decrepit they would want to remember their days of robust drinking and sunburn, their feats of daring. If there was a shark, a cave marked Danger, a cocktail, they wanted to be in on it. "Booze cruise," someone, different someones, kept saying. Four tall men were challenging each other to shots of this and that. They sent over a trio of shots arranged in holes in a miniature surfboard.

"All together now," one of the men said. They counted down, 3–2–1 and Stephen and Louise and Deborah shot the rum concoctions together.

"They're my daughters," he said to the tall men. "Aren't they beautiful? A blonde and a brunette."

"They're beautiful," one of the men agreed hungrily.

"Your wife must be a good-looking woman."

"*The* good-looking one," another said. Male banter. They were all tall and good-looking themselves; they would never have wives who fell in love with women.

"C'mon, Daddy. Let's go home." Deborah was next to him, taking his arm.

The girls helped him into the boat and motored him back in the black dark; they were lost for a while without their navigator.

THree

Spring came slowly that year, held back by cold rain. In May it was still promising to arrive. Outdoors the air still smelled faintly of thaw. Louise had not gained enough weight to look like a woman. She graduated from college in the body of a girl. Deborah and Stephen and his parents, aged now, his father moving on a cane and breathing with difficulty, sat together at the ceremony. Bev and Joan and Bev's father sat apart from them, end seats toward the back. Bev's mother had dementia; she was too ill to travel. A celebrity had a nephew graduating. Necks craned; the celebrity's name was on everyone's lips. She was an avatar of the new plastic surgery. Everyone wanted to see the face in person, so as to have an opinion about whether or not it looked real.

In the fall Deborah would go to college, but not to this, her father's alma mater. She wanted to be far from home, anonymous; the campus vast as a small city. No one there would know her. She was going to Michigan.

There was a celebrity at the dais as well, regal and bored. Louise had wanted Ralph Nader or a Nicaraguan poet who worked for human rights. This man was a news commentator; one night a week he was on television. In his speech he charged the graduates with a responsibility. The wrong people were having children; it was time for the right people to begin doing their part. By rhetorical means he seemed to want to extract a promise from the audience. They would procreate; they would send more good people into the world.

Joshua van Gelden had been hired as a representative for a wine company. Louise had interviewed for editorial assistant jobs at some trade magazines. They put her in a room alone with a typewriter and some pieces of information. In an hour she'd had to make a story out of what they'd given her. She had believed she would fail. Her story would be fanciful or mocking; her contempt for the task would shine through in her prose. But that had not been the case. They wanted to hire her to work with them. They would give her a cubicle in a building in Times Square.

In the middle of the ceremony the rain of the past several months returned. There was no choice but to press on through the list of names. Many of the graduates, sitting in the front rows, were under the cover of a large elm tree. Others had brought umbrellas. Stephen opened his and held it over his parents. The afternoon was ruined, hundreds of people having traveled to sit here and now everyone only thinking about when it would be over, when they could get up and go indoors.

Louise went to her mother first. They embraced; Louise with the leather diploma holder in her hand.

"Let me see."

"It's just the case. We get them later."

Joan hugged her, and then her Florida grandfather. He was liver-spotted now from so much sun. Skin cancer had been gouged out of his head; he had none of his own teeth and wore none. His mouth curled in like the edges of a piece of dried fruit.

"Your mother is very proud of you." Joan had a spiky haircut and was wearing a shirt with a mandarin collar, jute linen, a spacious shirt, it was not tucked into her pants. She wasn't shaped like a woman. She and Louise were females who were not shaped like women.

"We want to take you to lunch."

It was her graduation day. This once.

"I don't want lunch."

❖

The campus had a certain feel the morning after a celebration, sub-dued, nearly silent, half-full plastic cups on the stone ledges, in the stairwells. The sheets announcing the parties in spray paint hung over the arch at Hamlin Hall and the arch at Jarvis—now they bil-lowed in the morning wind; now what they announced was history. Almost. "Come . . . and Come Again" were the words in blue on the Hamlin sheet. It was the best arch, the most foot traffic. The first party was over now, Saturday night, people were sleeping it off. The brothers had handed out condoms at the door, had thumbtacked condoms filled with water to a cork board beside where the pledges worked the keg.

"We're raising AIDS awareness." They were straight-faced when the assistant dean of students arrived to question them. She was Asian, serious, wore glasses big for her face. Heidi Chu-Anderson, her name was.

"Heidi who?" they called as she retreated from their property, back to campus proper. "Heidi Chu!"

Brunch was the Come Again, Bloody Marys at eleven. Louise woke in daylight, in the back bedroom of the fraternity house. An Indian tapestry was tacked over the window but still the sun shone through.

He turned over and faced her. The leonine head, the eye. He had ridden her when she was drunk. She had never been entered from behind before. Now she was ashamed of it, of being ridden like a mare.

"You're so fucking skinny, I love it."

She had seen Caroline in aerobics class; this year Caroline had gained weight, most of it in her hips. Caroline looked like a woman now, ready to be a wife. Already she was no longer a college student; she wore sweaters draped over her shoulders.

He ran his hand down Louise's flank. "You have a great little ass." He pulled her toward him. His skin was warm; he smelled of beer and Canoe; she loved the smell of him.

"Let's go again." He rose up over her.

"No, I can't. I can't."

"Why?"

"The sponge won't work anymore, it's too late."

"I'll pull out."

Her period hadn't come in months; she acquiesced.

"Now you go on top."

She saw the image of herself riding him like a horse. Him the horse now, her the rider. "No. You go on top."

"I'll hold you. I'll make it good."

"No." As with lunch the day before, no.

There was a poster of Wayne Gretzky on the wall. She watched Wayne Gretzky as he entered her from behind again, again, again.

This was the last time. They would leave college, they would never lay eyes on each other again.

～～

They talked only about their daughters; there was nothing else to discuss. After twenty years they were strangers to each other. But strangers who shared a past. They could not think of their lives without thinking of each other. No reverie was pure.

Bev and Joan lived at the edge of a beach community. In Suffolk County now, farther out on Long Island. The Pine Barrens dense with trees that would burn before the end of the century, sand in drifts on the roads, dunes in some places on either side of the two-lane highway. Out here the weather was less predictable, the names of the towns exotic, Indian. Quogue, Moriches, Mastic.

There were times Bev longed for her other life. There is ease in being the wife of—the mother of—. In not having to present any other form of self.

"There were fewer choices," she told Joan. She had not forgotten that she had wanted to write a book. What she could no longer feel was the intensity of her desire then. She had wanted to prove herself someone who could step above merely managing the disorder of children and households. That was what all women did, daily. Had she come upon the avid notes in the margins of the Goffman book she would have laughed the harsh laugh of one suppressing tears or anger.

There was always an outside eye on her now. The neighbors were curious. Maybe they were disgusted, wanted to keep their children away. She couldn't tell which were her own feelings, which interpretive errors. The woman across the street drove a school bus. It was parked in front of the house. She had two boys, lanky, addicted to basketball. They played at any hour.

"Do they have to do that at eleven o'clock at night?" Joan got out of bed and put on a sweatshirt.

"Don't get into anything with them. We're already on their shit list."

It was one thing for a straight person to tell you to knock off the basketball, another for a big old dyke in a sweatshirt.

Straight people seemed to resent you the way married people resented single people. You were doing something they hadn't thought to do, or that they had relinquished.

They were all the time now in the company of women. For Joan this was nothing new but to Bev a life had opened inside life. They made parties for women; they grew flowers; their house was full of photographs of women, their bodies, their faces. Marilyn Monroe on the hall closet in her glamorous upblown dress. In the bathroom, a nineteenth-century woman bending to her ablutions, the curve of her back to the viewer.

"I love our life."

"We'll make it go on forever."

They wanted to marry each other, they bought each other rings, they were married in nearly every sense.

Bev called Deborah in Michigan. Another woman's voice answered the phone.

"She's not here, she has lab until six."

"Will you tell her, her mother called?"

"I'll tell her."

"Will you tell her to call back?"

"Is it an emergency? I can try to find her."

"No, it's not an emergency."

She and Deborah hadn't spoken in two months, since before Deborah went off to Michigan. Now Bev began to have episodes of panic, shortness of breath. On the way to work she had to pull off to the side of the road, push her seat back, force her head down between her legs, try to breathe.

Oh god oh god oh god. They were the only words she could get out.

Music was the worst; she never knew what would trigger it. James Taylor, Donna Summer, Crosby Stills Nash. *Hot stuff baby this evening*—she remembered dancing with Deborah, age six, pony-tailed, in the living room. The two of them whirling in skirts, Louise curled up on the sofa. Bev listened only to morning talk shows on the radio and then to news on the way home. Howard Stern was on the radio for hours; she became a fan of Howard Stern in spite of the breast jokes, in spite of the Lesbian Dial-a-Date. It was good to laugh; she tried to do it often.

Stephen called her one Saturday afternoon, just before Thanksgiving.

"She's not doing well. She failed some of her midterms."

"I don't understand it."

"I think she's angry at you. She wants an explanation."

"An explanation for what?"

"For what happened with you." He was searching for the word but all that would come to mind was 'conversion.' He didn't want to say 'conversion.'

"For you and Joan, what. Getting together."

"I don't have to provide her with any sort of explanation—"

"I'm not saying you do, I'm saying she wants one."

"Has she been to see a counselor?"

"No."

"Maybe she should go see someone."

Blank air, dead air, on his end. "That's your way," he said finally.

"It's the way of a lot of people; anyone on the street goes to see a therapist!" Her voice rose, shrill; she was losing control, the way she did sometimes when she was driving and a James Taylor song came on the radio.

Deborah was finding her own way. She tried varieties of Protestantism, avoided anything having to do with Jews. She went to the Newman Center. There wasn't a shred of Catholic in her but Catholicism fit her best. There was order, there was beauty, she liked the Madonna's upturned face. One day she would go to Florence and see the friezes, see the church that held Michelangelo's tomb. Her roommate, Angela Eckers, was Catholic, tormented, clever, bulimic. Angela's parents sniped at each other; her father kept a mistress. Rotating mistresses. Angela had met some of them; some of them she liked. Sometimes, if she especially disliked one, it seemed her father dismissed the woman; she was never seen on Angela's father's arm again.

They didn't speak of the bulimia. Deborah didn't tell Angela about her mother and Joan. These taboos held them in place with each other, forces in equal and opposite directions. Angela knew Deborah knew she vomited her meals; Deborah knew Angela knew about her mother.

"Growing up I never had a religion."

"You can see how much good it did me," Angela said.

"You don't think it helped you?"

"Christ did." She was sitting on her bed, pensive, a notebook in her lap. "I always liked Christ."

The martyrdom, the flaying, the crown of thorns—that was what Angela liked.

"Yes, well. I do admire his sacrifice."

Whereas Deborah liked everything but the Christ dangling from his cross. It was the opulence of the Catholics that appealed to her, the architectural grandeur. She would have liked the main icon hanging in the front of the room to be a picture of Jesus and Mary with the baby Jesus and maybe a dog.

He had no ritual, no moorings or tethers; he invested himself completely in boats. On Saturdays he drove to boatyards all over Long Island, in Connecticut, in New Jersey. There was always a forlorn or abandoned trawler to be rescued, a skiff, an old wooden Chris Craft with a hole punched in the hull. "Beauty," he would say to the boatyard owner as they stood together surveying the boats out of water, their hulls cradled in wooden ribs.

"You want it? It's just taking up space here."

"You don't often see a honey like that." He accumulated them. He couldn't turn one down.

"You have to make him," Deborah told Louise. "You have to say look, Dad. There's no more room for these boats, you've gotta start clearing them out of here and not buying any new ones for a while."

"You tell him. You're better at it."

"Christ Almighty. Isn't there even one thing I can count on you to do?"

No. Louise too was tetherless. She had taken one of the Times Square jobs. The magazine's offices were on the seventeenth floor.

She had a cubicle that blocked the light from the windows. *Sporting Goods Business* was the name of the magazine. Her boss was overweight and picked at his nails with a hunting knife. She wrote a brief on a new sports tape you could use to wrap your ankles, another on banana clips. She had to look up the definition before she wrote the piece. It would never have occurred to her to put *banana* with weapons.

She claimed she walked the twenty blocks and then across town for the exercise. But it was also true she was afraid of the subway. Turnstile jumpers, panhandlers who hassled and wheedled for money, a fear of being pushed off the platform. Another fear of missing her stop and ending up taking the train all the way to Brooklyn. All the way. As if she would have to swim back to Manhattan, or as if she would be engulfed by the people who lived in Brooklyn. She had never been so afraid of rape and robbery; she hated the city; at night, when she cleaned her face, the cotton ball came away gray with soot.

Uptown on the East Side, Hinderly was amassing a lifestyle. He was a sugar trader; he drove out to the suburbs on the weekends to buy his liquor in volume, the vodka and whiskey bottles with handles and pour spouts. He took her to a restaurant in the Village with a one-word, one-syllable name. Fashionable. She was too drunk to remember it later. Bam? Doom? Maybe something minimalist: Food. Room. She remembered eating endive. Champagne. Back in his apartment, he never seemed to tire of working her over.

"Autumnal drink."

"We've already done this."

"We've never done *that.*"

Slouched on his crimson sofa, amid what she called his treasures of the orient, maps and trunks and tapestries, she looked up at him. His face appeared prismatic, chubby angles. If angles could be chubby. He was all in pieces.

"You don't want to do *that* with me."

"Why not?"

"We're friends."

He was off and running with it. "Friends who sleep in bed together, friends who do things for each other, friends who make each other feel good." He plunked down beside her, stroked her hair.

He was embarrassing her, even beneath the drunk layer. "No no no."

Why? A million reasons.

She wouldn't have to go into them.

"I'm leaving the city."

He would never leave the city. He was already a fixture; to her he was like the lions outside the public library, a minor Manhattan landmark. He lived the life here as life here was best lived. His door-man knew his name. That was nothing. Twice a week his doorman placed his order for mixers at the deli down the street. Tonic water arrived at his door, cranberry, OJ. He never shopped; his refrigerator was spotless.

❖

"*It's sort of* a bachelor pad," Stephen said.

She surveyed the apartment. A guitar in a sticker-covered case, a sheet music holder, a harmonica with a headset attachment that allowed the wearer to play guitar and harmonica at the same time. In the one bedroom, a photo of a recumbent woman, face obscured, body sensuous and feline as a cat's. Part of *Hai Sing*'s polished hull hung on the wall over his bed. She didn't think she'd want a hull hanging over her head. There was a big Heineken bottle cap, the size of a Frisbee, hung low on the wall next to the living room sofa. The books on the shelf from the living room at the old house. He still had the book about healing mushrooms. Books on weather, books on the tides, a book on extending one's life span. In the freezer, in foil, mince pies made by his mother ages ago. Literally: a year? More? His mother's hands were now so arthritic she had trouble baking. There was a bottle of colloidal silver in the refrigerator. He had heard it provided minerals leached from the soil by contemporary farming methods.

Did he want to live forever? What did he want?

The drawers in his house were filled with old bills, magazines, photos of contact lens manufacturing machines he'd built or fixed in Puerto Rico, Brownsville in south Texas, the Philippines, Vienna. Other photos of her father standing beside bespectacled or squinting people who looked like foreigners. The engineers he worked with in those places. Louise studied them. It didn't matter where you were from; engineers everywhere had that vague rabbity look, as if they would prefer to run off under the cabbages.

She had never thought she would return to Soundview. It seemed shrunken to her, as do all childhood places when one returns as an adult. She could jog the whole circumference in less than an hour. In the mornings she passed the children climbing on the school buses. Her old bus stop—all the faces were new there now; she didn't even recognize younger siblings of people she'd known. But there were still awkward girls as she had been awkward, though in different fashions, with different satchels, neon colors. Girls who wore glasses, who slumped and read standing up while they waited for the bus, whose braces snagged at their lips and made them bleed. Things tumbled from memory: a case study on the sinking of the Lusitania, a novel they'd read in ninth grade social studies about apartheid, that word knocking around intermittently in her head for a decade, too abstract for her to understand it; a report on the Puritans' colony at Roanoke in eighth grade. The teacher had taught them to burn the edges of the paper, to make the document look aged. Someone's had gone up in flames, the teacher's feet stamping it out. Probably you weren't allowed to have fire in a classroom now; the rules were tighter; there was fear in schools now, the threat of guns.

While her father was at work she cleaned the apartment. The division of belongings between him and her mother had been in the end haphazard. He had two salad spinners, two crock pots, a surfeit of salad forks. But he had little in the way of bedding. She had to improvise with sheets when she made up the sofa bed; there were no fitted sheets at all.

"There's a waitressing job down at Poseidon's that just opened up," Stephen said as they sat on stools at his kitchen counter and ate take-out Chinese food. Louise would touch only the broccoli in garlic sauce.

"You should try some of this General Chang's Szechuan chicken."

"I'm a vegetarian," she said.

"Do you want me to ask about the waitressing?"

To picture herself a waitress was no easier or more difficult than to picture herself on a narrow platform high above a crowd, ready to grasp the bar and sail forward in a sequined leotard on a trapeze. This was how it was to envision herself in black and white, a skirt, sensible shoes, her hair pulled off her face, her manner brisk and decisive as she announced the specials, took orders on a pad, carried a tray at her shoulder past the large aquariums and murky lobster tank, the lobsters scrabbling despite their tied claws. She was fundamentally a sleepy and plodding person, given to doing one thing and then another. She was not brisk and decisive; all that had gone to Deborah.

"I was thinking of applying for a job at that health food store in Glen Cove."

Stephen shrugged. "Waitressing would be a lot more lucrative, I mean for the time you'd spend."

How could she explain to him? Never a waitress; it would expose too much of her, strip her down to her white bones. There were so many things she could never imagine herself doing, all in her mind involving certain exertions beyond what she was convinced made up her core self. She could never see herself stage acting as her father had done in high school, the new karaoke craze terrified her, she was equally unable to imagine herself selling anything, but particularly cars or homes. Selling those required a persona; waitressing required a persona. Most jobs did.

Jogging again the next morning, it began to rain. She kept running anyway, her shirt soaked through, her face slick. She was not a lazy person, but she was very afraid. The only kind of job she could imagine excelling at was repetitive, solitary, the work of factories or libraries.

⌐⌐

She saw old friends from high school now, the ones who had stayed. Not bona fide friends, only people she had known by sight or sat near in chorus or math. When they met in the pharmacy or grocery store they spoke warmly to each other. Some had babies already, some already looked tired by motherhood, their hair pulled back hurriedly, their bodies ruined. Tired at twenty-one. One named

Barbara took to her especially, clung when their paths crossed, detained Louise in the drugstore when she was contemplating new formula Dexatrim.

"I *thought* it was you."

She was married to the man who owned the fresh seafood store in town.

"Nicky Liantonio. You remember him?"

She did, in connection with Rosalie. How Rosalie had gotten a hiding from her father after talking to Nicky.

The store, Barbara said, was a basic place, chilled as the inside of a refrigerator, with fluorescent lights, cement floors. With a fish store you didn't spend money on the décor. Nicky had taught her that, when she tried to spruce up the place with dried flowers arranged on a wooden table.

"It's okay. Except the work's seasonal."

Louise recalled driving past one day and noticing a chalkboard outside announced the day's specials. Little Necks, Tuna, Flounder.

"I can't get the smell off me, no matter what," Barbara said. "Even the kids smell like it." She bent and lifted the fine hair of one of her children. Both were towheads, their hair nearly white. There was a single wrinkle under each of their eyes, from illness or sleep; they looked like tiny old people. They had the wise look of the aged in their faces, as if they knew with the parents they'd got they were doomed. Or doomed insofar as they were destined never to leave here. They would pick up their old-age prescriptions for blood pressure and palpitations at this counter at Twin Harbor Drugs just as their mother was picking up their medicine now for coughs and earaches.

A scrap of a poem from college came to her. ". . . *even the dreadful martyrdom must run its course . . .*"

"You have beautiful children."

She didn't know why she so dreaded this town, why she felt herself being engulfed. Sometimes there came as if from the inside of her head a great rushing noise, like water.

Friends of the family had, after her parents' split, cast their lot with her father. He had not asked them to renounce her mother, but her mother had left. To leave a small town is to renounce.

"How is your mother?" some of them asked.

Bev was only her mother now; she was not any longer their friend.

A friend from childhood rocked on a porch swing at her own mother's house one day. Louise sat on a sofa in a metal frame that rocked back and forth. It had been here forever, this sofa. She had curled up on it and fallen asleep the Fourth of July of the Bicentennial. More than a decade ago. This was the house of Mrs. Qwee. That diminutive foreign presence moving about, small as a child, but with adult knowledge concentrated in her. She had seemed dense with adult knowledge, a kind of beatitude that comes of seeing the most terrible things occur and of surviving them, of watching the next stage come to pass.

Her friend was a lawyer in Brooklyn now; she had recently gotten her blonde hair done in cornrows, at a salon for African-Americans; she had been the only white person. People now stopped on the street to look at her.

"I don't think she's really a lesbian."

Louise felt dreamy, lightheaded, ill. "What do you mean?"

"It's a phase."

Louise said nothing; she was not prepared yet to contemplate her parents' phases. Of them she had only heard of the man's midlife crisis, when a sports car would be purchased. Hot flashes for women.

The cornrowed lawyer stood up, dusted crumbs off her skirt. "Or she's realized a man won't want her. It's better than being alone."

There were some like this one who shrugged at her mother, the new life, seeming conversion. Who cared if she attended the Pride parade, if she walked down the avenue with this new lover, no longer the mother her daughters recognized?

Others would not speak of it to her at all. Her mother in the next county with Joan Kellerperson might have been banished, imprisoned, dead.

She found an aerobics class at the Presbyterian Church in Glen Cove. After class one afternoon she went into the health food store and bought a carrot juice. She stood out front drinking it, her hair pulled up off her face. She was gaunt but radiant, her heart thuddering in her chest.

A man in a short apron with the store logo on it stepped outside and lit a cigarette. She turned to him. Pale, pale skin, naturally pale, with a puffiness under the eyes. A drinker, like her father. Thin lipped, glasses, cleft chin.

"You're allowed to smoke?"

"Out here it's a free country. In there's another story."

Not American. She felt almost gratitude toward him for it, without knowing why. What objection did she have to Americans?

"I just thought if you worked here you wouldn't smoke."

"Work is work, love." He tapped his ash; he had an expert way of moving with a cigarette; later, she would see, with a drink in his hand as well. Bars were his home base. For the Irish this is true of bars; whereas Americans are most themselves at work.

"What part of Ireland?"

He inhaled and answered her as he exhaled. "Not far from Dublin. A little town called Trim."

She knew nothing of Ireland. All her images were from literature, the Misses Morkan and the strains from the piano, Gabriel listening on the stairs, Eveline walking toward the gangplank and then turning back. The mad, garbled Dublin of *Ulysses*.

He had read one by Roddy Doyle that he proclaimed excellent. Another by Edna O'Brien, but only the naughty bits.

He was staring intently downward. "Those are lovely trainers you're wearing."

"Thank you." He bent and touched her shoes, a hand on each foot. They were just sneakers, though high-end ones. She felt the heat from his hands. In spite of the ludicrousness of the gesture there was a startling intimacy, to have someone touch her feet like that, even through shoes.

She remembered after a party at college, finding a pair of alligator skin shoes on top of a garbage can full of trash. It was one or two in the morning, she just back from one of the fraternities alone, wandering through the men's hall on the bottom floor. Maybe looking for someone else who was lonely. She lifted the shoes out and set them on the floor. Nothing appeared to be wrong with them. They fit. But she put them back, though they were elegant, sleek and reptilian. There would be a price to pay if the original owner recognized them clacking along on her feet. Belongings at college had been thrown away because they acquired bad associations, perhaps because they inspired an insult; because people were bored.

The Irishman cupped his hand and lit another cigarette. This was his second wind he was chasing, he said. After his shift was done here he would go caddy at the country club, then get his baby from his wife, who waitressed nights.

A nearly overpowering static in her ears, of disappointment, opportunity missed. She forced her mouth shut, pushed the conversation onward. "How old's the baby?"

"Oh, she's just a little tiny baby, barely old enough to lift her own head."

Clare. They had named her after a county in Ireland, though not the county they were from. "Meath's no kind of a name for a baby girl," he said.

"How long've you been married?"

He laughed. He was smoking the cigarette down to the very nub, so that he had to hold between two fingers like a joint and squint as he inhaled. "Too long," he said.

She raised her eyebrows. He looked young, nearly as young as she herself.

"Not long at all. Just a few months now."

He held the door for her as they went in. She found the owner and asked for a job.

"Fill this out."

She wrote everything she could think of on the application, her hand shaking. She had no thought of hiding anything so as not to be seen as overqualified. Recent college graduate, major in English. Phi Beta Kappa, summa cum laude, awards for writing about literature, awards for poetry.

The owner surveyed her precise handwriting, the eloquent statement about the value of natural foods stores in the community. A knowledge of macrobiotics, Buddhism (though this knowledge academic rather than experiential); a desire, Louise had written, *to learn more about healthy ways to live.*

Craig Gibbons was wearing a Grateful Dead T-shirt. He had a big crooked mouthful of teeth, good skin. The skin of someone who eats quantities of fresh foods, so glowing and radiant that it dimmed the effect of the teeth. "What have we got for you?" He rested against the wall beside the time clock. "I worry nothing that would be enough of a challenge." He lowered his voice. "You might be bored."

She had lost sight of the Irishman; he had gone back to stocking shelves.

"I could do a lot of things. I just left a job at the city. In the city."

He was looking closely at her application. "Wirth," he said. "Are you related to Bev Wirth?"

"She's my mother."

He brightened considerably. "Bev Wirth's daughter. I wouldn't have pegged you."

"No one does." This not said in a way, she hoped, that would lead him to any particular interpretation.

"How is she?"

She never knew whether or how to mention the divorce, complicated as it was by Joan Kellerperson. You couldn't well go announcing to people you barely knew your mother was now a lesbian, it wasn't the sort of thing one announced.

"She's good, fine. She doesn't live around here anymore."

"Oh?"

"Or she would be in here all the time," she finished weakly. She thought of her mother watching cable TV beside Joan in their big bed with the splashes of flowers on the sheets. Why that image? Why that one?

"Well." He folded her application. "We have cashier, deli clerk, maybe some assisting Janet, who's in charge of our supplements. But for someone who's been studying Faulkner—"

"No, it sounds good. I love it here; you have a good store." She made some disjointed remarks about her own diet, quoting brokenly from memory a book she'd read, *The Macrobiotic Way*. At one point later she would remember telling the owner how she had grated daikon or taro root for a sitz bath, it had cured a yeast infection. She had known it was the wrong thing to say, that she was babbling, overstating the case. But the Irishman, his hands on her feet. She would do anything to be near him.

Another autumn came, this one wet. Rain pasted leaves to the ground like splayed inert hands; to try to rake was futile. Deborah had not made a trip home at all that summer. She had stayed in Michigan and waitressed at a restaurant on the Leelanau Peninsula. Stephen and Louise had received postcards with color photos of The Cherry Hut on them. *People come and have cherry pie a la mode for breakfast at six in the morning.* Then at the bottom in a different pen, maybe an afterthought. It struck Louise as a little hint in some way of desperation: *Even I am getting sick of cherries.*

"We haven't heard from her either," Louise told Bev. It was almost true; they knew nothing of Deborah's life. Cherries wasn't anything. Did she have a boyfriend, where would she live in the fall, what of her academic pursuits? How she was wearing her hair was an unknown; Louise recalled Deborah mentioning in the spring that she might dye or cut it. She imagined her long-haired sister with a bob, or with her dark hair yellow.

"I don't see why—" Bev began. But didn't finish.

"I'm sure we'll hear from her soon," Louise said. But it was only conciliatory, to keep the conversation moving. On the other end of the phone she could hear her mother stuffing back a sob.

Louise became both daughters; she considered it her fate. She strove to be one with enough good in her for both. *Moiety:* the word came to her, one she'd had to look up when she read the Austen novels in college. *One of two approximately equal parts.* Now she would be both to her mother. Both moieties. In the early autumn, the first weekend in four when it wasn't wet, she met Bev and Joan at the Fire Island ferry dock. It was Indian summer, a glistening day with a high strong sun. They had a red and white cooler between them and a canvas L.L.Bean beach bag with Joan's initials monogrammed on the pocket. Only initials; no Kellerperson. On both their T-shirts was the same word, *Provincetown,* Joan's blue and Bev's purple.

Other friends showed up. Louise hadn't known there would be other friends. Donna and Donna, Charlotte, Carol Miller.

"Lezfest," someone was saying as they climbed the stairs to the upper deck of the ferry. It was repeated, the day's first joke, lezfest, lezfest. Though Charlotte wasn't a lesbian and neither was Louise.

Still, she felt a shrinking from them; she wanted to be small, step out of giant shoes and creep away. To become so small she could recline in a pocket as if it were a hammock. Eamon, the Irishman, wore on cool mornings a nondescript gray windbreaker. He kept his cigarettes in the pocket, Irish cigarettes called Majors in a green and orange box wider than American ones. Even the box seemed elegant and substantial, the smoke from the cigarettes richer. The lining of the jacket smelled of him, beer and baby talcum and his own peculiar sexual smell of perspiration, many labors. She had slipped an unsigned note in his pocket in answer to his question. As the ferry crossed to Cherry Grove she stayed at the rail and looked down at the churning water. Would he call her or was it a bluff?

A large crowd met the ferry on the other side, men kissing men, people of indeterminate gender kissing people of indeterminate gender. A person with breasts and a small, tended goatee. Men with the articulated gestures and manicured fingernails of women.

The wooden boardwalk creaked underfoot as they made their pilgrimage to the beach. Mecca, someone said, and one of the Donna's dropped to her knees and salaamed in the direction of the sea. That prompted more jokes. *You don't need to get down on your knees with this crowd.* As they reached the end of the boardwalk where the sand began, Bev lunged theatrically at the beachfront bar, gasping for daiquiris.

"Oh if you must, before lunch." Joan handed Bev her wallet. "Uncivilized brute."

"It is you who are uncivilized."

Early daiquiris; in the sun, from alcohol on an empty stomach, Louise could feel her heartbeat ticking in her temples, an unpleasant pulse and pulse. Their chairs were arranged in semicircle. Six women with their feet stretched out in front of them, their elbows propped on the metal arms of their chairs. They presided over this stretch of beach like a panel of judges. Two women further down, one young and brazen in her preening, the other subtle as a gentlemanly European adulterer, lounged languidly on a blanket.

"The little chickie's wearing a thong."

"At least she has a beautiful ass."

A bag of pretzels was handed around. Then popcorn. The young woman sat up and removed her bikini top, took off the kerchief on her head and shook out her hair. She had an exotic look, as of the very wealthy or the racially mixed.

"A model from Montserrat," Charlotte said.

"Oh, get off it. I bet she's a little Jewish girl from Brooklyn. Her name's Lisa Steinberg."

"That's actually less of a show than I thought we'd get," Joan said.

"They're well aware we're watching them."

"We're the whole point."

The Donna who was heavier, who with her broad shoulders and strong thighs and the rooted to the ground way she stood reminded Louise of a bouncer at a nightclub, threw back her head and laughed. "I remember the first time I came to this beach. I was seventeen and terrified, all these bodies and freedom. I was just this little uptight high school kid, I didn't know shit."

Everyone was sitting forward now, the lovers on the blanket forgotten.

"I left the group I was with and went for a walk by myself. I was just wandering, it was like my mind had left and my body was walking around on its own. I must have been drinking or drugging or something. Then at one point I was up in these dunes." She gestured behind them, "I came to the crest of this one dune and I look down and there are these two men with their arms wrapped around each other, tongue kissing. It was like something hit me right between the forehead, I mean right in the forehead. Right between the eyes. I knew what was going on with me, I was like, duh, of course Donna, you're gay."

"That was what seeing two men tongue kissing taught you?"

"I don't know how to explain it," Donna said. "But yes."

"That's some story," someone said.

Her mother was wearing sunglasses; Louise couldn't see her eyes.

"I'll cook a turkey," Stephen said. "The whole nine yards, from when you and Deborah were kids." He would make the improvised stuffing with pretzels that Aunt Beck had invented; also the waxed turnip the English called swede that he had eaten so often in his childhood in London, when there were meat shortages. Real cranberry sauce, and he would cook the turkey slowly, overnight. It was the only way to do it right, cooking the bird slowly.

Louise no longer ate turkey. She was now a vegan as well.

"Eggs are off limits now, too? Cheese?" Stephen was aghast; there were only so many meals in a row at which one could eat brown rice. But in spite of this regimen Louise had gained a little weight. Without knowing it Eamon had swayed her. It was the great joy he took in eating. He and Louise would try to take their breaks at work at the same time, sitting on empty bulk tofu containers behind the store.

"Don't they ever use chopsticks in Ireland?" She was laughing as she watched him try to negotiate his lunch between the wooden sticks. The food kept slipping through them; finally he dug in with his fingers and pushed a whole croquette into his mouth.

"A Chinese back home I'd eat with a fork and knife, like anything else."

"Or your fingers, more likely."

He ate like a savage, a delighted savage with good manners, a napkin tucked in his shirt. He licked his fingers. "You should try this millet croquette, it's good." He lifted another one out of his Chinese food container and held it out to her.

"No."

"Half."

She opened her mouth. From his fingers she would eat.

In this way, after four years at college of starving on Diet Coke, she began to inhabit the body of a woman, though a slight woman, bird-boned and delicate. Her jaw and cheekbones were still prominent in her face, so that her head was the head of an older woman on the body of a young one.

His shift started and finished before hers. He smoked out back by the dumpsters, the latest issue of *Natural Foods Merchandiser* in his lap.

He fell into step with her. "Will I walk you to your car?"

"It's across the street, behind the bank."

He took her arm at the curb, in exaggerated gentlemanly style.

She could smell the perspiration and talcum; his cigarette was still burning in his other hand.

At her car he asked for her keys and opened the driver's side door for her.

"Get in." His voice was hoarse.

It was ridiculous but she obeyed him, climbing in behind the wheel and sitting primly with her hands in her lap, waiting for the next command. He shut the door, then motioned for her to roll down the window.

"Yes? Can I help you?" Beaming up at him she was a character in a play who hadn't been told her lines.

He swiveled to survey the parking lot, then knelt and held her face in his hands. It was not a game. She let the smile she'd been holding go slack. He was looking searchingly into her eyes, back and forth from one to the other.

"I have come to care for you very greatly."

"I have, too—"

He stopped her with a look. "I know it has not been much time, but I feel very deeply, I feel . . ."

He could say nothing more; his eyes were filling.

"I know."

"I have married the wrong person," he said.

"I know."

"No, I mean not just a wrong person, *the* wrong person. She'll never let me get away."

With some effort Louise reached her hands through the window of her car and took hold of him. His shoulders as she held him shook.

❖

"Tofurkey."

"It sounds like a curse," Deborah said. She held up her middle finger. "Tofurkey you." She was just off the plane and had about her the velocity of someone who has been traveling by air. Roving, unsteady. She could not sit still in the apartment. Instead she wandered, lifting objects and inspecting and then putting them down in slightly different places. A metronome, a can of beer from Austria, a yellow embroidered pillow: *Never, Never Question the Engineer's*

Judgment. It would be hard to see the apartment through Deborah's eyes. She loved Stephen with partisan zeal, absolutely.

"I'm making it," Louise said.

"You'll be the only one eating it."

"I don't care."

"And then of course you don't eat."

But now Louise did eat, though the added weight was muscle, from jogging. In the basement of the store she packaged bulk Medjool dates, raw and tamari roasted almonds, Turkish apricots. And Eamon, interrupting his inventory came over with his clipboard under one arm and fed her from his hands. She was returning to food as a child comes to it, fed from the hands of those who love her.

"What's it like living with Dad? Does he bring that girlfriend here?"

"He goes to her place. It's only on the weekends, she has kids and works."

Deborah was still traveling around the room, surveying. Who was her father now? The books alone sufficed to make one wonder. Bertrand Russell's *Wisdom of the West, The Horolovar 400-Day Clock Repair Guide,* what was he doing with *The Fountainhead* on his bookshelf? Or *Psychedelic Drugs Reconsidered*?

He was their father but now first and foremost he was a man. The role of the father was secondary, something from before that now was fading.

Deborah found an open bottle of white zinfandel in the refrigerator and splashed some into a glass. She too had grown in this year away at college. She drank casually now, though never to inebriation. She would sometimes smoke one cigarette.

"Who eats kippers?"

"Dad. He makes kipper sandwiches on rye."

"Is he still drinking a lot?"

Louise considered. "A fair amount. Not as much as before."

"Probably because of you."

Louise couldn't tell whether or not this was a reproach.

Now Deborah was looking at the collection of cassette tapes beside the stereo receiver: Cabaret, Brubeck, Grieg, something called *Ice Flowers Melting* and another called *Golden Voyage* with a mandala on the cover. *Bette Midler: Live at Last.* That one must have escaped when Bev was packing. "When are you getting out of here?" "I don't know. In a while. I think he likes having me around." Louise didn't know whether or not this was in any way true. Her father said nothing and he asked nothing about her life except whether she had read anything recently that she liked. She had said *The Bell Jar* by a writer named Sylvia Plath and he had snorted a laugh and said, "Well, don't get too involved in that. It wouldn't be too far-fetched to say your mother's problems started with her or Anne Sexton." He knew nothing of Eamon, though she believed they would like each other if she put them together in a bar. No one in her family knew anything of Eamon, anything of this new self in her coming to life.

She could not even call him. If he called her it was from a pay phone or from work. Then she rushed for the phone; if her father picked it up the line would go dead.

Stephen arrived home late in a suit, a raincoat folded over his arm. Deborah was the spitting image of Bev at eighteen, even down to the doe eyes and down-turned laughing mouth. All the gestures were Bev's; he could hardly look at her.

Louise and Deborah shared the fold-out couch. At least Louise had gone out for a proper set of sheets.

"Sleep tight, Eskimos," Stephen said as he went into his own room. When they were children he had told them stories of his beagle who hated cars and then got hit by one. The dog hadn't died, had only come to hate cars more. Sometimes in those days when he was their father first, even before being himself, he left cartoons he drew under their pillows. A family with large trapezoidal heads. "You have to put *hair* on them," Deborah said once. So that the trapezoids would be like their family, a father and mother and two daughters.

"I thought they'd end up having a bigger house, on the beach, and we'd stay in the guest rooms," Deborah said as they lay in the dark.

"It's not the end yet," Louise said.

"It's my end."

She was not renouncing everything; one's family can seldom be so completely renounced. But her sights were set in the future now; she was planning already for her own family. Children, a husband. Herself, steady at the helm.

⌒⌒

Thanksgiving morning they awoke to branches clattering against the windows.

"Up, up!" He pushed at the metal bed frame with his foot. His daughters lay facing away from each other on the sofa bed, the covers pulled taut between them. "Get up, get dressed. We'll go for a walk on the beach."

Breakers rolled in and crashed against the sea walls. High tide. In some places there wasn't any strip of sand on the beach to walk; the sea had completely taken over. At the big new restaurant built on the water some people were sandbagging; there were shouts of "Here!" and "There!" and some cursing. Maybe a great wave would come in and wash the whole business out to sea, blonde wood and expensive glass, nautical flag plaques on the bathroom doors. In the thirties a nor'easter had blown in and flooded the town. People were rescued by boat from second-story windows. There were black-and-white photos of people navigating the streets in rowboats.

"Do you think we should help them, Dad?"

"We could ask."

They followed his yellow form toward the sandbaggers. He was in his foul weather gear for boating; in this costume he looked authoritative, though his voice didn't carry in the wind. Louise wore an anorak with a hood; in only a windbreaker, Deborah had an exposed head. Sea winds had plastered her hair to her face and neck.

"They're set," their father shouted to them. "They say we should go home, batten down the hatches."

Back in the apartment he made tea. "Very dramatic. That's what I like about living in this town." Sea air whipped against the windows, clouding them with salt spray. He'd invited two of his engineers to join them for dinner, one from England, the other from India. "I thought we could show them an American Thanksgiving."

"American's the only kind there is," Deborah said. Her parents' habit of welcoming; why did it always have to be freaks and strays?

"They don't know people in this country. Me and each other's all they've got."

It was an echo of what their mother had said to them about Joan Kellerperson. She was an orphan, had divorced her husband, had no children.

But whose fault was that? Deborah thought. These people, if they wanted families, they should go out and make them.

Stephen was breaking pretzels for the stuffing. "Your Aunt Beck's in California now. You should go visit her sometime."

"She must be like a million years old."

"But a solid million. She still works. She volunteers for Head Start."

Deborah made a grudging noise of assent.

"You should go visit your mother. The two of you could go out there this weekend."

"I'm not going to her house."

"Deborah."

"I'm not. There's no law that says I have to go there."

"Maybe you could meet at a roadside McDonald's."

"If I wanted to."

Stephen was speechless. He had not believed Deborah would object this strongly.

"Did *you* ever go there?" she asked.

"No, but I'm her ex-husband. She doesn't want me there."

"If she wants to be with that woman then she must not want me there, either."

The engineers arrived at four. Awkward men in ill-fitting clothes, squinting and smiling. To Louise they looked sex-starved; she pictured them pushing down giant erections that bounced back up at them. She and Deborah shouldn't sit too near them. They looked at her but they looked more hungrily at Deborah, who had fixed her hair but still wore her close-fitting sweatpants and an old shirt with a neckline that showed cleavage.

The men had hydroplaned in their little car in the storm. There was an animated discussion of hydroplaning. Some cars had driven into the middle of a vast puddle on the main road and gotten stuck.

They had brought a bottle of black currant liqueur.

As they were passing the serving plates at dinner, Louise explaining tofurkey, the phone rang.

"Wirth residence."

"Can you talk?"

"No."

"Can you meet me?"

"Yes."

"Where?"

"You say."

"The deli."

"Which?"

"The million dollar."

She was thinking wildly as she hung up, at the same time not sure why she had to lie. She after all was not the married one. They didn't need to know he was married. But she hadn't told them she was dating; she couldn't just drop that in casually now.

A story developed as she said it. A friend, despondent on the holiday over a death. Death of a mother. Thanksgiving a difficult time.

"I'll be back soon."

"What about your dinner?" her father said.

She had a brilliant idea, took a plate loaded with food. A drumstick, dark meat, a mound of potatoes. The friend was alone, had nothing for dinner.

Stephen was scooping the swede he made every year on the plate, remembering as he always did when he made swede how back in England in the war when he was small, swede had been a meal. Swede, a head of broccoli, a head of cauliflower with a bit of butter or cheese. "Why don't you ask her to come here? The more, the merrier."

"She's very depressed." Louise pictured Eamon setting his infant daughter on the floor in the bedroom to change her diaper. No changing table, Eamon on his knees with the baby, the two of them looking up at her as she stood in the bedroom doorway in her anorak, her heart pounding the fight-or-flight pound. His wife had been away waitressing that evening; he had called and begged her to "pop by." "Doesn't get out very much," she said to her father and sister, the engineers who looked glad at least it wasn't Deborah leaving. She shrugged her coat on and scanned the room for the car keys.

"Avoid that vast puddle Jivan was talking about."

"I'll go the long way, through Oyster Bay." Though she had no intention of being cautious. That part of herself was finished; maybe she had starved it away or was gradually eating recklessness back into herself.

⌒⌒

It was Eamon who became truly reckless.

Standard procedure for anyone cheating on a spouse included washing often, but the smell of Louise on his hands and his mouth either resulted in temerity or caused it. He slept with his hands next to his face, fingers that had been in her mouth, that he had slid up in the welcoming between her legs when they met and sat in her car. To wash it off would be to wash off the touch of a saint. If you were ever fortunate enough to encounter a saint you wouldn't wash your hands. Not that Louise was a saint but Louise was Louise and loved him. He felt it as surely as a believer feels the benevolent presence of Saint Jude.

"The walls have ears," the vitamin woman at work said. Her name was Sylvan; she had given herself her own name that fit her better than MiLynn. He didn't know what kind of a name MiLynn was. She wore long necklaces made of dried corn and claimed psychic powers. He was learning there were many kinds of Americans, many more than all the varieties of Irish put together.

For Mairead's birthday he surprised her with a leather coat, glammier than the usual birthday fare: a night out, a bottle. He didn't want a night out with her. She was his wife, which term he now equated in his head with *cop*.

"They're called *gardaí* in Ireland," he told Louise. They were in her car in the bank parking lot, early morning, half-undressed. Their shirts were in their laps.

"Because they guard you?"

"It's an Irish word."

"You're my gardaí," she said. She had gained four pounds. And she had discovered sex. What all the fuss was about. Sex was no longer being told to put your legs up higher, Wayne Gretsky on the wall in his hockey togs. Sex was this whispered moaning abandon, this peaceful daylight climb that then went scrambling, as if you were climbing a mountain and then fell flying into bright air, knowing you wouldn't land hard, wouldn't die. For the only bad thing about falling was when you hit, not the fall.

When they finished they pulled their clothes on and she lay with her head in his lap. He lit a cigarette from the car's glowing lighter.

"We should go live somewhere together," she said. "We would be happy."

He knew this; he never contradicted her.

"But Clare," he said.

"We could take her with us."

"Mairead would take her back to Ireland; I'd never be allowed to see her again."

In Louise's eyes the baby was so young as to be a generic baby, with cries and needs like any baby. It had not yet acquired its language, its personality. Even the way she thought about it was as an it; the gender as yet unacquired. There could be other babies. Louise caught herself before saying all this; she did not make that mistake.

But Eamon made mistakes. He failed to wash his fingers and mouthwash his mouth. In a dream he mentioned her name. In the morning Mairead asked him, "Who is this Louise?"

"Someone I met. She must have had an effect on me."

"At work?"

"No. Yes. Back home, when we were at Super Quinn."

"There was no Louise at Super Quinn."

"She was a manager's wife, in Balbriggan. You wouldn't have known her."

Now he had dug himself in, reminding Mairead of how he had been offered a promotion and she, in spite of her better record and more time in service, had not. That on top of this Louise business.

He was surprised when she rose up in her nightgown, batting at him with her fists.

"Fucking, fucking wanker!"

He leapt out of bed and backed away from her. She had always been the more volatile of the two of them; he was never certain of what she would do.

They edged down the hall into the kitchen, he at a disadvantage because moving backwards.

"Where's the baby?"

"Don't try to distract me."

He made psychic contact with many objects in the room. His gray jacket, a packet of crisps on the counter, this week's issue of the *Irish Echo* folded in half on the table. He was feeling around for clues; the mention of Louise's name didn't seem enough to set off this many alarms. Maybe something had been in the pocket of his coat. Sometimes Louise left notes.

An object within his reach that could be used for defense? On the counter was the packet of crisps. Useless. A can of beans he'd planned to eat with an egg or two. The beans at least were heavy in metal.

Mairead backed him up against the counter. Then he couldn't see the beans or reach for them.

"Tell me who it is and what you're doing with her."

"Nothing, nothing."

"Eamon." She put her hand into the pocket of her bathrobe. Out of it she drew a knife. But a foolish kitchen knife, the blade small and dull.

"I could stab the heart out of you. I would, too."

"I know it."

"Louise, Louise. Tell me about this Louise."

She was right up in his face, her teeth clenched. Probably the closest they had voluntarily gotten to each other in weeks.

He spilled it, shouting at her, the meaning of the words forming not as he said them but after they were said, giving him no time to consider what he was going to say. She heard what he said at the same time he did. They reacted together, spraying words like hoses in each other's faces.

The worst: that he cared for Louise. It would not have mattered had he just fucked her.

With her dull knife Mairead managed to put a nice gash in his hand. That ended it for the time being.

Behind the locked bathroom door he sat on the edge of the tub and cleaned the foolish little wound. She had done it to humiliate him and he had known it and let her. Had she gone for his heart he could have wrenched her away from him, hauled off and hit her in the face. But this way was better; he could still hope to get away without putting a mark on her, without leaving a dent. That way no explaining to do. He didn't even have a bank account; he was paid in cash off the books and emptied his pockets into his bedside drawer. Without a green card he wanted to live in America clean, not making a mark on anything.

"You won't go back there." This through the bathroom door. The baby was awake now, screaming.

He looked at the door and spoke to it. They paid him well, far better than the caddying and it was far more reliable than bartending. "It's my job."

"Well find another."

⌒⌒

Emigration. Why was leaving so much more romantic than arriving? Immigration made her think of processing, paperwork, cholera, destitution. Whereas emigration had about it the aura of flight. Birds migrated; emigration was leaving as birds did, for better climates and eating.

For the second day in a row he didn't show up for work.

Outside, Craig was angrily checking in the Tuesday order. His gestures, every action was precise and neat. The point of his pencil broke, broke again. He could draw and quarter a steer.

He only glanced at her. "What can I help you with, Louise?"

"Did Eamon say why he wasn't coming in?"

Craig counted bottles of liquid acidophilus, tapping them with his pencil eraser. "Eamon gave no information whatsoever regarding his absence."

"He didn't call in sick?"

"He didn't call period."

She couldn't surmise the vector of Craig's rage, whether it was all directed at the absent Eamon or whether her boss knew about her and Eamon and blamed her.

"Maybe something happened with the INS."

"In the future all will be revealed, I'm sure. That's what's great about the future."

She felt sick to her stomach.

"Why don't you put on a jacket, Louise, and come count these breads?"

Bobby Sands had died of hunger. She remembered that, her first glimmer of any real Ireland, beyond Saint Patrick's Day and singing one verse of "When Irish Eyes are Smiling" as a character named Kathleen O'Something in her fourth grade play, in which a male innocent travels to countries all over the world and everywhere he goes gets sung to by someone in native costume. It had taken Bobby Sands a long time to die. He had written screeds on scraps of paper, poetry with his own shit. Before he died everything in him had lived. He had left no stone unturned. He had made of his body a resource, a way to speak instead of a way to silence. She had read that they made him bend over so they could check inside his anus. He had kept the screeds in there.

Still, she couldn't eat. Even though she knew it was not political, it was stupid, it was not even about her or her looks or her oppression by advertisers or the cultural ideal or anything.

She called Bev.

"There's this man I was seeing." She began to cry.

"Oh god, don't tell me, you're pregnant."

"No, Jesus, I'm trying to tell you." But then she was ashamed of herself, going for a man with a wife, a man with such a young baby and no green card and no degree. Someone who drove a van and drank his paycheck. Illegal Alien. Even if he managed to get legal his card would only say Registered Alien. She was seeing him as her mother would see him.

"Is someone hurting you?"

"Does that have to be the first thing you ask me?"

"I asked if you were pregnant. And anyway it's a thing I have to ask."

"I'm not one of your clients. I can take care of myself."

"My clients say that, too."

She remembered their conversation in the car after she'd lost her virginity to Joshua van Gelden. How excited she had been about his big leonine head, his prep school life, the damaged eye. That was nothing compared to this. She had found in the most unlikely of people someone kindred after all the dark days in college, a thousand little humiliations. *Public or private?* It still stung; college done now, those people scattered, and she was still pushing out of herself and away.

One night she had driven over to Eamon's while Mairead was at work. He came down from the apartment with a bag in his hand. It was raining as they sat in his van in the bucket seats and listened to the radio. He had gotten a bottle of champagne. "I love the cheap stuff the best," he said. His mouth was wet, his saliva faintly metallic. His body often gave off whiffs of some underlying deficit, signs of poor health. She understood it was not so much a particular illness as the more general crisis of difficult living. Life without health insurance, without regular dental care or even proper over-the-counter medication. Hot sugared whiskey was a favored remedy for any number of ailments. He'd once had a tooth pulled with pliers or string, she couldn't remember which or whether it was both.

The cork rang against the van's metal ceiling. He hadn't brought cups; they traded swigs from the bottle and held hands. It would all be maudlin in the telling; she couldn't tell her mother about being in love or how she was afraid he had gone and disappeared in a magical whoosh like something delivered in a dream that receded instantly upon waking. The Love That Dare Not Speak Its Name, someone had told her love for someone of the same sex was called. Bev had never come right out and said she was a lesbian or that she loved Joan. All that left for inference and conjecture.

"We broke up," she told her mother.

There was a long pause on the other end of the line.

"I'm sorry, Lou. I hadn't even heard about this person. It must not have been very long."

"Oh, no. It wasn't."

"Well, then. You probably wouldn't want to get too attached to anyone now, with your circumstances. Before you know it you'll be leaving."

Louise dreamt that night that they found her body on a slanted roof in winter, the snow piled up on her. She'd been sunning in a bikini when a blizzard came in and covered and whited her out.

⌒⌒

The year turned, also the decade. 1990. Each of them spent New Year's Eve alone, though that had not been the intention. Deborah went skiing with a group of people, college friends she knew vaguely through other friends, brightly colored and talkative, she the only one needing to rent her skis. The rest of them had learned to ski as children in Aspen, Wyoming, the Alps. That she was inept and had only skied once on an icy hill in Vermont wasn't cause for courtly derision, the way it would have been among Louise's college people. This group saw in Deborah a cause and a challenge; they wanted her up on skis by midday. By midday she had sprained her ankle; she went to bed early in pain while the others in fleece and sweaters drank from steins at the ski lodge bar. In the woods the night felt darker and more muffled, though she woke at one and heard the sounds of someone puking, crying, in the hallway.

Stephen drove into the City and went to First Night in Grand Central Station. It was billed as a family event, with games for children and costumes and face painting. It had come to him to avoid drinking. It came to him in a manner almost occult, though later he thought perhaps some people got these messages all the time, maybe Christians were Christians because they got envoys from God telling them what they should do and what would happen to them if they didn't. It had come to him simply as a message from an intercom would, were an intercom implanted in his head, that he shouldn't drink this New Year's Eve, he would end up in jail or a coffin. He got a hot cider at First Night and wandered along the train station's cavernous passages, marveling at the architecture. If given a wish he would choose to build something of this scale and utility in the world before dying. To be Robert Olmstead and plan Central Park, or Robert Moses with his highways and big beaches. Instead what had he done? He had concentrated on small things, contact lenses, nothing that would dome over people like this magnificence. Contact lenses were the littlest domes, barely visible. It had been a mistake to work so small.

In Stephen's apartment, Louise paged through *Soma: The Divine Mushroom of Immortality*. Why mushrooms and immortality? Her father seemed to be drinking less. He had been talking about Religions of the World in the way some people talked about makes of cars they were considering buying, often speaking wistfully of Buddhism and Hinduism the way one who can't afford the Jaguar speaks of the XJ7. On the stereo she played and replayed Don McLean's "American Pie" and half-sang to all the words. *Them good old boys were drinking whiskey and rye, singing this will be the day that I die. This will be the day that I die.*

She didn't want to die anymore. She wanted to move to Ireland, emigrate.

Joan was down in North Carolina, visiting her aging friend who had given her money, the old woman in whose house she had lived before she and Bev got together. Bev stayed home alone. It was bitter and snowing. She lit a fire and opened one of the good bottles of champagne. For Hanukkah-Christmas, she and Joan celebrating the holidays now as hyphenated, part of each other, Joan had gotten her a book by her favorite writer, Alice Hoffman, about a child dying of AIDS contracted from a blood transfusion. A whole literature was springing up. They'd had three friends die this year.

At ten p.m. there was a knock at the door. A man in a sports jacket and striped ski hat hugging his elbows to him, stamping the snow off his tassled shoes. Snow turned to water ran down his glasses. She recognized him but not how she knew him.

"A friend of Joan's," he said.

"Joan's not here."

"Not on New Year's Eve?"

"She's out of town."

"She told you I might be stopping by?"

"No. She didn't tell me anyone—." She stopped, bewildered. Hadn't she been trained to handle just this sort of occurrence? But the phone was miles off, all the way in the kitchen. The police miles from that. There was no chain on the door; she would have to close it to lock it.

"I'm afraid you'll have to come back."

His hand jammed at the door as she tried to slam it.

"You know damn well who I am."

Jim Kellerman. Of course.

"Let me in."

Snow fell off him in clumps; he stamped more in the foyer. Her teeth were chattering, her whole body shuddering with a child's fear.

"I'm not going to hurt you, I'm not fucking stupid."

"What do you want?"

He took off his glasses and wiped the water from the lenses. How blind was he? Would taking a swing at him gain her anything? She measured the chances. If she hit him she would only provoke him. But she had to do something. She offered coffee.

"That's a bizarre thing to do, I just pushed my way into your house."

"You said you weren't going to hurt me."

"I don't want any coffee."

She looked at her glass of champagne on the table over by the fire. That seemed a long time ago already.

"Why do you have a tree? I thought she said you were Jewish, too."

"I'm not talking about that with you." Her panic had gone for a moment but then in a wave it came back. How angry Joan said he had been when she took "Kellerperson" legally. In a confrontation once he had said he was not done with her, he would make her pay.

"You like living with her?"

"I'm not talking about that, either. I want you to leave."

"I'll leave in a minute." He was moving around the living room, but carefully, never turning his back to her. As if he knew she was looking to grab a heavy object and brain him.

"Are these your daughters?" He had paused in front of the table with the framed photographs on it; Joan called it the Shrine. Bev didn't answer him.

"A brunette and a blondie."

Still she waited. Soon it would be over and she would be alive or dead. Either way, he would be gone from her.

"What do they think of this arrangement?" He gazed at her. She didn't meet his eye.

"Don't want to tell me?"

How this man's penis had been inside Joan's vagina. Her mind racing, racing, a movie played in speeded up time in her head of Jim Kellerman bucking atop his wife Joan Kellerman when she was still a wife. Wrong, wrong. Make it stop. She made it stop; she came back to the living room and endured him.

Jim Kellerman was holding one of the framed photos. She wouldn't learn which until later.

"You tell her I've had enough of this situation, it's humiliating."

Bev waited.

"She can use her own last name." His lip curled. "Or yours. The true feminist liberation marriage."

"Please go now."

He moved toward the door, blithely, light on his feet. He was small but wiry and very strong; she could see it even in his hands just holding the framed photograph, but tensed. She didn't ask for it back. Let him take it, let him have it.

"Tell her a new decade, she can turn over a new leaf and stop this nonsense."

She was choking on her own air.

He stepped out into the snow. "Good. Cunt." He slammed the door.

She went to the phone, miles away. Hours seemed to have passed and yet it was only 10:13. Minutes had passed. She dialed the number in North Carolina. The old woman answered the phone on the first ring. She put Joan on.

"I thought I was supposed to call *you* at midnight."

Bev was close to incoherence, close to sobbing. "Jim was here."

"Jim?"

"Kellerman."

"Oh, god. What the hell did he want?"

There was a silence while Bev thought about what he wanted. Stephen was alone walking the corridors of Grand Central, Louise and Deborah alone in dark rooms, skiers in the cold country with their leg muscles pleasantly aching. "I don't know, he wanted to intimidate us."

"Did he bring a gun?"

"Fucking Jesus, is he the sort of person who carries a gun?"

"Not usually. I don't know. I'm asking."

"I didn't see one."

"Go lock everything, make sure the windows are latched. Then call someone."

"The police?" Crying now, she went from room to room, turning on all the lights. There should be no dark corners. Even the insides of the closets should be blazing with light.

"No, a friend."

"It's New Year's, no one's around."

"Call Louise. What's she doing? Or Stephen."

"The last thing I'm doing is calling Stephen."

Though later she thought of all people he would be the most help. He would be a realist about the laws and secure the premises. He had an ancient metal toolbox he carried everywhere, for emergencies.

In the heart of winter, brief dim days that dropped into interminable chilly evenings at four in the afternoon, Stephen took a girlfriend to the Caribbean. Bright water, swaying palms, the old forgotten joy of sweat. In Charlotte Amalie the air conditioning blasted from the open doors of the shops into the dusty streets. The girlfriend's name was Janet; she had a head of rich auburn hair like hair in a shampoo commercial. Her hair was the most beautiful thing about her; she was squat and had a slightly disfiguring scar on her chin. She was younger than Stephen and had four sons. The injury her scar marked had been made by her former husband. Stephen did not have to so much as ask. He met the man one Saturday when he came to pick up the boys for his weekend. "He seems to have a chip on his shoulder," Stephen said later.

"You could say that." She was looking off into the middle distance, the dent in her chin prominent. Her ex-husband's violence was a net that lay over her life; at any moment he might take it upon himself to kill her.

Their day on the island was hot and dry; the light reflecting off the white buildings and pavement made the light even flatter, more relentless. Stephen thought of the beach as described by Camus in *The Stranger*. He had read the book in a Philosophy class in college, a slim black volume in his hands, the radiators hissing and wooden floorboards creaking in the old classroom. In the front of the room the professor lectured, but Stephen couldn't listen, he could only reread. He was on the beach with Meursault, running, running, the sunlight blinding. It was like that now, only he was sitting on one of the benches where the shopping tourists rested.

"Can't you do anything about him? A restraining order or something?"

"He doesn't *do* anything anymore." She wet her finger and worked on a stain on her white culottes. "He hasn't laid a hand on me since the divorce. So he tells me he wants to cut me up in little pieces. What am I going to do, call the cops?"

Stephen was silent. Around them were the competing shouts of vendors, their crescendos crisscrossing in the air like birds. Of course, a restraining order would do nothing. Bev had taught him that.

"Are you documenting the incidents?"

"It's not 'incidents.' It's the inside of his brain."

"You should still keep track."

"What, and tell the police, 'He wants to slice me longways like a cut of meat.'"

"He said that?"

"He's crazy, he says everything. But he holds a good job, he acts like an ordinary guy."

It was market day in the town's main square. Several women, large and black, were setting up to braid hair. A folding chair, a box of beads, bottles of scented oil.

"Have yours done." Stephen pointed at the one who looked like the mentor, old and magisterial, with fine dexterous hands.

The cost for a whole head was forty dollars. Far less for just two or three braids, a small adornment.

"Go do it. Get your whole head if you want."

"That's too expensive, forty dollars for braids!"

He was feeling expansive; he wanted to make things happy for Janet, blot out the plot to cut her up longways. "They're artisans; the braids stay in for weeks. And it's for a good cause, it supports them."

He led Janet to the woman's folding chair. With her smooth hands she oiled Janet's scalp, saying in her clipped island English, "I will make you like a queen." It was a performance for tourists that made them feel sheepish but nonetheless pleased. When her head was covered with braids sealed at the ends with beads, Janet looked ten years younger, exotic. Now you could see the exquisite bones in her face; the braids distracted from the deformity on her chin.

"You do, you look like some kind of island queen," he said as they departed from the square in search of a meal.

"Oh, stop."

But he was so pleased with her happiness that he bought her mother-of-pearl earrings, then a watch.

Weather instigates changes; people shrink or expand. In the bleak midwinter of New York he had felt pinched and tight. Twenty-four hours in the tropics and he felt broad and optimistic as a suspension bridge. Bridges always made him feel optimistic—it was some combination of engineering and artistry with oh it would sound like bullshit to say it but the human spirit. That was what he felt every time he encountered a bridge. But in New York two of Bev's friends were dying. Both men, emaciated, worn through by AIDS, would be dead before spring. One of them she and Stephen had been close to in their married days.

In a week Stephen and Janet returned to New York transformed, tan in the airport among so many pale people bundled to the neck. Even the skin of black people here looked gray and ashy in comparison with the shining black skin against bright fabrics they'd seen in St. Thomas, the vivid coloration that was dead here or dormant. Janet had a white straw hat on top of her braids. People in their parkas and scarves smiled at them with their tans, Stephen's peeling nose, his tropical shirt, Janet's beaded braids.

Louise met them at the baggage claim with coats she helped them into, black and wool, as if helping them back into their winter skins. And the next day they awoke to the careful work of an ice storm that coated each branch of each tree as if with glass. The broom on the porch had its coating, the porch railings; everything was encased, as if it had been decided this was the moment in history to preserve.

Why this moment? Why any? The human goal was to preserve oneself and collect the moments. To keep those and not lose them, not forget. Forgetting the dreaded damnation, worse than sicknesses of the body. For the mind was its own separate entity, in the body but not of it, like a monarch among the people. In a notebook Louise wrote every phrase of Eamon's she could remember him uttering. Once they had gone in his van to a fast-food drive-through and in the driver's seat he had wolfed his food from the box on his lap. Wiping his hands on napkins, he'd exclaimed with some dismay he'd forgotten to eat his Mild and Spicy sauce and in that moment she had loved him completely, for reasons obscure certainly to anyone but her; he had food on his face and a box of chicken bones in his lap.

No one could explain with any clarity why love of this person and not that, why this person now and not that one now, why that one before or later. Hence Bev with Joan, Stephen with Janet and her dented face. Not even love could be preserved, and certainly not the reasons for love, which had no rationale or map.

The goal of the world was never to preserve itself but to keep burning along. The world didn't believe in anything. By midday the ice on the trees was melting.

⌒⌒

Applications were due by the first of February. Louise used onion skin paper slid into the Smith-Corona Selectric she had used in college to type her papers on Auden, on Plath, on George Herbert's poem shaped like a bird's or a butterfly's wings, on *Madame Bovary* with its odd heretical descriptions of religious icons as if they were dandies or hookers, the Virgin Mary with her rouged cheeks. Was this the sentimental tug people referred to when they spoke of their alma maters? Were they remembering their Modern Novel seminars, their introduction to the Metaphysical Poets? She was inclined to think not.

She thought she might want to be a writer; she thought she might want to live in the west. Her oeuvre consisted of a story based on her cousin Petra losing her hair to leukemia, another other about a young woman who has an affair with an illegal Irish immigrant, the third about a man who learns that his wife is a lesbian. They were well written from sentence to sentence but baldly autobiographical, deficient in invention.

What of literature for the ages? She should be writing about suffering, about God. Yet she had known little, comparatively, of suffering. For a while she had starved, but she had starved amid ample cafeteria food, among the bins full of gorp and licorice at Edward's Food Warehouse. She had starved at Hinderly's fraternity dinner with a steak on her plate. She hadn't in any way starved as the victims of the Great Famine had, their tongues rupturing the roofs of their mouths at the end, their bodies ruined sinew thin as lace. She had not even starved as Bobby Sands had starved: for a cause, hurling his food against the wall of his prison cell, hiding his writing in his body cavities. A far cry from laxatives (she had tried those, too) and grad school.

As for God, she had nothing to say but of God's absence. She didn't like television and she didn't think she believed in God. Eamon had once told her she made a terrible American. *When you are raised without religion, all religions become the occult,* she wrote in her journal after Eamon described kneeling in his living room in Ireland with his family every night of his life in childhood to say the rosary.

"Did you like it?"

He knew swaths of the Old Testament by heart. Even if he got in a terrible car accident he guaranteed he would be able to lie there with a drain in his head and recite Our Fathers and Hail Marys.

"I would have liked something like that," she said.

"A catechism?"

"A code to live by. Something."

"You have a code to live by. Your intelligence. I don't have that, I'm just a fucking eejit."

"You're not." He had told her the meaning of the word *abattoir*; his knowledge of geography put hers to shame.

They had been at his local that night, the Dribble Inn, next to the train tracks, with its awful light and a smell in the bathroom Louise associated with drugs. But it was only the one time she saw a needle on the floor. Other times just vomit or once, oddly, a hank of hair.

She longed for those times now. She had not seen Eamon in

months and hadn't heard from him since the day before he failed to show up for work. At the store, Sylvan clucked under her breath and said only that she'd heard Eamon's wife found out he was having an affair and threatened to take the daughter back to Ireland with her for good. Louise asked nothing and said nothing. What was there to ask or say?

She wished she believed in a religion, so that she could talk to God. A few times she knelt beside her bed, her hands joined, head bent, and whispered. *Please, please, please.* But there was no force behind it; they were purely gestures, futile as a child's wish for magic.

Sylvan made a decoction for her to drink. "It's no good to cry all the time," she said. Louise drank it eagerly; she was willing to sign up for any anything that would ease the pain of heart. It seemed to her the one man she loved had slipped away from her and now, as her father moved more deeply into the lives of Janet and her sons, that her family, too, had slipped away, had reconfigured in their separate shapes without her. Deborah had a boyfriend now who was wealthy, from the kind of family that traveled with the seasons. Winter in the Alps, summers on Nantucket. They had a flat in London; Deborah was going to spend the next summer there. And then Bev and Joan were talking about moving south. Warmer weather, and Joan's elderly friend was ill again, this time maybe for good. They didn't want to live on Long Island anymore, they said. They were convinced now it was unsafe.

"That shooter on the Mineola train," Bev said.

"That could happen anywhere. You don't even take the train."

"It's very overpopulated here. People get tense."

"Calcutta is overpopulated. Long Island isn't overpopulated."

"Everyone's entitled to their opinion."

Fine. She put the application sheet in the typewriter. Tasks themselves can be a shelter, as love can be a shelter, books, art, the learning itself, even rote memorization. She did not need religion; she did not need family.

In the spring the letters came. She could go now to Pittsburgh, to Colorado, Arizona, Utah.

On a Sunday afternoon she drove out to Bev and Joan's house, the letters in the zippered front pocket of her anorak. There was a new dog, skittish and little, that her mother and Joan fawned over. It had a middle name. When they called to the dog they used the first and middle names, as if the dog were their beloved child.

"I could go to any of these places." Louise reached into the pocket and fanned the letters out on the coffee table. Bev was pouring champagne.

"And leave me?"

"But I'm not with you, I'm supposed to be going out on my own. And away from Dad—"

"You're my only one left, Lou. She hasn't talked to me for a year."

"Maybe if you could just explain—"

"Explain what? I didn't do this from a fucking *kit*."

"How to Be a Lesbian in Three Easy Steps." Joan had a Coors Lite. She put them in the freezer until they got ice in them.

"That's what she thinks? That I did this to get her goat?"

"I don't know what she thinks, Ma."

Though Deborah had told her: under no circumstances, none, would Joan ever be Aunt or Grandma Joan to Deborah's children. She had already planned that part of the future; it was in her mind already, immutable as if it had happened in the past.

One of the most difficult things to part with is an idea of your life that you have clung to beyond its obsolescence.

Stephen thought of himself as the good child. Parker's intelligence had been vaster, but he had been the better son, with a beautiful wife and children who brought his mother pleasure. In the tradition of his father he had carried on with boats. And he was no longer the drinker he once had been, whereas Parker was ruined now by alcohol, his face bloated, broken blood vessels threaded along under the skin.

Stephen drove up to Connecticut to visit her one weekend a month. In her cottage by the sea, his mother moved through her small rooms on two canes.

Though he always suggested they go for dinner at one of the inns in town, she considered it a failing if she didn't prepare a small feast. Steak and kidney pie, crabmeat quiche, pigs in a blanket. Recently it had been lobster, though one time when she made him duck he praised it extravagantly, in the hope it might supplant lobster in the future. Had she forgotten his allergy to shellfish? The last time she sprung it on him he had been forced on the way home to pull the car to the side of the road and vomit on the turnpike near Stamford.

This time it was lobster again. His superlatives in regard to the duck seemed not to have penetrated.

"When will your girls get married? Have they brought home anyone you like?"

Sometimes in his dreams Louise and Deborah showed up at family functions sitting on women's laps. And sometimes he knew the women on whose laps they sat: old girlfriends of his, the one with the membership in Mensa and the one who was a scientist and smarter than he, with frowsy hair and a mole like Marilyn Monroe's. A house full of women, him the only man.

Then he fretted over his fretting. Why should he care who his daughters loved, as long as they loved people who loved them? He didn't think he had categorical objections to lesbians; it had only hurt that his wife left him for one.

Bev herself was baffling to his mother. That any woman would leave her son, but to leave him for a woman? But she was a career woman and a Jew; she had always been baffling.

Often in conversation when he and his mother made reference to Bev they used the old nickname she had gone by in high school.

"And how is Binky?"

"Same as ever." But of course she was not.

"And her health is good?"

He didn't know how her health was. He said it was excellent.

It was as if they had to invoke Bev in her previous incarnation—beautiful, heterosexual, the sheet of coal-black hair, though her hair hadn't been coal-black or straight since sometime in the middle of the mid-seventies. They didn't hate her now; they only loved who she had been and couldn't forgive her for having become something else.

He went around the cottage, winding clocks, inspecting the television and the new VCR his mother hadn't learned to operate.

"You put in the video here and press this button."

"Which?"

"Play. And then it plays."

"Not when I do it."

She was putting the video in backwards. He turned it around and had her put it in the right way with her arthritic hands.

"When I won the Lord Mayor's Prize . . ." His mother was starting in. It was the version of herself to which she always returned. She was twelve, in England, precocious, still a child. She was at the age when precocity in girls is still looked upon fondly. Later, a liability. The war had not yet cratered out London; there were no scores of soldiers needing to be put back together with catgut or to die quietly with morphine.

There was a sharp rap at the door.

"Let me in, you rapscallions!"

Parker strode in; he had a bottle of Dewar's in a canvas bag and was wearing duck boots and a flecked oatmeal sweater. His hair, disheveled, was patted down to one side; he had clapped on a handful of water and tried to smooth it with his hands.

"Hello, Parker."

"You didn't tell me you were having a lobsterfest. She won't make it for me, you know."

"You won't eat it. He drinks his dinners."

"I'll have you know I'm a die-hard fan of the oyster cracker." As he said this Parker was settling himself at the table, taking off Stephen's plate the lobster meat he had tried to conceal. "Drink, anyone?"

"I'm giving Mum a lesson with the VCR. She also needs some lightbulbs, the next time you get to the store."

Parker was searching the table. "Where are the olives? Where are the onions? I mean the ones in brine, not the salad onions. How's Binks?"

"Well, recently I haven't spoken to her."

"She and Deborah talking again?"

"Not in over a year."

Parker whistled through his teeth. "You know, it was hard for me to believe about Binks. She's about the last person I would have pegged. It must be hard for the girls."

"You never know, I guess." Stephen's standard answer. People rarely got him to join them in trying to pinpoint or analyze what it was that made Bev "cross over." He hated talk like that.

"I never knew Caryn was going to crack up. One day she was fine and the next Conran's was delivering three living room sets."

"You must have had an inkling. Wasn't there mental illness in the family?"

Parker lifted the lobster off Stephen's plate and danced it upright, the claws moving back and forth like arms in the air. Before Petra's death he had the patience for opening up the appendages to get at the meat. In the death of his one daughter that kind of patience had evaporated. He had once been a devotee of the crossword puzzles in the *New York Times*. Now who knew what he did with himself.

Their mother slowly lowered herself on to the edge of the sofa, her hands slack on their canes. All week she had been waiting for this Fred Astaire movie. Now it was in the VCR the right way; at last he was dancing.

Stephen joined his brother at the table.

"He's wonderful on his feet," their mother breathed. Then she seemed to come back to herself. "His face looks like a clothespin."

"You wouldn't throw him out of bed," Parker called to her.

"Get your mother a vodka collins," she called back.

"I don't know," Parker said as he fixed the drink in a green glass. Only he would know it was their mother's favorite glass. The drink wasn't to be too cold, only two cubes, the small ones. Now he and their mother were co-conspirators—he had joked with her about bedding Fred Astaire. Stephen had not known his mother to joke or to drink vodka. He wanted to ask Parker about it. The questions were dry in his mouth.

"You don't know what?"

Parker glanced in the direction of their mother. When he spoke next he lowered his voice. "She's been talking a lot. She wants to be cremated. She has this idea her ashes will blow in and rest on our noses or in our noses."

"Did you tell her we're keeping her urn corked? I don't want her in my nose."

"Really, Stephen. The noses seem to comfort her."

"Fortunate for her we got big ones. I used to tell Bev if the girls' noses were this big I'd get them nose jobs."

"Remember when we met them? I wouldn't have believed they weren't perfect even if they told me. Even if they tried to show me they had extra toes or a double vagina."

Stephen tried to remember when he'd first met Caryn. Someone was playing the guitar and trying to sound like Woody Guthrie. People were smoking pot and cigarettes, complaining. It was a pot luck dinner, Parker repeatedly saying "pot latch" and someone insistently correcting him. Caryn wore a short skirt and knee socks. Someone else saying, "The president has been shot" over and over again in a newscastery voice, the voice getting smaller and smaller each time the phrase was uttered.

That was all. The memory had haze at the edges as if he had retrieved it from celluloid rather than his mind.

"Remember Binks's hair? I told her it was black like coal. I thought she was going to hit me."

"And Caryn? Before the kids she had the most beautiful breasts."

When the end of August came, Bev flew west with Louise. At the airport in Utah crowds of people held banners and signs, balloons, pinwheels, small squirming children, flash cameras going off, shouting, anxious disarray, women in pastel sweatshirts with doves or seagulls on them. Their hair was gray, sculpted. They had given over the whole of themselves to mothering; there were no other parts of themselves left. All of the attention seemed to be directed at the young men in dark suits with nameplates on their lapels. The ones who filed off the plane in front of Bev and Louise stood with their heads held high, backs stiff. "Welcome Back Elder Hammerstrom" was printed on the largest of the banners, held at intervals by tow-headed children and at either end by an adult. Heads held high and backs stiff as the backs of military personnel, they were engulfed. Moments later they were hoisting small children on their shoulders, bending to embrace the mothers in the sweatshirts, who wetted the shoulders of the dark straight suits with their tears.

"Is that him?" the adults asked each other. "Is that him?" the children asked the adults.

So this was Salt Lake City. This airport the airport of missionaries, leaving to and returning from all corners of the earth.

The streets were clean and wide; the sidewalks seemed scrubbed. An unforgiving light fell on every surface. The West: land of open spaces, new religions, big sky. Land of possibilities; Louise could see how in a landscape like this you could erect a temple, make new rules for living and call it a religion. The land felt like new land, just manufactured, waiting for an imprint. In the shops and restaurants large women in clothes like the clothes of children moved slowly with their own children in tow. Women in bibs and pinafores, in pale shades of yellow and pink, always in skirts.

"Stepford Wives who went off their diets," Bev said.

Louise laughed. "Oh, I knew you would say that."

"Well, c'mon Louise. You have to admit."

"Maybe they're happy. They have their whole families around them."

Louise had never been west of the Mississippi. Other than California, Bev thought, why? She worried they would swallow up Louise. Her daughter alone in the middle of some western fundamentalist neo-theocracy in an unfurnished apartment, the refrigerator empty but for bottled water and Diet Coke. They would marry her to one of these bland upright men. She didn't even have the faith to believe Louise would stop them if they tried. She seemed pliable; her will was liquid, whereas Deborah's was the proverbial iron. Why was it Louise couldn't put together a life for herself? She owned almost nothing: a plastic jug with a filter in it for tap water, her favorite paperbacks from college, the anorak, running shoes with the soles worn down. Whereas Deborah with her hair care products and suede skirts hanging in her closet with the store tags still attached. Deborah's wardrobe, with its leather coats, umpteen barely scuffed shoes, cashmere scarves. Louise didn't have any kind of wardrobe. Nor did she ever have money or food. Once, when Louise was eleven or twelve, Bev came home early from work and found her working with a pair of tweezers at a charm bracelet Bev had been given in high school. One of the charms was a tiny gold-edged box with a dollar bill folded up minutely inside it. With the tweezers Louise was working it out of the box. To buy a ballpoint pen, a pack of gum.

"Please," Bev said now at the grocery store. "It'll make me feel better if you let me." She pulled from the shelves boxes of raisins, prunes, Familia, Cream of Wheat, Alba shakes in three flavors, Diet Coke. "You should also get some staples, pasta and sauce."

"I don't need staples." Staples were for families. Louise hadn't observed a regular mealtime for years.

The first day of teacher training she felt nearly ill enough to faint from the nausea as she sat in one of the bathroom stalls and tried to make herself calm. Some of the other women in the class came in and stood examining their faces at the mirrors above the sinks. She could see them preening through the crack between the stall and door as she sat on the toilet. Probably they could see her, too. There were times she had glimpsed women sitting in the stalls. That you could glimpse a person in a private moment seemed wrong, an architectural disaster. Stalls should be sealed; there shouldn't be the gaps and cracks to view other women. Though with men it was worse, peeing right beside each other in a casual way. At sports arenas, Joshua had once told her, the men peed in trenches that ran along the floor. She couldn't see women ever agreeing to that. Women were private beings. Maybe it was the uninflicted bleeding that made them private. Men only bled when inflicted.

Louise's hands and feet were nearly numb with cold. She wasn't eating the raisins, the Familia. It all stood neatly in the cupboards as if meant for display only.

"Do you think he's gay?" one of the women at the mirror asked.

"Is he Mormon?"

"He is definitely not Mormon."

"Well, there's something weird about him. I can't put my finger on it."

His name was Temmy Wezbyrt; he was the one in charge of their teacher orientation. What kind of name was Temmy? He was a representative of the new breed of man, his age and sexual preference indeterminate, his profile the profile of a model, the nose and chin chiseled as if from some fine material, soapstone or marble. From the front his face was not nearly as attractive, but from the side he was a knockout. He wore his black hair combed straight back from his forehead, usually pulled into a ponytail. His fingernails looked tended, he wore dark boots regardless of the weather, he was from California and liked to bike and cook and surf. He was vigorous, with a narrow waist and broad shoulders; on campus he could be seen walking many times a day. Always he seemed to be striding somewhere—to deliver a lecture, to collect on a bet. When it was sunny at midday he could be found reclining on one of the benches outside the Languages and Communications building, one arm slung across his eyes. In the sun he basked like an amphibian; he didn't seem to mind that his colleagues walked by, that his students saw him. If one stopped to speak he sometimes replied without lifting his arm from his eyes. He had decided he liked Louise. But not everyone; some of them he had no patience for at all.

"He's a flamer, is what he is."

"You're out of your mind."

Louise looked down at her arms. The shirt she had chosen was meant to highlight their thinness. No one cared about the thinness of her arms. She saw this for maybe the first time since she'd acquired the body of a woman. No one cared about her arms. It was a revelation.

Temmy Wezbyrt had once been a Mormon, but he was a Mormon no more. He had been raised in rural Idaho, one of eight children. His father a sociology professor now at Brigham Young University, but his father was getting older.

"A little bit cracked," Temmy told her. They were having lunch in the cavernous student union, with its smells of oily food and bleach. "He thinks the government is out to get him, for his religious views."

"I thought he was a Mormon."

"A kind of renegade Mormon. A Mormon with political convictions."

Temmy had gone on his mission to Madrid, but once there he had refused to proselytize. "They put me in an old age home and made me empty the bedpans. I did them one better; I got the language and learned a lot about Catholicism. And I lost my virginity twice."

"What do you mean?"

"Once with a woman, once with a man. Thank you kindly Joseph Smith."

"Were they both missionaries?"

"Only he was. She looked like a princess, but she practically lived in the streets. I met her on a bench in the park when I was getting a little sun one day. She prevented a thief from stealing my backpack. I felt I owed her my life."

"So you had sex with her."

"What more can you give someone, I mean if they're willing to accept it?"

Louise blushed deeply. She had not expected ever to speak of sex with Temmy. In fact she pictured him like a Ken doll, male but without the lower anatomy. Why did it please her to picture him this way? Sometimes she pictured Joan's body as unencumbered by sexuality as a doll's, so she wouldn't have to think about Joan and her mother engaged in the act of having sex. But she had been all wrong about Temmy. He was not blank; he was omnivorous.

"Did you ever tell your parents?"

"I came back speaking Spanish with my hair long and no longer Mormon. That was enough."

She wanted to ask whether he still made love to both men and women. That was what was different about him; he was a man who would make love to you with the same casual joy with which someone else might discover in conversation something in common with you and chat for an hour.

Temmy sipped his milk from a straw. "They were both bilingual. I thought that was appropriate." He smiled. "Don't make me explain why."

None of her fellow teaching assistants was Mormon, but most of the undergraduates were. It was the era of the culture wars. She was charged with teaching them why some people were in favor of the Western canon, others ardently or bitterly against it.

"What is it?" That was their first question.

"What's what?"

"The Western whatever, cannon."

"Canon." She wrote it on the blackboard.

Her students knew nothing of the Western canon but they knew the Book of Mormon. They knew a story of the world's beginning sifted through the teachings from stone tablets discovered near Poughkeepsie. They knew the angel Moroni and the seagulls who had saved their land from the crickets. They knew of the rules of their faith, which guaranteed them to be sealed in marriage to one person for all eternity.

She had a Vietnamese student in her morning class who grimaced when they spoke of their beliefs. There was a large contingent of male predental students. They spoke knowingly of their graduation plans, careers, of who they would marry and the children they would bear. How arrogant they were, how foolish! But she couldn't avoid seeing the Mormons dressed in white and paired neatly, lounging on clouds looking down at the motley assortment of everyone else below, herself alone and her mother and Joan in overalls and doomed to toil for the devil, maybe holding the long bags that draped on the ground like the ones the slaves once used when they picked cotton. Why should she picture the next life that way, when she didn't believe in the devil or a next life? Still it plagued her. They were so certain, and she was certain of nothing.

On her desk in the room of TA cubicles she found the Book of Mormon bound in white imitation leather, embossed in gold. Certain passages were marked in yellow highlighter. Another day there would be another Book of Mormon on her desk, different passages marked or underlined.

She was known to be unmarried.

She loved their devoutness, their certainty, the clear-eyed way they looked at her as she tried to explain to them the culture wars. To them, in their ideal city with every street named according to its proximity to their temple, the culture wars were already settled and won.

"But you see here how bell hooks is arguing that certain voices get excluded," she heard herself say. She had written the black theorist's name on the board and explained to them how bell hooks was a woman named Gloria who renamed herself bell hooks, small b, small h.

"But if she wants to be equal to us what's she doing spelling her name in small letters?"

They believed they were the chosen ones, the ones God had saved for best and last.

In the mall there were shops that did a roaring business in luggage, others that sold only white clothing, dresses for ceremonies and the ceremonial garments they wore under their clothes, to remind themselves they were God's first and foremost, their skin sealed off from human hands, even their own. Did they shower naked? Were they clothed when they made love? She knew these were an adolescent's questions but all the same she wondered. A sandwich board outside the luggage shop was printed with the words MISSIONARY SPECIAL. Eamon would like that but Eamon was gone. Gone from her life, maybe gone even from the world. He might be dead and she wouldn't know it. Was it possible he could be gone from this earth without her getting the slightest sign?

The phone rang one morning at six-thirty, while Temmy was shaving in the bathroom. They slept together casually, almost always on weeknights. Weekends would have implied dating. They were not dating. On the floor in the living room they read magazines in the late afternoon, made love, put their clothes back on, walked down to the grocery store and each bought what they needed—razors and granola bars for Temmy, hair conditioner for Louise, maybe green grapes. It was on Sundays that Temmy sometimes stayed overnight, the two of them sleeping beside each other on Louise's futon like friends sharing a bed in a hotel room to save money.

"Is that Louise?" the voice in the phone said.

There was some static or an echo on the line. "This is she."

"How the hell are ye, Louise?"

She had imagined him dead and here he was, or at least his voice; she would not believe him alive unless she saw him again in person. She had all this time been imagining him dead. It was easier than imagining him alive and conducting himself in the world away from her. That he might be putting his clothes on and making love and eating chicken from a box on his lap without her was too much; better to think of him as dead. Now he wasn't.

"Where are you?" She could barely get her voice out.

"At work. I've been trying to track you down for ages. Finally Craig found your mother. He told her he had back pay for you."

Of course. Her mother would never have given her number out to Eamon.

"I still have your note. I keep it in my wallet. Mairead found it all folded and refolded."

"Which note?" She had forgotten what she had said in the many notes she had sent him, had forgotten how extravagantly she had written what she felt. It would have shocked her to see what she had written, how completely she had declared herself. All that she had stowed away from herself in order to keep going forward.

He was thanking her for what she had said. "We're getting a divorce."

Temmy was calling from upstairs. The hot water had run out, he was shouting from the shower.

"Do you have someone there?" Eamon asked.

"No!" She was frantic; she did not want him to catch her in a lie. It was crucial that everything she said to him was the closest to the truth she could get. "No one important," she said. "A male roommate. We share a bathroom."

"I'm staying with some friends. On their sofa." He gave her the number and she wrote it on her hand.

"I have to go now, the delivery's here," he said.

She knew his phone habits, how when he got off the phone he got off quickly. She shouted his name.

"What?" he said, alarmed.

"I was making sure it was you."

She was standing in the kitchen still when Temmy came down the hall, his wet hair in a ponytail, his body scrubbed and strong. He smelled of pine as he leaned and kissed her cheek.

"You're burning up. Did someone call?"

"A former love, lover."

"Someone you still love."

She didn't have to answer; it was on her face.

"You should pursue that." He touched her back lightly. "Come see me off. The sun's just coming up."

Outside, his bicycle stood chained to a narrow tree. He took a granola bar out of his pocket, opened the foil, kissed Louise.

"Did you ever read Plato?'

"In college. I had this female professor, with a space between her teeth, like Lauren Hutton. She taught Plato and Aristotle. I was amazed by her. And another professor I had, in this course on the Enlightenment. She was tiny and wore blue all the time, blue tights and even shoes. She was like an elf and then she would open her mouth and all this business about the Age of Reason would come out of the mouth of this elf."

"We've had some good talks," Temmy said. "I've enjoyed them."

"The talks were the best part, weren't they?"

The sex hadn't been the best part. Shouldn't people who talked that easily be able between them to have sex with distinction? But their sex had been like their trips to the market for items each needed alone, the walk pleasant, uncommitted. Was there no passion in them?

It was not that there was no passion. Rather that he had passion for everything equally. He was the new man; all options were open to him. He might be a composition teaching associate and an outdoors enthusiast this year; next year he might go to law school, take up pottery, move to Vegas or Nice.

He took off down the long boulevard on his bicycle, eating his granola bar as he turned to wave goodbye. He was the new economy, he could change his habits daily, he had been born into the world the way a bird is born into a nest and before long grows and flies away. There was nothing he could not live without, not even home.

four

They were married in the late spring. Donna and Donna were in attendance, wearing denim jackets and boas, bottle cap belts. Some of the neighbors came, Ed and Maria from next door, Maria with a tray of ziti, Ed with cannoli. Bev referred to them as *very traditional but very accepting.* Others were not. The people who lived across the street with the basketball-playing sons did not speak or look at them. Aunt Beck flew in from California; by now she was old and gnarled, her speech slow. Her mind was still intact. She wore all purple and answered Joan's questions about what the girls were like when they were young. Joan felt a new and ardent sense of mission. It was time for all of them to be a family.

The old woman from North Carolina came, leaning on her cane, telling stories about Joan in the wild years, when she was married to that penis with arms. "Don't talk about him," Joan said. But it was already a coined phrase, *penis with arms,* for everyone to repeat. Evelyn from the old days, too; she had come, it seemed, out of the woodwork, reappeared in Bev's life via a drug rehab program Bev ran at night. She was still in love with Bev, though Bev was the only one who couldn't see it. In her red sweater dress, the first dress she'd worn in decades, and her black ankle boots she looked like a groupie, a little supplicant, starry eyed and disappointed. Watching Evelyn move so carefully in her dress moved Bev almost to tears. She was a lonely woman with all her emotions tamped down but on this day they were right on the surface with that dress and those boots, her ankles thin and unsteady like the ankles of a newborn colt. She managed somehow to be both breathless and gruff.

"How are your girls?" she asked Bev.

"They're beautiful, they look like movie stars."

"Deborah looks just like Bev," Joan said.

"Only younger, and thinner."

"And straighter!"

Everyone knew about Deborah, the long silent feud, the empty

Christmases. It had been years. She and Bev sent each other cards at the holidays and birthdays, nothing but their names under the printed messages.

"Isn't Louise here?"

"I didn't tell her. She doesn't believe in marriage, whether it's recognized by the state or not."

"But you do. That's the important thing."

She didn't know what she believed. Her ring was an amethyst teardrop; they'd gotten it from a jewelry maker in Provincetown who wore a cravat and seemed to chuckle at them as if to say, why do you bother with these rituals? But maybe that was her projection. He had put the ring in a velvet box.

Still, it was not so many years ago that she had sprinkled rose petals on Stephen's head at their reaffirmation of vows. She remembered how Stephen had called it a reaffirmation of views one day by accident while they were having a second or third drink on the deck and she had laughed, saying Not as if we could ever have any affirmation of *views*. He had looked at her strangely. Hurt that it was so obvious to her and, she had thought, not to him? Or hurt that she would laugh and say it, not even pretend they had anything in common? And yet she had liked that marriage for a long time. Unlike him, she didn't see its dissolution as a loss or failure. She had her own house now; her name was on the deed. She and Joan had written their own vows, incorporating a Navajo story and some of the goddess ritual from a book from the old woman Joan now considered her guardian. Stephen would have balked at a goddess ritual, though, just on principle. It wasn't as if he believed any less in a goddess than a god.

And still she was not sure she was doing what was right. This marriage was only one in heart. Was she foolish holding Joan's hand and being showered with flower petals again? Enough with the flower petals; let the flowers have them. She was wearing a pale orange drop-waist dress; Joan liked her in orange. Joan was wearing a suit. In Polo cologne she smelled like a man and in her suit she looked like one. As she had begun to age or perhaps to identify in public more fully with men her breasts seemed to have flattened down as if in sympathy or shame or some awareness of their obsolescence. Now Joan didn't wear a bra, only a sleeveless undershirt, like a man or a child. Sometimes people mistook Joan for a man, though when she spoke she had a fine clear alto voice that was clearly the voice of a woman. In the car she sang along with her favorites when they came on the radio: Whitney Houston, Celine Dion, Bette Midler singing "Wind Beneath My Wings." When Bev drank too much at a dinner party and that song came on in the car as they were driving home once, Bev, slumped in the seat said, "You're the wine beneath my wings" and the two of them laughed at that. They were big laughers. But it wasn't always funny, Bev's drinking, and sometimes she went off to the bathroom for stretches by herself as well. She had gone in this morning and rolled herself a joint and smoked it before the mini-quiches went in the oven.

During the years with Stephen she had tried to be practical, conventional, discreet. Now there was no incentive to be like that anymore. She had begun to eat whatever she wanted. She kept a box of saltwater taffy in her bedside drawer, she got stoned for breakfast. After three glasses of champagne at the reception she reported how she and Joan sometimes ate hamburgers in the morning, challah bread French toast with powdered sugar for dinner.

"Don't tell people that; it's our secret," Joan said later.

It was no secret that they were gaining. In the months after their wedding they ate as Bev imagined peasants ate, tearing hunks off the loaf of bread and swabbing the grease off their plates. Meals took over their evenings, the preparation and then the sitting for them, one course after the next. There was a lot to watch on TV all of a sudden—Whoopi Goldberg always seemed to be on, a show called *Ally McBeal* with a number of female lawyers, Roseanne Barr with her show, Oprah as always, and then a comedian named Ellen DeGeneres, clearly a dyke but a lovable one, thin, with an impish sense of humor. They put the TV on a cart and wheeled it into the dining room. Didn't it seem as if it was all of a sudden that their reality was up on the screen and in some way mattered? The question of "Is she or isn't she?" was of course still at the forefront, but it was astonishing to Bev nonetheless. A television movie about Eleanor Roosevelt remarked on her affiliations with women, romantic affiliations. The wife of a president maybe a dyke. *With a face like that,* Joan always said. Ugly women were always suspected to be dykes, for obvious reasons. But Eleanor hadn't been rejected. Neither had Bev.

They believed they had seen Jim Kellerman in the neighborhood. Bev had glimpsed him out the window once, then Joan thought she saw him drive by in a sedan. After a stormy night some of their flowerpots out back were overturned. Certainly pots could be knocked sideways, but overturned? They ate licorice, fudge, more taffy, frittatas for lunch on the weekends. The next time Louise saw them, at Thanksgiving, they had become serio-comic expansions of themselves. In her journal she wrote, "My mother and her girlfriend: two dough dolls." Had Bev seen it she would have cried.

She cried anyway, in her cold car, on the way to work. An hour on the parkways each way, five days a week. She only hopped onto the Sunken Meadow Parkway for a few miles, but each day when she did she thought, sunken meadow. Sunk in that meadow was her strong coal black hair that she had once ironed straight, the privilege of that body and that youth (she still felt inseparable from that younger self, though it was gone—how could she feel inseparable from it still?), the privileges of being young and white and the wife of a good husband and the mother of two girls with hardly a blemish on them. Louise as a baby had been pink-cheeked, good-natured, her eyes like blue marbles and her temperament easy. Deborah like Rose Red in the fairy tale, dark eyes and pale skin, the daughter everyone said was lucky to be the copy of her mother. Now all of that gone. Sunk. Who was she now? Her bra straps cut into her back and chafed. She was less herself, bigger than ever.

It was the era of pharmaceuticals. *Prozac Diary, Prozac Nation.* Everyone, it seemed, was taking the new drugs. But was there more happiness around? Deborah went to work in midtown Manhattan for one of the big firms. She was in marketing; she chose the pink or lavender-bordered photos of women arranging flowers or walking beside children on bicycles, the fonts for the optimistic prose. *Feel Like Yourself Again.* In Evan-Picone suits, her hair pinned up on her head, she strode the long blocks to her office in Midtown. She herself had no need for the pills; the pills were for the downtrodden.

She worked at headquarters; the lobby of her building was a portal to the world. A designer came and feng shuied the lobby. Soon a sheet of water poured continuously down one wall. There were other Japanese effects, but this was the most dramatic. There was an arrangement of rocks in a box of sand.

She didn't so much mind the sand box. But the water on the wall went too far. Ostentation didn't bother her. Nor was she the type of person to perceive anything as malevolent unless it was demonstrably so. A snarling pit bull in an alley was malevolent. But the water-on-wall was irksome; it required comment. Did you approve or disapprove? From then on, it seemed any client she saw felt compelled to mention it. A lobby should be a lobby, not a conversation piece. She had noticed she also felt this way about sushi, particularly in the restaurants where a miniature train brought the plates of kappa maki and eel rolls and so on. She preferred a place near Grand Central with stainless steel counters where all they sold was soup.

She had begun to make money; she made more than Louise with her teaching stipend and more now than her mother as well. She was twenty-three years old and could afford clothing, good vodka, vacations. She bought herself colognes worn by women twice her age, jewelry; she got her hair cut at a name salon and brought home styling products in clear bottles. She arranged them on her bathroom counter as if they were liqueurs.

If her ads brought in the designated number of new accounts she got points toward travel, hotels and dining, rental cars. For Thanksgiving that year she took herself and her roommate from college to Puerto Rico. The bulimic roommate whose eyes were puffy and teeth bad, her abdomen concave.

"When I was a kid I came with my family. I had forgotten . . ." They were sitting on the patio at the Hotel Condado, drinking piña coladas. The weather was windy, changeable; they were both wearing windbreakers, their arms and legs crossed as they sipped from straws the pale yellow drinks in front of them on the glass-topped table.

Deborah saw in quick succession a number of images, lit from behind as if illuminated for visitors in a museum. Her mother holding up handmade bikinis in a shop on a narrow street here in San Juan now lost to her, she and Louise and both parents swimming in a lagoon during a rainstorm, the four of them, again, walking single file along a beach road where vendors sold the fried salt cod their father had introduced them to. "The food of the people," he said. Then of all of them eating dinner at a restaurant called The Green Room. It was New Year's Eve; her parents drank rum before the meal and spoke to the waiter in halting, bashful Spanish. Then her mother with her elbows on the table, sinking, her eyes closing, her hair in the sauce on her plate. "Ayudar!" her father shouting, so distraught he couldn't conjugate the verb.

The friend leaned over, flashed her ruined, translucent teeth. Her family had always been horrible, the father and irredeemable drunk, the mother cowering. "What did you forget?"

The lantern slides faded; she was back to the present life. "Nothing. Just that we were happy."

"That's not nothing."

Hair in the sauce. That one image wouldn't leave.

Was it still happiness if others so near were suffering?

"Or I was happy."

⌒〰

"They're sending me out for a vitamin conference."

Louise propped the phone on her shoulder. "A *vitamin* conference?"

"Herbs and vitamins. It's the medicinal herb capital of the country, don't ask me how or why."

She drove into the mountains to meet him, the car she'd borrowed struggling through the long climb up the canyon. "Oh Jesus please don't die on me," she said out loud. The heater didn't work; it was early spring and she was bundled in a parka, hat, gloves, long underwear beneath. Like the Mormons with their garments. Only hers were pink silk and meant for warmth.

Since the phone call she had been involuntarily shivering. She had not seen him in almost two years.

It was eleven at night by the time she found the hotel in the mountains. There he was in the headlights, a little heavier than she had remembered him, in his trademark acrylic sweater and jeans and "runners," his word for sneakers. He was not a clotheshorse, not like the men at college or now even the men in her classes at graduate school. Temmy with his ponytail, his suede and moleskin shirts. And yet he cared about his appearance. The sneakers were new and white; the sweater, too, was creased down the center, looked new. His hair wet from the shower and parted down the middle.

He climbed into the passenger seat and in one gesture took her head in his hands as if receiving something fragile for safekeeping, an infant, a giant intact shell from the sea. She put the car into park and allowed her head to rest in his lap.

"Remember?"

"I remember you used to put *your* head in *my* lap."

"I wanted it this way, too."

His hands were rough and smelled of travel, of airplanes and packaged food. His breath smelled of cigarettes.

"It's freezing. Why aren't you wearing a coat?"

"I didn't know it was going to be snowing in feckin' April!"

"It's a ski area here. We're in the mountains."

They were unbuttoning and unzipping each other's pants, their hands intent on each other.

"I've got about seven layers on. Let's go indoors." She pictured her body in the sagging pink silks. Soon those would be off and her skin would be against his, the smooths and the roughs, his ingenuous penis, uncircumsized—as she thought of it, blind. She was not like the Mormons, she did not have to hold on to her garments, she was free to partake of the flesh now that the flesh of which she wanted to partake was near.

"No, please. Once here." He hoisted himself up and climbed between the two seats to the back. "Ever since we were apart I've thought of you in cars."

She turned the off the ignition and headlights. Then it was completely dark up in these ancient mountains, except for the spotlights illuminating the hotel and conference center signs, etched in local, ancient stone.

He helped her out of her garments, parted her legs. When he bent to kiss her, saliva dripped from his mouth. He was not embarrassed; he admitted every symptom of nervous anticipation his body presented.

"The first time I'll come off in half a minute. We may as well get that out of the way."

Louise didn't want to get anything out of the way. In the morning they woke early in the first bed they'd ever slept in together and made love while still half asleep, awakening fully only as they neared completion.

"Now we have to go see how echinacea liquid is made."

"Christ Almighty."

A school bus took them from the hotel to the facility where the herbs were grown and processed. They spoke on the way for the first time as people who haven't seen each other in years. They had not spoken that way all night. Night was sacred; this daylight bus ride was profane. Their lives apart from each other could be acknowledged, invoked.

"Clare's three. I see her on Tuesdays and Fridays; she stays at the apartment with me and the boys." He lived with other emigrants who hoped someday to get legal. There was a Brian from Wales and another Brian from the north of England. They lived in a cottage behind a manor house in Sea Cliff, a couple of towns over from the isthmus where Louise had grown up.

"Our bachelor pad," he laughed. "Only there's trouble with the septic tank and our yard's for the most part a swamp."

Later they drank the local beer in the hotel bar and traded stories of what their lives had been like.

"Mairead was furious," Eamon said. He pressed one hand against the other, told the story of the attack with the knife.

Louise looked away. "Oh God, Eamon. I ruined your life."

"No, you didn't, you didn't. I did."

It was a time for making pronouncements. Perhaps it was the mountains around them, perhaps they felt cradled or felt how old the earth was here, how it outlasted all human vagaries. In any case her heart was in her mouth. She put her hand to the side of his face. "It ruined my life, too."

"You're in school," he said solemnly. "You're making something of yourself."

She drew herself up. She wasn't in the habit of drawing herself up, of making pronouncements. "But without love—." Here she faltered; she didn't know what she meant to say next. Had she known the Bible she would have known a phrase.

"Ah, Jaysus. A bank book'll beat love any day."

She looked down at the floor, at his runners. Someone nearby was ordering ostrich medallions.

"I left my cigs in the car. Want to walk out with me to get them?"

They dawdled in the parking lot, swinging their joined hands in broad arcs like indolent teenagers as they walked toward the car. Everything was better in the car; there they dismantled the elaborate punishing architecture of their different classes, the vast distances between their cultures. If they could live only by driving a car from place to place, if there need be no permanent structure. But that was a thought for children.

They parked the car at the far edge of the lot and removed only the clothes on the lower half of their bodies. After they made love he braided her hair; he'd braided his daughter's and was dexterous and precise. He called them "plaits"; he called a run in a stocking a "ladder."

"I could get you a job."

He was still wearing only his sweater and white underwear, his jeans in a tangle on the floor of the car. He rested his elbows on his knees and then hung his head in his hands.

"Louise."

"What?"

"What are you thinking? To take up with me?"

She nodded her head back and forth, setting the braids swinging. "Why not you? I'm crazy about you."

"I'm shit, peanuts, crap."

"No."

"Yes, Louise. It's a mistake."

"Don't say that."

"It's true."

When she was a girl she could always at least refuse. The joys of a permissive childhood, of a childhood without the absolutes of religion to hem one in. Even parental authority had been negotiable; with Bev and Stephen it had never been law. Of all the choices available it seemed most unfair that the one choice not offered was a return to childhood. That time was lost to her now, those small and willful beings she and Deborah had been were gone. Like Deborah in Puerto Rico, she was still mourning their disappearance.

⌒⌒

"I think we're being stalked," Bev said.

"Seriously?" With the phone pressed between shoulder and ear, Stephen reached for his gin and tonic. He wasn't much in contact with Bev anymore; he liked to keep it to business, their daughters or money.

"Joan would do this herself—I mean she will—but I want to know if it's okay, if she's installed it right."

"Check her work."

"Yes. She's very competent. Only she's emotionally involved, so."

"So you're worried she'll do something wrong."

"Stephen, she's a wreck. This man is not safe."

He took the lime out of his drink and examined it. The wonders of nature: limes, the mind, the brain, its waves of resentment and indifference and rage. The terrible mess humans could make. If this guy was serious, and maybe he was or wasn't. With Bev's tendency to believe men capable of the worst he wasn't sure how much to believe. How many bashed faces of women had she addressed? How many accounts of men gone mad—hurling women in the eighth month of pregnancy down stairs, backing cars over their slippered feet, rearranging their pretty faces into patterns of cartilage and pulp—had she been charged to summarize and document in triplicate? Of course, of course he would check their new alarm system.

When he and Joan were thrown together they discussed technical things. It made him think of that little woman in overalls so long ago when they lived in the split ranch, what was her name? The one who had helped him with his carburetor and then left without saying a word. He couldn't think of the name. Something about women who knew carburetors and the like gave him a bit of a jolt, the energy almost sexual. It was too bad all the ones he'd met were dykes. He should have taught Louise and Deborah how to fix cars.

"Do you think you could come sometime this week?"

He stood awkwardly in the foyer. He recognized the framed Province-town poster, the mirror with the stained glass fairy resting her fairy elbows atop it, the slatted coffee table, its wood deeply scored in some places. By children's toys, his children's.

"Nice place."

"It still needs improvements." Joan paced in the living room, arms crossed over her chest, over the *Provincetown* on her sweatshirt. They sure liked Provincetown. "I want to install speakers so we can play music in the kitchen."

"Another project."

"Yes. Always another project."

At this they laughed together.

The bathroom smelled of men and of women, of neither and both. A blurred painting of a woman at her bath, a nineteenth century sort of painting, when people probably referred to bathing as their ablutions, hanging on the wall above the toilet. He regarded the naked back, the dress bunched at the waist. The back looked pink and tender, as if recently immersed in hot water. Bev's back long ago when they'd stepped from the shower together in his apartment in Hartford. That little yellowing tiled box with its miserly trickle of water. They had showered in it anyway, they had presented to each other their trembling imperfect bodies with wordless promises to improve them, each ashamed at first, each then reveling in the devout gaze of the other's eyes upon the imperfect body that stood white and trembling in that shower stall. In the mornings Stephen drank Wate-On shakes with raw egg and in the apartment she shared with her friend Mary Lee, Bev drank a cup of black coffee and then another cup. If only they were made of clay and she could pinch handfuls from her waist and thighs and press them to his skinny haunches and narrow stabbing shoulder blades. Would that not be the ultimate act of love?

No. The act of love had been each devout gaze each had cast.

It seemed he had loved her for so long and then, so suddenly—for when you love someone for many years the course of a single year seems sudden—it was not his province to love her anymore. Nor was her body the same body he had loved, nor her gaze the devout gaze that had bathed him in its heat and light.

Shells in a dish, soaps in the shapes of seashells, a sign made of driftwood that said *Gone to the Beach*. Everything placed just so and dusted.

This was her life now, this larger body she inhabited. And a body so like her own was the body she loved.

He could not imagine loving any man that way.

In the living room he excused himself, went out to the car for his tools. He brought the black metal box everywhere he went, even on business trips and holidays. He had brought the box to St. Thomas when he went with Janet; he would bring it to Bonaire, where he would go next, after getting his scuba certificate.

He and Joan checked all the windows, the garage and sliding doors, every method of ingress and egress.

"I installed a motion sensor light out by the garage," Joan said. "Come look."

They walked out together in the fading light of late afternoon. Bev had disappeared into one of the rooms of the house he had not been invited to see. Her and Joan's private rooms, places he wouldn't want to see. The one bathroom had been enough. Their little lap dog followed agreeably, its tail in the air.

"Bruiser," Stephen said.

"Yeah, right."

They stood just outside the pool of light their motion triggered. Their noses and mouths sent out white gusts when they spoke.

"Bev is not to know that I told you this."

"Maybe you shouldn't tell me, then." Why was he being called upon to be part of them? It was his wish to be separate.

"For my own peace of mind I need to."

"Okay, then." *Her* peace of mind. He was surprised at the thought. He had never thought of her as a rival, never even as an equal. And yet he was the first husband, Joan in a way the second.

"You know about my husband, Bev's told you about him."

"Jim Kellerman. Bev told me about an incident."

"Jim hasn't been a very happy man the past few years."

"About the name thing?"

"The name's part of it. He was probably already going downhill but my lawsuit didn't help. There was an appearance I made on the *Donahue* show a while back I now regret."

He had heard about that *Donahue* show.

"He's capable of a lot. I think he still has a drug problem. I'm not sure where he is with that now. But if anything happens to me, promise you'll take care of Bev."

"Joan, that's ridiculous. We live in a law-and-order society; there's not just a bunch of vigilantes living on Long Island. This isn't the South Bronx."

And yet as he said this a picture flashed in his mind of the young woman, still a teenager, with a gun shooting the adult woman with the frosted hair point blank in the head. That woman still had a bullet lodged in her brain, spoke with an impairment; it was amazing she was even alive.

"I'm watching my back but there're only so many precautions I can take."

"Tell the police!"

Joan knelt and helped the dog climb onto her, then perch with two feet on her chest and two on her shoulder. She didn't say anything, just petted the dog. He remembered now his conversation with Janet about her ex-husband. Was there nothing the law could do about these people?

"You can't arrest a murderous wish."

"Bev says stalking. You ever see him out here?"

Joan looked out over her yard. New suburbs, old trees. These were the new suburbs, houses without histories, a swath carved in the woods for developments that sprung up practically overnight. The new families were settling among the old families. Women and women, men and men, the blonde single mothers with their Chinese or Romanian daughters. Joan and Bev had just gone to a baby shower for one of the new mothers, whose daughter would be arriving soon on a plane. There was already a photo of her on the refrigerator, a swaddled baby held in China by hands belonging to a person not shown, maybe someone at the orphanage. The mountains of paperwork. All those documents completed for the possibility of love. But still the old families, old rivalries. She thought of her wedding to Jim Kellerman, her mother crying, Jim smearing her mouth with white cake. She had been a virgin when she married him, had thought he was serious when he said he would show his father her blood smeared on the sheet.

"He's around."

He drew himself up, stepped into his role. "Well if there's anything else I can do, you just let me know."

She stepped away from him, gave him a perplexed look. "I told you. If anything happens just make sure she's cared for. That's what I asked, that's what I said."

She was looking at him as if he was a halfwit, an asshole. Maybe just a deaf mute. He had noticed their identical rings but he wouldn't ask her. The rings meant one thing. He could be done. Done with that part of the marital journey, for even after you divorce you must continue to travel for a distance with your spouse, the way even if a car turns suddenly the bodies in it will continue to travel forward in the trajectories already begun.

Done, now, with the pretend equanimity, the ingenuousness— *yes, well it certainly was a surprise to me, but different strokes for different folks is what I always say* (had he really said that in conversation, at backyard barbecues and dinner parties, when people asked him about Bev? Different *folks*? Jesus)—the middle ground he had staked out as his.

He drove home in the dark. He is an artifact; he is made of solid matter, not fluid anymore. See how he can walk with his toolbox, how he can come to the aid of the damsel? It was a new era. He sees how it is no longer his time. He with his toolbox will remain part of the old one.

On Louise's birthday that year, her twenty-eighth, the three of them called her in succession from their common time zone, their incongruent lives. Deborah at work in Manhattan couldn't speak long; she was headed on a business trip to Toronto.

"Canadians don't seem like an easy market for anti-depressants."

"Why do you say that?" Deborah asked.

"I never met one who expected to be happy."

"That doesn't mean they reject it when they get the opportunity."

Once, briefly, in the days before Temmy, Louise had met an

effaced older Canadian author with a head that reminded her slightly of Joshua van Gelden's, though his age and, she was convinced, the fact he was Canadian softened him, made him humble. When he was younger he had been a sprinter, but he had damaged his legs with too much running. His looks had once made him a prince; he was aware he was a prince no longer. But this awareness, a certain tremulous apology for the notching down of his looks was what made him appealing. The years had begun to hobble him. He fought against it, ran each day on a bum knee he nursed at night as one would nurse a baby. He had been traveling through town on a book tour. Both nights he and Louise had lain together for hours on the striped coverlet in his B&B, eating corn chips, drinking red wine, and talking about the books she'd been assigned to read: *The Decameron, Gargantua and Pantagruel, Don Quixote.*

"It's all so far away from my experience."

He had kissed her closed eyelids. "Maybe it's not. It doesn't have to be about people like you to speak to your experience."

She had not understood him. Americans wanted the world to look like them. What was a world of plagues and beasts and windmills? For AIDS had not touched her as it had touched Bev; a distant Italian plague would not strike a chord. Nor beasts; she had never been struck by a man, though she had lain coldly beneath Joshua in the later days, after parties when they left together, she hazy from diet pills and liquor.

She and the Canadian had only slept beside each other. Literally slept, not making love beforehand or afterward, neither of them waiting for the other to disrobe. It was not a disappointment; each the second morning confessed to waking during the night and watching, unbeknownst, the other sleep. When the author got on a plane back to Canada she knew she would never see him again; she knew also that when she was dying the image of him sleeping, his mouth open and slack, was one in which she could take refuge. She was already collecting images straight from life; she didn't want to die thinking about TV. Images of Jesus were no refuge, her parents were not a refuge anymore. When she died she could think of the Canadian's face rich with sleep, luxuriant in its wanting of nothing and taking of nothing. That was the true wealth, the only one: not to want.

Her birthday was a Friday. Her parents had canned things to say. When one is waiting for the voice of a lover all other speech is static and noise. Her mother told her again the story of the day in the past when she was born. How it felt when her water broke in bed. The Long Island Expressway, their blue Valiant with the hole in the floor through which she watched the pavement blur past, icy patches they skidded on, icy rain. Stephen's nervous hands, and then how he had, after great diffidence and silence in the months leading up to her birth, bestowed on her a name. Louise Michelle.

Her father called while eating a sandwich from the Italian deli near his office. He described the meats, the bread, garlic aioli. She did not want to hear about his aioli. Why was she allowing this conversation to prevent her from receiving a call from Eamon? Because he was her father, because he had named her.

He told her she should look forward to growing older. He had, he said. He never looked back.

"So I won't, either."

She felt desperate as she hung up the phone. She would not be a writer, after all. She would be a prognosticator, she would predict the next trends. People having their faces fixed, people getting entirely new faces, with movie star features. A mouth like Marilyn Monroe's, a gap between the teeth like Lauren Hutton's.

She waited the better part of the afternoon for Eamon to call, then in the early evening went out for coffee. There was a shop several blocks away in a liberal enclave: independent movie theater, bagels, a novelty shop that sold feather boas and dildos. The coffee shop was owned by a man who wore a skirt. He was known in the neighborhood; the deliverymen waved to him. He stood outside his shop smoking, petting the dogs tied up while their owners studied or played chess or chatted and leafed through the newspaper inside his shop. No one knew it was her birthday. To contain this fact made her feel separate and packaged away from people, as if she was the only one carrying the knowledge of her eventual death. How childish she was: birthdays meant nothing.

Why hadn't he called? She thought they had declared themselves to each other. She had begged him to pack up his few things and move west.

When she returned to her apartment she called him. His answering machine picked up. What jollity, what ease his voice conveyed. You would not guess the dismal coordinates of that answering machine, of the life he lived. She listened once and then, punching the buttons a second time, again to the voice. He lived now in the basement of a house owned by a British couple he knew, the man an owner of a bar Eamon frequented, The Rose and Thistle. There was no heating in the basement, no lights other than bare bulbs dangling from the ceiling. The floor was cement, his furniture scattered haphazardly through the one vast room.

She had known the neighborhood as soon as he mentioned it: the same area where her mother had lived right after her parents separated. Not so near to the main road and the all-night convenience store as her mother's apartment had been, but still a sad neighborhood, the houses deteriorating, the lawns dotted with For Sale signs. It was Louise who had told Eamon the sociological designation: white flight. Eamon had laughed at that. Maybe the term was funny; she had never stopped to think about it apart from its implications.

"Where are you, fuckhead?" But she said it after she hung up the phone.

That night she dreamt of a vast dental operating theater presided over by the orthodontist from when she was a child, the woman whose clean hands had installed the metal bar across her upper palate and told her mother to turn it with a key. Dr. Whalen wore jeans and a pink open-necked shirt, a gold Tiffany locket hanging from a chain around her neck, tennis sneakers. The floor was covered with sawdust and all around were sheep tramping and lowing, peasants in hemp smocks tending to them and some peasants hoisting skinned and pinkly bleeding parts of sheep onto wooden dowels. Four of Louise's teeth had fallen out; she had saved them in her pocket and presented them to a woman wearing a hygienist's pastel smock. Then on two chairs pushed together she lay and opened her ruined mouth.

"What can we do here today?" Dr. Whalen asked.

From her mouth Louise extracted an ancient, rusted retainer, clogged with dietary embarrassments. It reeked of sour breath, old food.

They studied her teeth.

"What can we do?"

⌒⌒

The basement had been emptied, the one rug rolled up against the wall and abandoned. The digital display on the answering machine on the floor blinked its red zero and one and then two and three and four.

He had meant to arrive in Utah that night and surprise her, but on the layover in Chicago the plane got socked in by early snow, a blizzard. Could he call her? The noise and echoes of the airport would reveal him. He drank in the airport lounge, smoked one after another as he hadn't since Ireland, bought rounds with some salesmen with dark suits and matching shoulder bags. It wasn't clear what they were selling even after they explained their line of work. Something with computers; everyone involved with computers seemed to be pissing silver and gold. As the night and snow went on he slept near his gate with his head on his duffel, his dreams shot through with footfalls and intercoms announcing the new delays. His childhood in County Meath had been such stasis, such containment and habit, the days falling one into the next without incident or scenery to distinguish one from the next. All scenery and incident the same, all part of the predictable tapestry. Now in adulthood this movement over such vast spaces, his destination unfixed.

He had been born in midsummer; his astrological sign was the crab. At thirty-one he had used up nearly all of the nomad in him. To survive in this country he would have to settle. That or give up, return home to the days he knew. Burrow as the crab burrows.

⌒⌒

La Cage au Folles. Pricilla, Queen of the Desert. Paris is Burning, Angels in America, The Ryan White Story. She couldn't get away from it. The actor from *Starsky and Hutch* had a wife and kids sick from a blood transfusion, a basketball star announced he was infected. From promiscuity, not men. Not gay. Gay was the plague, not AIDS. Or they were one and the same. On the plastic side panels of bus shelters and on the tiles in the subway stations the pink triangles appeared. Slogans and slogans, rainbow flags outside the bars in Chelsea, Silence = Death.

She didn't believe that AIDS was a scourge on homosexuals; she wasn't sure she even believed in the category of sin. Had she been born into another family, it is likely she would have embraced these tenets, the virgin birth and resurrection and the snake and Adam and Eve. But she didn't possess the infrastructure for that. By the time she came to hear them, the stories in the scripture sounded like an Alice in Wonderland story without the grinning cat and Tweedledee and bottle labeled *Drink Me.*

She was tired of hearing the rants and shouts, she was tired of the pink triangles plastering the city's public walls. She was one of the few young women who truly would have been happier in an earlier time. Aprons, pearls and cameos, the household of the fifties with its new appliances. She had a figure that looked better in skirts. She wanted to have several children, to make of her home a fortress. Large cars appealed to her, men in movies who wore hats they removed when women passed, flirtation by the water cooler, mixed nuts in a tiered dish, maraschino cherries, swizzle sticks, place settings as dictated by *The Joy of Cooking*—she belonged to another time. It is a curse to be so and know it.

Had her mother been ill or infirm, suffering the ravages of cancer, even mad, Deborah would have risen to the occasion. Had the corpus callosum been cut, had electricity been wrongly fed into the brain. Oh Deborah could have pushed a wheelchair, soothed a madwoman, bathed a stump where once a leg had been. It was her mother's love of women that was beyond her. Her mother's love of Joan Kellerperson, whom she could not learn to like. A stump would have been easier.

Bev and Deborah met now for dinner at restaurants off the highway, equidistant from Bev's home on Long Island and Deborah's in the city. TGIFridays, Ruby Tuesday, the servers in suspenders and hats with propellers or cloth flowers on them presented sugary drinks in giant parfait glasses. A margarita for Bev, a piña colada for Deborah. They were made with corn syrup and dye; they gave the satisfaction of neither booze nor dessert.

This one time, she would go to the house. She had news.

"I'll go do errands," Joan told Bev.

"This is your house. We've been together for years."

"I'd rather do errands, really, than make a point."

It was Sunday morning. Joan went to the Garden Spot and looked at the zinnias, a greenhouse full of cacti, a small pond with frogs clinging to the undersides of driftwood. Who cared? It was April and she was in the April of her life if December was death, or at least she was not that far gone from April, and she had found love. She had borne no children, her friends were few, she had been an orphan since the age of fifteen, her ex-husband would not if given the option object to her death; he would not even object to being the one to cause it. Yet there were zinnias and Bev.

On the way to her mother's Deborah missed the Wading River exit and had to double back. Why hadn't she just agreed to meet at Ruby Tuesday, eat the bad eggs, let their feet get stuck in the gook on the floor, drink the thimbles of orange juice? Because that was not the place; you didn't talk about important things at chain restaurants, the servers in suspenders hovering over you or god forbid overhearing and then going back to the kitchen to crack jokes.

She would do this in her mother's living room; she would be gracious as Oprah with her hands folded in her lap.

In front of the house someone had already mulched. Soon the rosebushes would go in, the one named Ingrid and the ones named Marilyn and Bette. Deborah wouldn't know about those; they had only told Louise about their pantheon of rose goddesses. A driftwood *Life's a Beach* sign hung on the front porch. One of Bev's favorite slogans but what did it mean? Bitch, beach. Always the invocation of the embarrassing, the unseemly. Could she not be a normal mother like some of the other ones and put van Gogh's sunflowers on the wall? No, it had to be Provincetown, mandalas, *Life's a Beach*.

She rang the doorbell, greeted the asthmatic dog, breathed the smells of patchouli and marijuana in her mother's hair.

"Thanks for coming."

"Sure."

"Do you want something? Decaf? I've got the makings for mimosas."

"Decaf would be good."

"Joan's out. She had errands."

They walked across the terra-cotta floor of the kitchen. The floor from Bev and Stephen's last house. Though of course not *the* floor. A floor like that floor. A sliding glass door led to the forested back yard, where Bev and Joan planned to put in an herb garden, ornamental grasses, eventually a swimming pool. Photos were magneted onto the refrigerator, photos of Louise and Eamon next to the sign in Emigration Canyon, of Deborah and Scott at Niagara Falls, of Bev and Joan in front of a Provincetown B&B, the rainbow flag curling in the breeze behind them. Deborah accepted a glass of water and a glass of juice while the coffee brewed. She spoke freely, told of being sent to the great cities of the world—Barcelona, Madrid, Vienna—on business trips where she never saw anything of the great cities other than the insides of conference rooms. She spoke freely but she did not look around. Her incuriousness was vast and protective; she looked neither left nor right, as women walking through unsafe neighborhoods keep their eyes fixed forward.

"Want the nickel tour?"

"Not right now."

"I want to show you the afghan I'm knitting."

Would she be tricked into visiting their bedroom? These months, these years, she had made in her mind an image of their bedroom as a place that would alter her if she saw it. She needed to believe there were two beds. Why after so long this grasping after fantasy?

The afghan was yellow and green; it was for Joan to put over her feet when she needlepointed.

"Joan needlepoints?"

She was shown the embroidered pillowcases, Joan's plastic box full of spools of thread in the colors of the rainbow and the increments between. So it was she saw Joan's collection of baseball caps, her Yankees jacket, her autographed baseball and Yankees plaque.

Then they sat in the living room, Bev with a mimosa.

"Scott and I are getting married."

"I'm thrilled, Deborah. He's such a nice man."

She had imagined all the ways she would say this next piece.

"He doesn't know yet, about you."

A pause. "How can he not know?"

"We've never talked about it. He's very Catholic."

"He doesn't seem very Catholic."

"The family is, they're very Old World." She loved the sound of "Old World," she loved to think of the traditions cemented, the grandmothers with crooked fingers presiding, the dresses lifted out of lace and let out in the waist for the new brides, the recipes passed down from generation to generation. She wanted lineage. What could she pass on to a daughter? Her mother's bracelet with its bullhorn charm for cheerleaders, its empty gold box, mangled from when a desperate Louise went after the dollar inside with tweezers? What kind of legacy was that?

Bev leaned forward in her chair; Deborah was speaking quietly, it was important to hear. "What do you tell him about who I am?"

"You're my mother."

It was a reminder: As a mother your passions are of no interest to us. Your passions, your foibles, the joint you smoke and the Jordan almonds hidden in your bedside table. Your many weaknesses, your loves, your bodily needs and markings. The scar under the eye is a fact but not a mark with history: We need not hear that in high school Richie Salerno hit you, we need not hear of high school. Those days were scored in the book of time so long ago they have now faded. They are not our times. And do not speak of the tattoo. Tattoo? Bev and Joan had gotten interlocking halves of hearts on their backs. They lived for each other; they did not live for themselves or anyone else. Though in the days when Deborah was young and Bev's hair was long and heavy as rope, her face mistaken for Natalie Wood's—in those days when everything was on offer to Bev—for at a certain juncture in a woman's youth and beauty all is on offer to her, though all is not easy or good or free—she had lived only for her daughters. There had been the one deviation, with Pattie Jankowski, during the Bicentennial. How they had sat in the small sewing room at the top of Pattie's house those long mornings when the older children were at school and the younger ones napping. Quiet beside each other they sewed the spangled costumes for the many galas and parades. It seemed the whole country was celebrating. All of a sudden history could be invoked. History as a birthday; the country's age was all the children knew, the spangled two hundreds in the store windows. Then hand on hand and for some moments lips on lips. Those quiet hours together had bound them, each isolated from other adults. Caring for children isolates women from the larger world and from their husbands, who wait in vain for the mothers of their children to return to their identities as wives. For once a mother you never return to that thin-shelled egg from which you hatched a wife.

After the Garden Spot Joan went to the On Parade diner in Syosset and had matzoh ball soup and buttered toast, the dollar-ten Bottomless Cup of coffee. She read *Consumer Reports*. She checked her watch.

So it was Easter. Anyway she was a Jew.

The wedding was Trevor's, one of the men Eamon had lived with in The Swamp. Trevor worked as a bartender. In England he had been a linguist. His girlfriend Benna arrived from England later; the two of them took care of Eamon's daughter when Eamon was working or when his van broke down. Now that Eamon was in Utah they went to Mairead's and took Clare to pizza on Saturdays or to the movies or the mall.

Clare would be the flower girl. In art class at school, she had drawn a picture of herself sitting on Benna's and Trevor's lap all of them wearing the same pants and shirts. She loved them with the totality and exuberance with which we love all that is unattainable.

On the plane Eamon gave himself over to sleep as a bank teller hands over the money to the thief. Louise tried to puzzle through an essay called "Is the Rectum a Grave?" for a theory course she was taking. Sometimes her fear of AIDS was great; she was convinced Temmy had infected her, for it was obvious now Temmy had been promiscuous, Temmy had made love to women as others drink from fountains. His remarks about the upshot of his Mormon mission in Madrid rang in her ears. Men and women both: he was omnivorous. She would have liked to come of age in the seventies.

She hadn't told her parents or Deborah she was coming home; it would be enough to go to the wedding and to meet Clare. And perhaps also Mairead. There might be no avoiding it. Clare was seven years old; it had been seven years since she and Eamon had been in love. She remembered driving to his apartment in the rain, hurrying up the back stairs in her soaked shirt. How she had been too vain to wear a raincoat. In those days she had wanted to make of herself some dreamy filament. A Long Island accent was no dreamy filament. If Mairead stabbed his hand with a knife, she had wanted to enfold him. She had stood in the hallway while Eamon changed the baby's diaper.

The wedding was large and Catholic. Giddy and shivering, Clare walked down the aisle clutching her flowers in white-gloved hands as if they might fly out like birds and roost in the rafters. She was a skinny child with freckles across the bridge of her nose, Eamon's dark hair cut in a thick bang across her forehead, Mairead's close together eyes, Eamon's blue.

Skinny but not fragile, and alert to the adult nuances taking place above her. Of that first visit the image of Clare's head tilted back to catch the eyes and words of adults would be the one that stayed with Louise. There are some children who live in the world of children and others, ever more now, whose eyes are fixed beyond themselves, who have learned early that their fate rests not in the hands of gods or monsters but in the whims of the adults who care for them. Not just Mairead and Eamon but Benna and Trevor, and then other adults who had looked after Clare. Some had come and gone in a couple of months, others stayed on, slept in bed with her mother, bought her things. One old woman, Irish, a drinker who slurred in the late afternoons was gone suddenly, before Clare knew what "died" meant.

"She's gone to Heaven," Mairead said.

"Can I go?"

"Eventually. Not now."

Adults were at the core of it all; they paved the way to Heaven and furnished the earth. Sometimes rice pudding appeared in the refrigerator, for Christmas there was an indoor tree, tinsel. Wonders never ceased. Clare gave herself up to them fully; her childhood fears were not the childhood fears of Louise, who had been gated and protected, afraid of adults who weren't her parents, afraid to sleep in any bed but her own. Clare was from the new and different age. Her parents had parted before a memory formed of them together. She had slept in airports and cars, on sofas, in the basement Eamon rented, in a trundle bed beside his own. From a chair in the reception hall Clare leapt onto Louise's back. She was unafraid. In this she was nothing like her parents, who still crept as they walked on American soil. Louise carried Clare to the buffet, to the bar to fetch a glass of wine, to the dance floor, where Clare egged her on to whirl around until they both got dizzy and Clare let go of her and fell, biting her lip so it bled.

"Again, again!" Clare shouted, scrambling up off the floor.

Louise had not guessed that Benna would be black. Elegant, wispy, of many opinions she held quietly but firmly. This was evident even at her wedding, when women are most silenced by the attention called to their beauty or the illusion of it. And this was a woman beautiful in her looks and gestures both. She did not like America yet but predicted she would. Someday. The food confused her. What was catsup and how did it differ from ketchup? Currently she was waitressing at The Barefoot Contessa. They had to bring the bread to the tables in wide baskets; they were required to wear aprons and flowered skirts. Louise imagined Benna taking an order, bringing the plates. Even in bringing a loaf from beneath a cloth in the basket she would be elegant. There was no shame in her. There were not many people like that.

"Are you required to go barefoot?" Eamon asked. He had taken off his navy blazer and tie; his white shirt was translucent from sweat.

"I'm barefoot now." Benna lifted her vanilla colored dress and revealed her two brown feet, each toe tipped with opalescent polish. Sea urchins, pearls. She was blinding to look at, she was so herself.

They found their table with their names written in calligraphy on vanilla placards and introduced themselves to other guests through an elaborate flower arrangement dense with not just flowers but herbs and sachets and chocolate coins in gold foil. It seemed possible to put your hand in and pull out a wriggling bird, a handful of ripe berries. Someone had spent a fortune and a good deal of time. Benna seemed like a person with money. Clare sat on Louise's lap. Nearby stood Benna in chiffon and silk, Trevor barrel chested and curly haired, disheveled as a pirate after a capture. At their table, another English couple. They seemed to hate each other and like everyone else extremely, in direct proportion to the hate expended on each other. Robbie and Sophia, though everyone called her Soph. They glared at each other, seemed inclined to spit when they even turned in each other's direction. But when they turned away each got charming. Soph had a chip in her front tooth, a china doll face with blue eyes made of glass, a bosom she pressed with her hands when she spoke. Her dress was a brownish rose color.

"So this is the Louise we've heard about," she said.

"Ah, no." Eamon lit a cigarette. "This is a different Louise."

"He wrote letters to you. He would show us. I would say, send that; just post it right now and off it goes. Then Trevor would say no and talk Eamon out of it. He'd tell him you'd probably met someone else."

"I never would." Louise barely breathed the words. Then both of them saw how desperate she was in her love for Eamon and laughed at her, as jaded couples who have made their own indelible choices in such a state laugh. Soph was pregnant.

Louise and Eamon drank to great excess, dancing and tripping over each other's legs, kissing in the hallway that led down to the bathroom.

"Clare loves you," Eamon whispered in her ear.

"How can she love me? She doesn't even know me."

"She knows what you think of her."

"What I think of her?"

"That you already love her."

In one way children are like dogs: they are willing to embrace love from any quarter. It is only as we age that the beam narrows its focus. When we are young the beam casts itself wide. Love may be in any corner.

All year round, there were decorated trees in Donna and Donna's house. Their three dogs were sometimes kept in cages, to prevent them from destroying the trees. At Valentine's Day the tree had red needles and was trimmed with felt and hearts, retyped poems by Gertrude Stein glued in their centers. In spring out came the blue tree with ornaments shaped like boats. Tugboats were one of the Donnas' favorites, though there were also sailboats and clipper ships, a rowboat with fake barnacles and a tiny outboard motor. Christmas was the only time the tree was real, a Douglas fir weighted with angels, Santas, Marys. Donna and Donna had grown large on steak and sauces, Ben and Jerry's specialty flavors, Fra Angelico with fudge cookies late at night. Eating was their pleasure and their shelter. They cooked in their capacious kitchen, labeled leftovers in Tupperware with the name of the dish and the date and the chef. In the freezer sat containers labeled *Donna H Mali Kofta, Donna S Manicotti.*

These days Bev and Joan went to eat at the Donnas house more frequently. They had been paying for one of the weight loss programs that required them to drive to a storefront in a strip mall and be weighed behind a curtain by a woman in a white coat. That fell away.

There had been diet meals, low-cal cacciatore stacked in the freezer. Cookies called Healthables, low calorie, low fat. Each of them had lost some weight eating these foods, for a while there was even a system they followed. A point value was assigned to every food they ate. During the day they had to tote up the number of points used and make sure neither of them went over her allotment. Bev had less to work with at dinner because she spent points on wine.

She plunked a head of lettuce on a plate one night.

"This is all I have enough left for."

"I'm making chicken and rice and you're eating it," Joan said.

Whose eyes were their bodies for if not each other's? Joan planned to wear a black suit with tails to Deborah's wedding. At first Bev tried to dissuade her.

"What, you want me to wear a dress? Believe me, that would be the true spectacle." Joan hadn't worn a dress since her wedding to Jim Kellerman. She was one of those very few people who projects a self into the world apart from a gender. Most people are ensconced; their selves are inseparable from gender. Bev was this way. She dreaded a death from a disease that would strip her of herself: breast cancer, any cancer that took her hair. She feared most losing her hair, her breasts. Age was already taking enough, almost more than was bearable. To die suddenly of a heart attack or car crash would be better than any slow deterioration, anything that would make of her in the end just a body with its errors and effluvia. It was not enough to die a body; she wanted to die a woman.

At Donna and Donna's they ate for hours; it was the occupation of a day. Brie in pastry with apricot preserves, warm artichoke dip in a bread bowl, later aperitifs, T-bone steaks, rich desserts with drizzled chocolate, blueberry brandy. Joan then rested on the living room carpet with the dogs. One Donna's father lived with them in a room at the top of the house. He was infirm and only surfaced occasionally, looking for his newspaper or baseball cap. He didn't know Donna and Donna were a couple; he thought they were friends who roomed together. Homosexuals weren't an idea that had ever become current with him. They had decided it was better for everyone not to mention it.

"Greetings, Mr. H.," Joan said as he passed on his way to the kitchen.

"Well, hello. Don't you look comfortable resting on the floor like that."

"Come have some dessert."

He got his glass of ginger ale and wished them well as he went back upstairs. He was friendly but never used their names.

"All your friends and you don't think he knows?" Bev asked.

"I think he knows."

"He knows we're different," Donna said.

"But then *he's* different," said the other Donna, the man's daughter. "You should see how motivated he gets when the seasons change and we bring out the new tree."

"He wants to put up a golf one next year. I told him he could have June, before the Independence Day tree goes up."

"He loves our nutcracker collection." The other Donna pointed to the rows of them arranged on shelves. "He practically nuzzles them."

"Nuzzles nutcrackers?"

They were all smiling.

Why couldn't Deborah get into the spirit of it? Bev wondered aloud on the way home. Couldn't she be more like Mr. H.?

Stephen brought his mother on his arm to Deborah's wedding, Janet walking behind like an elegant servant, her purse on one arm and his mother's on the other.

His mother grasped his elbow and pulled him down toward her. She was vague and hunched with age, hardly able to walk on her own. Still she had a hawk's eye.

"And how did she get that terrible scar?"

"Look at the beach this time of year, Mum. Remember *Hai Sing*?"

She had asked about the scar before. Other times he had told her it was an accident.

"What sort of accident? It must have been terrible."

Autumn on the beach in Long Island feels forbidden, as if one has trespassed into Paradise. Sometimes when he stepped on the beach in fall Stephen thought of Romeo climbing onto the balcony to join Juliet. Or the fire escape, in *West Side Story*. It was the balcony and fire escape themselves he loved, though he would have said it was the lovers and their story. He was wearing a suit with a cummerbund; per Deborah's request he had gotten a dentist to whiten his teeth. On his own he got his hands taken care of. The unspeaking Asian woman had pressed his hands in soap, in dishes of warm oil. She worked at his cuticles and under each nail with a set of instruments, shining and smoothing as she went. He felt a camaraderie between them. Hands were important.

"Now they look dignified," he told the woman.

She didn't know "dignified."

He folded a five and handed it to her. "Thank you."

She only nodded; the next customer had already arrived at her station. He'd wanted to explain that his hands were everything to him. Now they looked the part, now they were distinguished objects he was able to showcase. The blunt, even nails, the shine on them.

The care given them stood as evidence of his health and well-being. He wasn't drinking as much; he had learned to downshift after the early companionable gin and tonics. He went to beer, and less beer at that. Like all alcoholics he had his own arcane, beloved system. Nothing made sense if explained.

The Tides Motel, Amagansett. It had a new paint job and the splintered boardwalk had been replaced, but other than that it looked the same as it had when he and Bev brought the girls out in summer. The motel was a squared U-shape, every room facing the ocean, only sixteen rooms in all. In one of them a woman held the dress so his daughter could step into it, as one stepped into a capsule. The day was overcast and breezy. It would not rain. So little went wrong for Deborah. Little had gone wrong for him in his life, either, but the difference was crucial: he had expected tragedy at every turn. When the girls were young he had been so fearful they would fall down stairs or be hit by cars he had shadowed them relentlessly. With wooden gates Bev had penned Louise in their first house; Deborah had removed the training wheels from her bicycle in secret, coming home triumphant, her knees raked with scrapes and gravel.

Now she wore the triumphant modesty of a bride: she had been chosen. Quietly she commanded a photographer and two videographers, all of them surrounding her, dressed in black.

"Where's Louise? We're going to be moving down the beach, with the bridesmaids and groomsmen behind us."

Louise and Eamon sat close together on the divan, the television on with the sound turned down. The room was quaint and depressing in the way that rooms built for summer habitation can be when the season is over. A fusty smell from the carpet, from the linens, and chilly drafts that the heat Louise had blasting didn't banish. Both wore their wedding clothes. Louise's hair was wet, her face pale, even teary. She had eyes that drooped downward like her father's, giving her a look of dreary endurance.

"Your sister wants you on the beach."

Louise moved awkwardly in the long dress. Stephen studied the stiff synthetic material with his engineer's eye. The body and the material that covered it were not well made for each other. He always thought he would be good at designing women's clothing.

But it was not something men of his ilk did. Queers were designers. He remembered his father saying that.

Each of them was here to perform a function. He had only to look down at his cummerbund and the authoritative lapels to remember he was the father. The patriarch, the only one Deborah could look upon with her ideals intact, her fervor for normalcy.

"Will you have a beer with us, Steve?"

Eamon with a cigarette and can of beer in the same hand. He was wearing black pants and brown shoes. Stephen took a can of beer and drank it as he headed back down the boardwalk toward the beach. The three forms in black still surrounded his white daughter, kneeling in the sand to adjust the folds in her dress and the bustle. The other bridesmaids and groomsmen were flocks of black and fuchsia, everyone color-coded like the electrical wire he used to bring home from work for the girls to make play jewelry.

Deborah was beside him, giving off perfume and agitation. "Where's Louise? Where's Mom? Stop spacing out. That beer can't be in the pictures."

Family configurations were assembled. Bride and groom with parents, bride and groom with groom's parents and sibling, bride and groom with bride's parents and sibling, bride and groom with all siblings. Janet and Joan stood on the boardwalk, watching, each with a can of diet soda. They were talking, but they did not turn to look at each other as they spoke.

How many things have happened to the institution of the family this century; what a shaken and unreliable property. But still a property, offering the possibility of shelter. Perhaps the only one. There was no shelter in communities anymore. The communities were old and broken, they were arranged from the shards, the oldness and brokenness. Alcoholics Anonymous, victims of domestic violence, Mothers Against Drunk Driving. He wondered if that was true too in the middle of the country or only here on Long Island, in such close proximity to the inflow and outflow of the changing, changing city.

There were all the old rules people were unwilling to break. Deborah didn't want to break them; she wanted them written on a granite slab with a consecrated stylus. Yet others were ready—Bev was ready, Joan was—to dissolve the family like sugar in water so that the family could remake itself. Was Stephen ready? He sensed his vote—*his*—was important. To others it was, if not to him. He remembered taking Deborah with him to vote for the president when she was seven or eight. At the intermediate school in Soundview, the voting booths with the curtains set up in the gym with its honey-colored wood floors. They had pulled the curtain closed behind them and stood before the levers. He'd wanted Jimmy Carter to win. It had felt like an average day all along, but when he got inside the voting booth with Deborah it felt momentous. His hands trembled; he was cotton-mouthed and needed to pee. The levers, the curtain. But he was only one vote. There were millions more, and there was the illegal money that packed and weighted the coffers. Democracy never worked properly. So many people didn't bother. And yet it had been important to cast the vote; it had been important for Deborah to see.

Janet with flesh-colored makeup that doesn't match the color of her flesh written on her scar. Joan in black dress pants and a coat with tails, a tuxedo shirt. She smells like Paco Rabanne and spearmint; she smells like a well-groomed man.

No photograph taken with Joan or Janet and the wedding dress. Stephen goes to retrieve the can of beer he twisted into the sand, so as not to mar the photos, so as to do what Deborah wished. He does not tap his daughter on the shoulder and say, "How about a photo with you and me and Janet?" Never mind Bev and Joan; he does not even ask for Janet to be recorded in what will become the annals of this family. If Deborah wanted it she would ask. She has asked for everything else she wanted.

He would not remember the day except in mechanical pieces and impressions—Louise's movements in the material of the dress that didn't move with her, the pleasing competent heft of the video camera on his shoulder when the videographer let him have a try with the new technology, the stippled leather cover on the steering wheel of the Mercedes Parker let him drive to the church, the hollow metal cane with the grooved handle he minded for his mother, determined to move herself from place to place.

When it was the moment in the reception when he and Janet were to play and sing a folk song for Deborah on their guitars, he would take his guitar in his hands and look down upon it as if it were a new and alien thing. This guitar, which had been with him since the days in college when he was thin and knew the script of *The Glass Menagerie* by heart, even the lines that were not his own, when television was still new and Bev spoke of the miniature people who lived inside it.

"You ready to start?" Janet asked under her breath. All the tables were silent; Deborah at the one small table with her groom was rapt, her chin poised on her tented hands.

Which chord? Which word?

His hands remembered; his voice went forward after his hands. It was a version of a folk song that had been playing in his head at the hospital when Deborah was born. He once said he was glad no commercial jingle had been playing in his head or maybe Deborah would be named Ivory. The folk song told of a swain who would love Deborah; Scott with his polite and serious family, his aspirations to gastroenterology, was now that swain.

His eyes swept the room while he played, caught Bev's face amid the other faces, continued their sweep. This Stephen he was showcasing was the one she had married those many years ago. Now this old self was dusted off and out of hiding; it made no difference that he wore a cummerbund and tux. Bev had always pleaded with him to let his hair grow out. Now he played his guitar again; now he didn't care so much for money, as he hadn't cared when they were first married and showered together, and sang for entertainment in the evenings and played cards and ate buttered toast with sardines and tomatoes for dinner.

It was not a mistake. He wished there was a way to tell Deborah this. His and Bev's marriage had ended, but it had not been a mistake.

Bev had been seated at a table with her father and cousins. Before the dessert she moved across the room and ate the crème brulee with Joan and the Jankowskis, from the old neighborhood.

Late in the evening Deborah and Louise sat beside each other. These had been silent hours for Louise; she had spent the whole day watching.

Deborah did not look the least bit faded. Her hair had been sprayed and modeled into a tight bun like that of a Spanish beauty, a dancer in the ballet. She had all the dignity. Beauty and youth and respectability were all now hers, and money. Stephen had spent all that he owned to give her this day. He had nothing left now; it was invested in the herbed potatoes some of the guests had eaten, the drinks and band and perishable flowers.

"What's with Dad's hands?"

"What do you mean?"

"It looks like he got a manicure or something."

"Maybe he did. Sometimes men get manicures."

"Well. Actors, maybe. Not regular men."

Finally, in Honolulu, Deborah cried. In the strange, beautiful bathroom with its chrome and sconces there was a white rug, the material too soft not to be the hair of an animal. In a hotel bathroom? Scott was off somewhere buying a higher number of sunblock. A book Louise had given her to read when they were young girls, she herself maybe just nine or ten, came back to her—a scene in a bathroom with a bottle of after-shave, the boy and girl negotiating about whether to put some on his balls. Deborah had not known what balls were, though she knew about the penis. She had not even been sure about aftershave, whether it was a lotion, thick or thin, or more like perfume for men. In the book the couple had agreed the girl should pat some on the boy's balls. But it had been unpleasant; she remembered a description of how it stung and that had ruined the mood. Why had Louise given her such a book? To teach her about the world? Was that her notion of an older sister's duty? Or to ruin something, as she believed her mother wanted to dirty the surfaces, marble the meat of life with perversities? Even her father had been infected, his hands like the hands of a prince or a homosexual.

FIVE

The economy climbed, climbed, precipitously climbed. Adolescents made money. Kids barely out of college lived in fantastic apartments overlooking Central Park, the sea. They could have any gadget they wanted; they invented new gadgets and sold the ideas for them the next week. They didn't even have to come up with a working model. Once Stephen had been featured in the Business section of the *New York Times* for a patent on a spin cast mold for contact lenses. That had been years ago, the photo with him and his Czechoslovakian counterpart jointly holding a wooden plaque. The plaque too small to be held between two men, it looked as if each of them was trying to pull it away from the other. A "Game Boy," that was how boys filled their time these days, that was how the young men could live in apartments with ocean views. Why the cheap plaque stuck in his memory like a hair in a glass of milk? How little it mattered. Now was there even a Czechoslovakia? All the borders were being redrawn; the maps were useless.

He still rented his apartment in the house overlooking the Sound. Hadn't he meant to buy property? In the evenings he ate soft-shell crabs alone at Wall's Wharf. He had at one time taken Bev and his daughters. Louise in her glasses and braces, homely in a way he knew she would outgrow but she didn't believe would ever change. She thought her looks were set, this was the person she would be. Deborah in some sort of majorette outfit, some uniform that conveyed her importance in the world she inhabited. Soccer cleats, a green junior varsity jersey belonging to a football player who was that month's interest.

Now on occasion he dated a hostess or one of the waitresses. They were nothing dates, weekends when Janet was busy with her boys. The hostess said she was happy going to Wall's on her night off; she didn't need to go to Poseidon's at the other end of town or anywhere new. She praised the croutons and cheesecake. "The best on Long Island."

"Don't you ever want to get the hell out of there? We could go have Indian food."

He didn't understand the restaurant was her home. Perhaps he had forgotten what home could be. She talked with the bartender, the owner, the other waitresses. Some of the drinks were free. If she got a Long Island iced tea it would be strong and she would he happy and talk about it on the way home.

He had really managed his drinking for a while but now he lost interest in managing; it drifted away from him. New bottles appeared. He got a bill in the mail for twenty-two thousand dollars, part of Deborah's wedding expenses. He put it in a drawer, on top of some other bills. When he drank now he often returned to the invention he considered his nemesis. Why hadn't he thought of it? Such a simple idea and it had made a millionaire out of someone. He pictured the millionaire: bearded, with smudged aviator glasses, overweight. Someone who imagined himself an inventor. The signs weren't even useful. They weren't functional. Was even a single car accident prevented by the presence of a Baby on Board sign? Careening into the back end of a vehicle, did one suddenly espy a Baby on Board sign and thus determine to swerve out of the car's way? Whereas had there not been a warning, would one sideswipe the car? And of course it had only been a matter of months before the legions of joke and novelty signs had appeared in car windows: Raving Lunatic on Board, Mother-in-Law in Trunk, Ex-Wife in Trunk. He had seen a lot of that last one.

In Wall's Wharf one night he got into a debate. The hostess' name was Elaine. She had a beautiful body but quite a homely face. His whole adult life, his overriding preference was for women with pretty faces. Janet's scar had been something of an obstacle, but her eyes and smile were so warm that he was able to overlook the scar. Like Bev, she had good teeth. He was glad her ex-husband had not seen fit to disfigure her mouth.

"You drink too much," Elaine said. "Have some water."

"Tonight are you the hostess or my date?"

"You don't want to hear it from me either way. I know."

Elaine had a tube of lipstick in her hand and was taking the cap off and putting it back on as she stood and spoke to him. Behind her, on the television, successive photos of the president greeting the same young woman in a variety of different locations were being shown. Often the woman was shown wearing a beret. He could see how someone might find charm in that.

"I'm saying this as a friend." She leaned toward him, so that her hair brushed his shoulder. "I care about you."

"I'm appreciative of your caring."

The look she gave him was carefully neutral. She turned and walked away.

Later in the evening, Elaine sat at the other end of the bar. Her shift was over; she was having clams on the half shell and vodka with some of the other workers. They talked about the president and his indiscretions. *A blow job in the Oval Office, it doesn't get any better than that*, one of the men said. The bartender and some of the other people agreed that was the maximum level of power.

"Maybe a blow job in the space shuttle."

"On Air Force One. Flying over Red Square."

"There are no Commies anymore; now there're just terrorists."

He had been given notice of the company's plans to restructure. All senior management were being dismissed; it wasn't personal. He reassured his boss that he didn't take it personally. He put what effects he had in a box. A framed photo of his boat and small framed wallet-sized photos of each of his daughters wearing makeup. The framed photo of his mother she had given him, he understood, for display in his office. So he had put it there, beside the several Lucite blocks, each with a bottle inside containing a cast-molded contact lens made by the machine he designed. Were the Lucite blocks his property? There was also a bottle of Goldschlager that had come into his hands. All he could remember was a dinner with some big-wigs in Manhattan at which he had expressed interest in the bottle with the gold flecks suspended in the liqueur. There had been just the sort of discussion of specific gravity Bev had lampooned when they were married. He had been given a bottle to take with him, pre-sumably to reward his interest in science.

The gold-flecked liqueur was part of the vast array of products and services, the invention of which had eluded him. He drove home with it beside him on the seat of his car. *Goldschlager on Board.* The car, too, would have to go: this Impala was the company's property. He would buy a beater car, maybe one of those old station wagons no one drove anymore now that sport utility vehicles had taken over. One with the paneling on the side, a woodie. In the back he could keep his tools and lug to the boatyard what he needed for the boat. Sport a tam, mismatched gloves in winter, become the town eccentric. He was old enough for that now.

Though anyone with the self-consciousness to imagine himself the town eccentric will never become so, lack of self-consciousness being the first and last characteristic of a true eccentric.

He gave the fine Impala back and bought an old station wagon. The upholstered ceiling sagged, the wagon became known around town for dying at intersections, the vents were capable only of delivering full blast, hot air or cold. He began to dress as he had always dressed on the weekends; he wasn't going to be like one of those Japanese businessmen who keeps up the pretense of having a job even after being fired, putting on a suit and getting on a train every day. He had read about the mirrors installed in Japanese train stations to try to prevent fired businessmen from leaping in front of the trains. Was a mirror all it took? To see oneself?

He hired himself out for odd jobs—getting a large piece of furniture up a narrow staircase, heating a garage, banishing squirrels from an attic. He had shirts made up with a logo on them and wore one everywhere. The logo had the face of an owl. A long while back he had bought a smoker so that he could smoke his own fish and meat, but he had never used it. Now he taught himself and smoked whitefish. He posted a sign in the rear window of the wagon, saying he had smoked fish for sale. *Also Boat and Small Appliance Repair*, he added. He fixed Walkmans, the newer Discmans, blenders, stereo components, food processors. He kept parts of many of these in the back of the station wagon. There were piles of detritus; every pile had its value.

He was absorbed in his work; if he was driving along Soundview Road and you flagged him down he would pull over to talk about a busted toaster.

He was working, his tongue wandering over his lips in great concentration. He had become an eccentric. He had no idea.

Louise went to Ireland with Eamon and Clare. The few times she had traveled outside of the United States she hadn't experienced anything of the discomfort she began to feel upon landing for customs in Shannon. She was in a state of unabated arousal. Her nipples ached; even her teeth vibrated in her head as if asking to be rubbed. She was slick, humid, flushed. She admitted it to no one, she didn't speak of it. It occurred to her that she might be pregnant.

They arrived in Dublin at seven in the morning and were taken back to Eamon's town by one of his brothers-in-law, a man in a stained white shirt with ham fists and hair the color of straw. His skin was deeply tanned.

"I didn't think people got tans in Ireland," Louise ventured.

The family was charmed by these remarks. They seemed to have no idea she was so greatly on the verge of sexual eruption. Her cheeks were always flushed.

"We'll go have a pint, we'll have lunch," Eamon said in the car as they spun through the little towns, along the tall hedgerows. Ireland smelled of smoky fires. And it was so small, the cars and houses and landscape seemingly in miniature. Only the people seemed the same size as they were elsewhere.

"It's eight o' clock in the morning."

In the back seat Louise and Clare slept collapsed on each other.

"She took pills for the jet lag. She wasn't supposed to take them until bed tonight," Eamon told his brother-in-law. "She'll be fucked all day."

"Better not to tell her."

"It'll only make it worse."

They drove to the hotel where Eamon's sister worked in the lounge, serving meals and drinks. She staggered glamorously in high heels, an apron tied over her miniskirt. Her shoes slapping against her heels made Louise notice the calluses, thick and serious as the calluses on an athlete, broken starbursts of veins above her ankles.

A table and five chairs were procured, set down right there in the parking lot. It was a special day. His sister brought out pints of beer, packs of cigarettes. "Crisps and sandwiches in a bit," she announced. They sat in the wan mid-morning sun and drank and smoked.

"Do you not smoke?" the sister asked. Her name was Martina. She still held Eamon's forearm, as if he might dash off into the brush and disappear. She dabbed at her eyes. "My God, it's been two years." She drank two glasses of a pale-colored beer Eamon said was what women drank. He gave it to Louise to sip. It reminded her of the Champale from years ago, the first time she'd gotten drunk and vomited.

"The Guinness is fine with me."

They liked that; she was brought another.

In her tall chair Clare sat drinking colas and swinging her legs. She ate crisps; she climbed into the back of the car and slept. It was the longest day of her childhood. At this time of the year the sun wouldn't go down until ten o'clock at night.

"You go on without me," Louise said at last, when they went back to Martina and Jimmy's house. They were only showering and changing their clothes so as to go out again.

"Come have a wash," Eamon said. He led her into the bathroom, removed her clothes.

"You stink of sex."

"That's travel."

He picked her up and held her. "On the plane did you have it off with someone in the jacks?"

They stood in the shower, a dim tiled box with a bar of soap on the floor and a purple lady's shaver. The water came out in a trickle; the pipes hummed as if electricity were surging in them.

"I did not."

They made love, him behind her, she crouching with her forehead against the tiled wall when she no longer had the strength to stand. There was a great deal of noise they hoped the running water deafened.

"Again," she said when they finished.

He soaped her affectionately, thighs and hips and shoulders. "I don't think I can go again now, honey. Later, before bed."

"Okay." A bolt of something desperate went through her. What was slipping away?

She walked out in the early evening, to try and get her strength back. The fields behind the houses were the color of hay, but she didn't know if that was what they were. In front of one house a handmade sign said *Jumble Sale.* In front of another a bush had been sculpted to look like a figure. A green and yellow Meath flag had been pushed into its bush hand. In some windows Meath jerseys on hangers twisted in the wind. Other windows were covered entirely with pages from the local newspaper on which were printed rows of faces and names of the Meath Gaelic football team, as if they were prisoners or martyrs. Two or three people who came along the lane greeted her with a tilt of the head or a phrase spoken as if they knew her.

She was thirty-two. Hadn't she planned to have a husband by now, children, a home?

No. She had not planned anything.

She was convinced her eggs inside her were growing sour or in some other way wrong or old. It was only an intuition but a very strong one. She might be a person meant to have children but her body was not the body that would bring them. Her body was not safe. How had she come to this conclusion? Her periods for years had come upon her like a trick childbirth, with cramping that made her writhe and vomit. Then the period itself a trickle of old blood. She had never gotten pregnant, never even with Eamon's sometimes Catholic birth control methods, when they ran out of condoms or couldn't stand ruining the moment to put one on. It was not safe to have children in America. There were guns, the people were too spread out and disconnected, the suburbs were doom. She had seen a documentary about a syphilis outbreak among preteens in an Atlanta suburb. It was an epidemiological blip, fifty or a hundred cases, from having parties after school in ranch houses with well-stocked bars, sectional sofas, the many bedrooms for learning or forcing or being forced to come to terms with the fact that humans are sexual, beneath all the layers and society. That the sex isn't often romantic, democratic, nice.

She met Eamon's other sister, his two brothers, all the children. Darren the star of the family with his footballer's thighs, the fame and clout he brought to the family and the town. The team had made it to the finals; the match on Sunday would be televised from Dublin. Another son, Declan, was quiet and blond and wanted to leave Ireland. Go to the States or to Australia. He would do that if it came to it, the other end of the world.

The girls were Kylie, Nollaig, Sinead, Nicola, and a word Louise couldn't hang onto that sounded like Caughtch. They played with her hair, sat in her lap at the pub, begged for coins to put in the juke-box. "We'll play mad tunes, the maddest," they said. They danced wildly, linking arms and spinning in circles, their hair whipping across their faces. Louise linked arms and danced with them, her face warm from movement and beer.

"Wouldn't you like to have one of your own?" Eamon's other sister asked. She was the eldest, practical, she already wore bifocals.

"Sure, sure, someday."

She remembered her own childhood, its seriousness and disappointments, the swift journey away from innocence once the journey began. Jumping in the leaf pile in corduroys and a Fair Isle sweater. Then childhood flatlined; she saw the child retreating indoors, to adulthood. Petra's strange cancer, her hair falling out in hanks until she was bald. A bald girl! And yet the cancer having nothing to do with the hair; the hair itself was not cancerous. So why did the hair need to go? She remembered going around with her mother on this one. Was the hair falling out a punishment for getting cancer? No, there was no punishment. Or the cancer itself was the punishment. For what? Not punishment for anything; it was just being alive. Punished for being alive? Then why were we alive? Why had we been made to live?

And by whom?

Up late one night, unable to sleep, she had heard her parents in the next room.

"We should have given them something."

"What? God?"

"I don't know, something. Maybe we were wrong."

"You think we should have given them religion?"

"I don't know. An *opportunity* for religion?"

"You can't give anyone God. They have to do that on their own if they want to."

"But it would've helped if we hadn't been so cynical. All that business about describing how their bodies would break down when they died. It's not very uplifting."

"Being strung up on a cross is uplifting?"

All the things she would have believed in. Family, love, work, money, sport. For God was not the only thing to which to attach one's faith. Six of them were crammed into a compact car, driving up to Dublin for the football final. Louise and Clare, Eamon, Jimmy, and two friends of Jimmy's, men from the town whose wives didn't care for football. The men smoked and talked of all the possible outcomes of the match: humiliation, triumph, a crushing defeat or a close one, a scruffy win in a final upset, the kind of win for which this team was known. The men wore green and yellow scarves or pompon hats, their Meath jerseys, jeans. In the dirt on the car UP MEATH had been repeatedly written with wetted fingers. When a car passed with a red-and-green flag on it the men announced "Mayo cunts" matter-of-factly. As with all religions, the enemy is known. Death cannot be the enemy, for death can never lose.

⌣⌣

Intimidation has its own quiet reign, subtle, discreet. It does its work by suggestion, part for the whole. One explosive can paralyze a nation. Any terrorist knows this.

Joan didn't see them until she was kneeling with a spade. They were scattered among the beds of waning impatiens. She traded a gardening glove for a leather one and collected them as one collects the fine things, seed pods that burst and scattered to produce more impatiens later. She had first seen the glint: sewing needles, razor blades.

On the ground by the woodpile, she came upon an Entenmann's cake. Chocolate coffee crumb, a variety known to be her favorite. Who knew? Cake and crumbs smeared the inside of the cellophane window in the box. She thought she could see the blurred imprint of a fist.

By degrees she and Bev came to walk cautiously in their lives, to tighten the circle of their activities. If one could have drawn the circumference of their existence with a compass, the concentric circles would have moved inward, as of the growth of a tree in reverse. Their house, work, market, pharmacy, home. In the cabinets stood containers of low-fat cookies, pudding, fudge. Potato chips cooked in imitation fat to avoid the sin of oil. Boxed and canned food in the garage, crowding the mulch and wood chips for spring. Stockpiling.

The new decade approached, the new century. Millennium was a word both of them spelled incorrectly. They appended it to everything: millennium fries, millennium flowers.

"I'm sick of your millennium bullshit."

"I've had enough of your millennial indecision."

They mail-ordered bulbs to plant from a catalogue. Daffodils, tulips.

"Millennial bulbs."

They tried all the new products: caffeinated water, fiery corn chips dipped in something neon, the new varieties of Hershey's Kisses with different nuts or stripes of white chocolate, a sugar substitute you could use for baking, better in some way than sugar. This was the next century's food. It made Bev think of the food once served on airplanes, identical steaming portions under foil, a faint chemical smell, more of the factory than of the kitchen. Now there was no food on planes but bagged pretzels. To recall those days on planes—with the bagged utensils, the anticipation of the meal and the sense of ceremony when the stewardess bent to slide your tray in front of you—was to recall another Bev. She saw herself as one sees the old sit-coms: reduced by the screen, the colors slightly distorted, upbeat bursts of music to signal a scene change, everything filtered through the muddy orange-yellow light she associated with the 1970s. All that was archived now. Her life, too. Only an episodic shape. There was no grand arc, any more than *The Mary Tyler Moore Show* had a grand arc.

It was said that when the new century came all the computers in the world might fail. The water supply contaminated, bank accounts frozen. It was conceivable they would be plunged into darkness again, a paper culture, paper and fire. Typewriters, abacuses, fires in the grate the only source of warmth. Bev pictured the spidery calligraphy of other centuries, sealing wax, a horse-drawn carriage. When Louise was a child she had come home with a book about Annie Sullivan, the girl who would become the great teacher of Helen Keller with grainy nodules on the undersides of her eyelids. In the crowded orphanage tuberculosis abounded. The ill, the dead were carried away by the Black Maria, a carriage with bars on the doors. Louise awoke with nightmares, crying from her bed and clutching at Bev as she described the carriage. It was a giant spider, a bulbous body from which sprouted not wheels but legs covered with hair.

"It's like the one in Cinderella, only not pink," Bev said. "I'll show you in the encyclopedia in the morning."

Though back in her own bed, trying to sleep, Louise's spider encroached, encroached, and won.

They slept poorly and woke early, five and then four, the house cold and foreign in its coldness, as if while they slept it shed its identity, became another kind of chamber, a catacombs. They ate quick pastries from the microwave, downed with hot cocoa or a sugared coffee that came in a tin. *Suisse Mocha*, they said to each other with European accents. Their dog sat on one of their laps and then the other, ate bits of pastry, yogurt, cheese. Again they were putting on weight. The dog too was growing fat. She felt their vigilance, barked more often, took up a sentry post on the back of the sofa, from which she surveyed the front yard. The appearance of a delivery man made her apoplectic; she had to be closed off in a room and placated with treats.

Work, errands. Their life outside their life together consisted only of these. Awaiting and dreading each other's departure, each then ate alone. Solitary eating, surreptitiously, in their cars or crouched in the kitchen, when no one was watching. In this they were not merely like each other. Each in this way became her own mother, long dead. Women who had lived their days alone in their homes with a broom and a magazine, meals to cook and no other avocation. To eat was to commune. They were ravenous. When the eating subsided, when each was full and loathing of herself, the longing returned, the great and irremediable loss. *My mother is gone; I will never see her again.*

At work Joan struggled to make the accounting system redundant. In case the computers went AWOL there would need to be paper copies of everything. She saw herself adding the old way, with the noisy adding machine, the scrolls of white paper and the numbers in columns of purplish blue. Perhaps they would return to a simpler time, before the machines. Before electricity: she pictured their home bathed only in candlelight, the television silenced, having said all it was to say. She could sew, Bev knit. Heat their meals in the fireplace, wrapping them in foil first; there was no need not to use foil, the point was not to reenact Old Williamsburg with calico and butter churns, for God's sake.

A key chain. Joan found it tucked where the windshield met the hood of her car. Double-sided Lucite frame, a photo of her and Jim on one side, a photo of her cut from an item in the newspaper when she won the case to change her name to Kellerperson on the other. She waited until she got to work, then slid the photos out. On the back of the one of her and Jim: Mr. and Mrs. James Kellerman. In her own handwriting.

Had she once been this person who loved Jim Kellerman? Who thought of herself as Mrs. *Him*? It was inconceivable. Yet here was the evidence.

She could no longer track that life, that vision of herself. She had turned fifty that year; she was willing to accept anything but having to reassemble her former life. She put everything, frame on key chain, photos, in the trash beside her desk at work, let it go out with the custodians, then on to a landfill at the end of a dirt road far from the water, where nonetheless the seagulls circled and dove.

"We'll leave Long Island," she said to Bev.

"Where would we go?"

"Anywhere. California, Florida. Or somewhere nothing happens. Some little town."

"Something's always happening everywhere. That kid was murdered in Wyoming, for Chrissake."

"Jim doesn't care enough to follow me to Wyoming."

Tears coursed down Bev's face. "My girls are here. I'm going to be a grandmother."

"Good, then. You want to report him? I have a bag with the blades he scattered in our garden. Take them to the judge and see if he gives a shit."

Bev was silent. Her mouth moved.

If they moved someplace anonymous, a place he didn't know and wasn't known. Carbondale, Illinois. It was near the Mississippi and the weather was milder. When she was a girl she had liked to read about the riverboats and imagine herself a captain. The great turning wheels that churned in the water. She had once seen a black-and-white movie in which a provincial woman fell in love with a riverboat captain and abandoned everything in her life to be with him. The river captain was her, Joan. She had never thought of herself as the woman trying desperately to get out of her town and life, scratching at everything. She knew how to do that.

"We'll leave after all this millennium business is done."

"If the world doesn't come to an end."

"We'll get a good price on this house."

"I don't want to leave this house."

"There are other houses."

In the delivery room, between the great rippling contractions, perspiration sprang to Deborah's forehead and rolled down her face, as if hers were the face of a garment worker, a laborer in the fields. A transformation was taking place: she watched the body that was hers become a machine that would become obsolete, the husk around another's.

She saw the face of her husband transformed by her pain, though he was a doctor, intimate with the many fine calibrations of suffering, raging and silent, devout and profane. He had broken and reconstituted the body, had administered the medicine that diminished the pain as well as the news that the pain would return. He had sawed through sternums. Yet toward the end, when Deborah was in great pain, his face went ashen, he swayed on his feet and was led from the room. Not when she was shouting, but when she could shout no more and lay quiet and blank as if struck, tears and sweat coursing down her face. She was expressionless, as a canny woman is at the moment before a flirtation begins. She hoped for the intercession of a god; she would not show it.

All these years and still only the familiar sour feeling in her mouth, the odd deflation and ticking silence.

"Mrs. Donadio? Are you okay?"

She wept when she saw her daughter emerge and again when she was given her to hold. It was purely a bodily elation. Could that be a sign of the presence of a god? She had not expected a moment of transcendence. When it didn't come, she suffered a great blow. For if we do not meet God at the birth of a child, when else might we hope to? What remained, it seemed to her, was only death. In death would she encounter the cause of all this and the judgment and the scaffolding holding up this life and giving it shape?

An image flashed in her mind. She struggled to perceive; perhaps it was a sign. A man on a bicycle, a rain-washed tunnel. Depths and deeps. She ventured further, to try to see. There he was. Warren Beatty in a movie she'd rented, *Heaven Can Wait*. He wore a track-suit. She pictured it all white and spotless; that was Hollywood language for "this character has returned an angel from the dead."

"You are not God," she might have said.

Scott's hand was on her forehead, smoothing her brow.

"Go to sleep, Deborah. Rest for a while."

Her daughter was born as she had been: easily, it was said, and long before birth greatly loved, as she had been. It was said of her own birth that she had come with great speed through the birth canal, the doctor catching her in midair as if she flew into the world on her own steam. So it was with Chloe.

It was easier to love a daughter; she felt she would have had to learn to love a son. It could not be denied: she knew the body the nurses placed in her arms; when she swabbed the tiny genitals they were not foreign to her, she was neither cautious nor afraid. A boy would have been different.

They lived now in Soundview in a house on the water. They would have money soon. Until then the banks were obliging toward surgical residents. The house was filled with windows and northern light. An enlarged and framed aerial photograph of the town hung on the longest white wall of their living room. When Deborah nursed she stared at it for minutes at a time. Over the course of a day the time must have added up to hours. How narrow the land was in this part of the world. It was everywhere circumscribed by water. The infamous rocky beaches that alone had prevented this town from becoming a resort. People resided here year-round. The abandoned shells of horseshoe crabs, prodigious seaweed in piles like shorn hair, shallow muddy channel of the creek. None of that visible from the air; from the air a pale jut of land around which swirled the greater watery world. It had been a wedding gift from her father.

It was a late wet autumn when they brought their daughter forth to be blessed. Deborah bent to shield her from the rain in the wind as they climbed the steps of Saint Gertrude's. The white gown in miniature, too long for Chloe; it hung down way past her feet. The white sweater with rosettes that warmed her would have to be removed for the photos, even if Chloe bawled.

It was a dowdy church, the crimson rug faded to a benign color that no longer evoked blood. The crucifixes high on the walls were too small for their venue; the body of Christ got lost on such walls, as if the body were a bug or smudge too high to wipe clean. Twenty years ago and more Stephen had brought the girls here for an encounter with Catholicism. Half a joke, to his mind; he wasn't sure what the other half was. Today each remembers the excursion differently, Stephen thinking of Pattie Jankowski, Louise of how she had felt nothing but awe when she entered she church, as she might have felt at a tourist attraction—Epcot, the roller coaster at Busch Gardens—or upon nearly slipping into a chasm between two rocks while hiking. It was Deborah for whom the memory of that day reminded her again of the great loss in her life. She still did not know, did not have the evidence to believe. Unlike the rest of them, she did not feel this merely as loss and sadness but as theft.

Had she been born to other parents she would have believed. Yet there could be no recovery of the item in question.

She stood at the altar with her husband and the priest in his vestments, with his great robes and authoritative gestures. The incantation over the living body of her daughter. Bestowing upon her a soul? No, he was only taking her soul under protection for the next some-odd years, until she passed off this earth.

Not pass off this earth. Pass into it. *What if there is just us, caterpillars, other insects and mulch?* She could hear her father's voice as if he were shrunk to the size of the crucifix and posted like a sentry inside her head; he sat at a table in the Soundview Public Library, thumbing through a book and telling her how it was most likely they would end up in the earth and part of it. Without consciousness, without pain. Without desire.

She could not have Chloe be mulch. Easier to imagine her with the angels in an imponderable heaven. Wings, haloes, Saint Peter at the Gate, the white tracksuit. All of it, anything but Chloe among the earwigs and waste. Even the loam was no consolation. Not Chloe's pink flesh corroding and falling from her bones. It could not, could not.

"Mrs. Donadio."

She was to give Chloe over for the rites.

"In the name of the Father, the Son, and the Holy Spirit . . ."

She tried. She set her face in all the attitudes of receptivity she could summon. Yet what passed within her as the priest concluded was the same astringent sting. It remained with her, this disbelief of belief. In this it was faithful as faith.

Louise's face during the ceremony was impassive. She wore a black sweater and slacks with a large beaded necklace that looked Native American. That was as ceremonial as Louise ever got. Bev stood with hands clasped formally in front of her. The posture showed strain, an attempt at various containments—of emotion, of body, of the force of her personality, which might impel her to protest this event in the life of their family. What ceremonies were hers, what rituals? She had never attended a baptism. After a friend's death from AIDS she had been charged with planning an event on the beach. Strong drinks in tall glasses, endless rum, neon swizzle sticks, his ashes sprinkled in the ocean by hands he knew. She had followed his orders down to the letter, to the neon; she *knew from those rituals*, as Joan said. These she didn't know from. The miter, the censer, the chanted words and dim nave. Catholicism frightened her; it was not a place to inhabit, only watch.

Scott's family milled and gathered, speaking in whispers, laughing with their faces, the women pressing their palms to their chests in quiet mirth. There were cousins that looked alike, aunts, uncles. They were of a piece; this was their ritual and their altar. Now Chloe would be brought into their fold.

It was an airy day in June, all soft sun and washed sky, as in a watercolor. Louise took the train into the city alone. Few passengers, without the legions of commuters: a Saturday, early. It was one of the new trains, which had replaced the diesel engines, slow and odorous, that had been traveling the island all her life, the windows coated with soot. Now a computerized voice announced the towns that flashed in red on the displays. Oyster Bay, Locust Valley, Glen Cove, Glen Head. It was a litany she knew. *Jamaica next station, Jamaica next.* The new train smelled of parts recently welded, a slight burnt odor. People smiled as they stepped on. The new train.

The prospect of being a commuter, her life given over to the trains—she could not do it. Eamon would return here, to be near his daughter. In the fall she would go to Kansas to teach at a small college, ride her bike to work in spring. She would be alone again, in the fall, Eamon back among the New York Irish, the pubs in Queens, satellite broadcasts of the hurling and the football of his country, the laughing and desolation at the center of immigrant life. The two of them would speak on the phone, one calling the other after too much to drink, the other sober and trying to make light of it, saying things to console. *Of course I still love you. You know how it is.*

From Penn Station she walked the long avenues down to the West Village. Glitter hats and glamorous excess, caricatured masks of the political offenders. From the accessories worn by the knots of people on the street corners and the steps of the public buildings it was clear that this was the parade route. In midtown the crowds were thin, but they got denser as she walked into Chelsea. Vendors were selling boas and wigs, bottled water, pinwheels. For seven dollars a woman in overalls and diaphanous blouse made Polaroid portraits and framed them at a folding table she'd set up at the curb. A single angry person holding a sign in his lap and calling from a wheelchair, moved along the street in tandem with a police officer. Would something erupt? The day was too airy for that, too bright. People sang by on roller blades, in costumes and shorts, devil horns on their heads and glittering tridents in their hands. Even shorts seemed a costume today, it had been so long since weather for shorts. Some women wore halter tops or the tops of bikinis; some men were shirtless, their nipples painted as eyes for the crescent of a smile rippling on their abdomens. Why was she not of this crowd? Was her life so distant from it?

She continued down through Chelsea, looking out at the city from under a baseball cap. Her hair was cropped short now, for summer. There was a chance her mother and Joan would be here, or friends of her mother's she had met, Evelyn, the many Donnas. It wouldn't be terrible to run into them so much as awkward. Even to herself she couldn't explain the impulse that had brought her here.

By Washington Square the crowd swelled, people sitting on walls and crammed on the sidewalks, lighter people hoisted on the shoulders of the heavier. Sometimes men on the shoulders of women. Though narrow, sickly men, their bones everywhere evident.

Who would she be now?

She had thought she would become a wife; she would wait still more years for that mold to encase her. For we learn that the real life begins in marriage; before then it is all promenading and rehearsal.

She would have an unlikely constellation of lovers. A dentist in the Northwest after saving a cracked crown late on a Saturday, men from offices who at the end of a day in the produce aisle of the supermarket or in line at the liquor store with a bottle of wine or bourbon in the crooks of their arms to bring home spoke to her. In their work clothes they were expansive in the way one is expansive when fatigued, when there is nothing else of the day to take or give. Single men with their unloved apartments awaiting them. Married men who had not spoken to their wives in years. The love was cold or defunct, irreparable. She did not wish to break anything. Whole years she spent alone, reading in the evenings. The great reading from the Americans. Who else right now is reading Welty? She would look up from the book and ask it aloud and picture the other solitary readers in their beds or college students puzzling through the paperback *Collected Stories* with a highlighter pen. She read Porter's strange fever dreams that had come out as books—to carry a fever in a knapsack! She longed to speak to someone about them, for there is no intimacy as pleasurable as to speak of books while lounging in bed, both heads propped up on elbows, both copies of the book open on the sheet and held open with a hand as the eye searches for the passage to read aloud.

There was the dogs' veterinarian, whom she would later see she loved for the way he succored the dogs, a tenderness in his face and hands as he calmed them, these animals she had not known would form the intimate inner pattern of her life. And young men, and older—men who would have been her father's friends and misunderstood her utterly. For it is charming when a person who belongs to another generation adores you and at the same time misunderstands you utterly, so that you must speak as if in a foreign language to speak at all.

I would have liked to tell her, this is the shape of your life; there is no other form. This constellation and succession, this uneven weave. She would not anyway believe in any other.

Some nights she would awaken in her bed alone or with a lover, the tremors running a disruption to her core. "I'll take an aspirin," she would say, climbing out from the warm bed into the dark and talking to herself as she did when alone. Or the lover would say it sleepily—"Take an aspirin." Because there are for us and us alone placebos and placebos are useful; they get us through.

With the aspirin traveling through her she would be able to lie on her back in bed and think. There might be no overall and final love as there might be no God. There might only be this provisional succession, each supplanting the last, none culminating, only the then and then and then until going as we all go to the grave alone.

It was no time to think about that. Nearby in the street a couple stood with their arms slung over each other's shoulders. One's ear gleamed in a shining crescent of gold, each stud, cross, charm catching the light. She turned her face with its pale beard and mustache and bent to light a cigarette, talking as she did so out of the side of her mouth. In her dexterity she gave Louise a pang for Eamon. She with a mustache, a beard. The woman wore a gray sweatshirt that had been cut at the neck with scissors. On her neck a welter of necklaces, gold chains that swayed as she moved. The other was a thin woman in a T-shirt and jeans, her hair clean and parted in the center. The sort of woman who didn't think about her looks, who is ordinary and accepts that she is so.

Above, the offices sat in their Saturday dormancy, other families ate breakfasts or looked out at the crowd gathering for the parade or closed their blinds. An Oriental rug in the middle of the floor, baby toys, light streaming through the slats, letters on the butcher-block counter ready to go out. Only a Saturday, for some.

She felt her ass get patted and removed a sticker from her jeans, advertising a political candidacy. There was everywhere an air of friendly audacity; she patted the sticker back onto her ass.

Music pulsated from an unseen source; people swayed and danced. Still no parade in view. Though more drag queens in platform shoes appeared, men with muscular, oiled chests. Dogs dressed in pink and silver accessories, someone throwing petals from a sack. Petals flew in the June air, a smell of burnt sugar and flowers and cigarettes. This was not the suburbs. Not the suburbs, not church, not dogma, Jews, not-Jews. People in masks of former presidents shook her hand, women's voices behind them. Some wore suits, the ties with tiny birds or ukeleles or interlocking bodies on them.

The codes were scrambled; the codes were to be eaten like eggs.

Then, all at once as if conjured, the parade was upon them, the street full of sound and color. Hands fluttered cardboard fans printed with words proclaiming the various and varying selves, heretofore quashed or hidden. *Dyke. Lipstick. Curious. Packing. Hung. Pervert.* Alone in the street between two groups of marchers a magnificent shirtless black man in clear plastic high-heeled shoes wielded a whip. He taunted the crowd, laughing with mock derision, turning cartwheels on the pavement. There was no derision, only a great chaotic hum of affection, as if a coronation were forthcoming.

Members of a South American contingent strolled by in straw hats and identical light blue cotton shirts and khakis. Each had a mustache, drawn on. Each was a woman.

If people did have it within them to transform. Not by faith in God but in others, the human experiment.

A float advertising a club in Queens came to a halt as the paraders regrouped and accommodated the whip wielder's pause for more cartwheels. It was this float from which the great pulsing music emanated down the avenues. In the June air people danced, in their colors and delight, straw hats, oiled chests. A woman reached to the woman next to her and pulled down her halter top, exposing her breasts in the bright June light. She looked down at herself, smiled placidly, pulled the top back up.

People on the float passed the stalled time by dancing, rousing the crowd by moving in sync, their arms raised in the sky, toward the predictable apartments, church spires, dead offices. As if to say, come be alive.